AF260698

SEEING RED
THE FIRST CALLING

WRITTEN BY

FINN

SEEING RED: THE FIRST CALLING

The dead leave clues. The living bury them. Ryan Red digs them up anyway.

Red was there when Casey Edwards died—and the official story doesn't match what Red saw.

Casey's life ran through the seams of the city: East-side respectability, West-side loyalty, and The Strip wedged between them. As Red digs, bodies start to stack up, rumours harden into patterns, and a new calling card begins to surface—numbers painted in blood like someone is keeping score.

With his oldest friend Dante trying to keep him on the right side of the line, and his family waiting at home, Red pushes deeper into a case someone powerful has already decided is finished.

Then the count goes up again.

ISBN 978-1-7645451-0-5

SEEING RED: THE FIRST CALLING
First edited and published by
FORTIFIED PUBLISHING

A QUICK DEDICATION

This one is for Ryan. Because I used his name for the main character when I couldn't think of anything else.

Thanks for being called Ryan, Ryan.

And putting up with me. That's a toughie.

1

The street looked like a block party if you ignored the police tape, the uniforms, and the fact that somebody had bled out on the nicest lawn in a three-kilometre radius.

The tape stretched across the front yard, slack in the breeze, with cops standing by it. Neighbours pressed in anyway, shoulder-to-shoulder, phones up, and whispers thick enough to choke on. Every so often, someone leaned too far and got shoved back with the firm, polite irritation of someone who'd rather be doing literally anything else.

Across the road, I sat on a bus stop bench watching the prying, nosy crowd in front of me. I had my phone in my hand, thumb hovering, focusing on more than just the sea of people.

A large house stood behind the yard. Shining windows and polished brick. A yard that looked pristine and landscaped to perfection. The grass was a perfect shade of green, trimmed within an inch of its life, except for the red stain spreading near the front steps.

The body lying in the middle of it was definitely an eyesore.

Through gaps in the crowd, I saw it all—arms bent wrong, the twisted leg, the shoe half off. The cops stood around the body—tight and careful.

Nervous.

It must be someone important.

I lifted my phone and hit call. It rang once. Twice. Then, a voice that had grown more tired over the years answered.

"What do you want, Red?"

I smiled into the phone. "I'm watching you."

I could picture him squeezing the bridge of his nose. Dante always did that when he was two seconds away from telling me to go to hell. He was always too kind to say it aloud, though.

"Where are you?" he asked, voice low.

I tilted my head toward the lawn. "Across from your little lawn party. Just sightseeing."

"You're not supposed to be here," he said immediately.

"Yeah, I've heard. You all run a very exclusive club now."

"Red."

"Dante."

"Don't do anything stupid," he said, and the tiredness slipped into something sharper. Fear, almost. Last year had left claw marks on the inside of his skull.

I leaned back against the bus stop glass. It was cold, gritty, and probably covered in all the wrong kinds of DNA. "I'm sitting. Calm and collected. Unlike everyone else, it would seem."

"That doesn't fill me with confidence."

"I'm sitting peacefully," I amended.

Another pause. Then a sigh. *"Again, I have no confidence,"* he muttered. *"I'm coming over."*

"Good. Bring snacks and—"

He hung up on me.

Rude.

I watched him cross the street a minute later, ducking between a patrol car and an ambulance like he'd done it a thousand times. He had the same build as he'd always had—solid, grounded—except now his shoulders carried a little more weight than muscle.

He stopped in front of me, hands on his hips, eyes scanning me thoroughly. "You're insane."

"Thank you. I try very hard."

"What are you doing here?"

"I need a favour."

He snorted. "This isn't how you ask for favours. Besides, I'm busy."

"I noticed," I said, gesturing at the crowd. "It's nice. Bringing the community together. Can't wait for the group hug."

He glanced to the tape. Then back to me. "Look, whatever this is, it can wait."

"I'd rather it didn't," I said simply.

Dante's jaw set. He wasn't angry at me yet. That came later. Right now, he was in that miserable middle ground where he was trying to keep everything together.

"I'll call you when the scene is cleared. When I'm off radio. When I'm not standing in front of forty people with cameras."

"Let's be honest, the cameras aren't going to be on you."

"Red—"

"You know what?" I cut him off and shrugged. "It's fine. You go do your job. I'll wait."

Dante raised his eyebrows.

"Okay…" he said slowly, knowing better than to push for more information. "Just… stay here. Don't move."

"I wouldn't dream of leaving," I said, and glided my hand across the seat.

Dante hesitated, eyes darting toward the tape again. Toward the body. Toward whatever politics and paperwork were swirling on the other side of it.

Then he stepped back. "Don't move."

"Butt is planted."

He turned and walked off.

I waited until he was ten metres away before I moved.

Because I'm a liar.

I slipped off the bench and crossed the road, blending into the crowd. The onlookers reeked of perfume, cigarettes, and that sour smell of people who'd been standing in the sun for too long.

A uniformed cop held the tape line in the quieter corner near the driveway. Not many people pressed there; it didn't have the best view.

He looked young, not fresh-faced exactly, but still carrying that polished stiffness, showing he hadn't been taught to relax into the job yet.

I walked up as if I belonged.

His eyes trailed over me and failed to place me. "Sir," he said, lifting a hand, "please stay back."

I stopped with exaggerated obedience. "Of course. How's your day going?"

He blinked, caught off guard by the fact that I was talking to him like a person. "Uh. Fine."

"Great. I love that for you."

His mouth twitched; he didn't know if he was allowed to smile.

I leaned closer, lowering my voice. "So… who's the schmuck important enough to bring the whole NBI for a lawn party?"

The cop stiffened instantly. His eyes darted toward the cluster near the body, then back to me.

"Like, the *National Bureau of Investigation*… what? That's crazy," I added, and he put his hand between us.

"Sir, you need to—"

"Stay back," I finished for him. "I got it. Keeping my distance."

His cheeks turned a faint shade of red. "This is an active crime scene."

I threw my hands up in an exaggerated shrug. "No shit."

I glanced around at the crowd before turning back to the officer.

"So, is there like a barbeque happening after… or?"

He looked like he was deciding whether to argue or just pretend I wasn't real.

I made the decision for him by pointing at an onlooker who had pressed forward at the far end of the tape, his phone reaching out as far as he could, practically leaning into the yard.

"Hey," I said, nodding. "That guy's about to break your line."

The cop snapped to action, stepping briskly along the tape line. "Sir! Back up!"

The moment he moved, I dipped down, lifted the tape, and slid under it.

Grass met my shoes. The air on the inside felt different. Quieter. Heavier.

"Sir!" the cop barked from behind me.

I ignored him because I have always had an issue with authority.

"What the hell are you doing in here?" Dante's voice hit me from the left, tight and sharp.

I turned toward him with a smile that said, '*I'm innocent*' and eyes that said, '*you knew this would happen*'.

Dante was already moving, closing the distance so he could physically pull me out of trouble before it became paperwork.

Behind him, a larger man stepped forward, moving away from the body. Broad shoulders. Thick neck. He looked like he could headbutt a wall and make the wall apologise.

Supervisory Special Agent Wilson Barnes. His gaze landed on me with a weight I couldn't describe. "Thought I said I didn't want you near a crime scene unless told otherwise," he rumbled.

"And yet, here I am," I replied automatically.

Dante shot me a warning look that I ignored.

Wilson turned away from me, massaging the bridge of his nose. "Get him out of here."

"Wait," I said, holding up a hand. "Just—"

"No. We're not doing this today. The mayor escalated this to us so we could do this right."

I glanced around at the officers and agents clustered near the body. Most of them looked tense. A few looked curious. One looked as though he wanted to be anywhere else.

And then I saw her.

She stood slightly apart from the group, arms crossed, posture relaxed in that way people get when they're in control. Hair neat. Clothes sharp but not flashy. Her eyes—dark and intent—tracked me with the calm interest of someone watching a predictable animal do exactly what they expected.

Mia.

I'd never met her before, but I knew exactly who she was because the bureau couldn't help but get her plastered on the front page of news articles when a murder was solved.

The psychic.

The consultant.

The replacement. *My* replacement.

Her mouth tipped into a small smile as if she already knew I was irritated by her presence. She moved to close the space between us.

"Oh," I said softly, and my smile sharpened. "You have a circus act."

Mia's brows lifted. "You must be Ryan Red."

"I don't do full names."

"Red," she corrected, as if humouring a child.

Dante muttered, "Don't," under his breath. I ignored that, too.

Mia's gaze slid over me, taking inventory. Not what I was wearing, but how I was holding myself. The tension in my shoulders. The energy in my hands. The fact that I was smiling too much.

"You're not here for Barry," she said casually.

I blinked. "Excuse me?"

"Barry Kieffer," she clarified, nodding toward the body. "The dead politician. You're not here because you care about the victim."

My smile stayed put, but it shifted. Less playful and more defensive. "And you know that because the spirits whispered it to you?"

"No," she said smoothly. "You wear it pretty obviously."

I opened my mouth. Then closed it again, because she wasn't wrong, and I hated her for it.

Wilson looked between us, trying to decide which of us he hated more. "Enough. Mia, I don't need a performance. Red, I don't need *you*."

"Performance?" I pointed at Mia. "A great idea. Host a séance—"

"Red," Dante warned.

I held up both hands. "Fine. Fine. You don't need me. But you've got a lot of people around. Cameras out. Dead politician. And just not a lot of movement."

Wilson's eyes narrowed. "And your point?"

"My point," I said, stepping closer to the body without actually getting too close—because I didn't need to—"is, I can solve this in five minutes."

Silence.

Then a scoff from somewhere behind me. Wilson stared at me. "You can solve it in five minutes?"

"Yes."

Wilson's jaw clenched. He glanced at Dante, who looked like he was regretting every choice that had led him to this moment. Then Wilson glanced at Mia.

Mia gave a small shrug; curious how much damage I could do before someone had to clean it up.

Wilson's mouth twisted. "Fine," he growled. "You get two minutes. And if you start making a scene—"

"I said five," I corrected.

"Two!" Wilson hissed. "And no making a scene."

"I would never," I said solemnly.

Dante made a noise that sounded like a half-hearted prayer.

I closed my eyes and lifted my hands slightly, palms hovering over empty air.

"Okay," I whispered, letting my voice drop into a dramatic hush. "Okay. I'm feeling… I'm feeling—"

Mia sighed loudly.

I snapped my eyes open. "Can you keep it down? I'm trying to work here."

Mia's smile widened. "By all means."

I turned my focus on the body properly now, and my brain clicked into clean lines like it always did when faced with blood.

Barry Kieffer was facedown, shoulders slumped, and body slightly twisted. The stab wound itself wasn't fully visible from this angle, but I saw enough. The blood pattern also told me what I needed to know. There was a dark stain spreading through the back of his shirt, soaked into fabric, clinging heavy.

One wound. A decision.

I looked at the position of his legs, the angle of his fall, the way the grass was pressed down beneath him. He hadn't run. He hadn't fought. He'd been close to his door. Close enough to feel safe.

And the surprise. It made for a controlled fall.

I straightened and scanned the front path, the steps, the doormat that looked brand new. Of course it did. Everything about this house did.

"Single stab," I said, voice normal now. "Near the kidney."

An officer shifted. "How do you—"

"Because that's where the blood pooled," I cut in, pointing at the spread pattern. "And one stab because the body looks like it was placed on the ground. Which indicates control."

Mia's eyes sharpened slightly at that. Not with surprise, but interest.

I kept going. "This wasn't random. Not a mugging or a fight that got out of hand. Could have been a conversation."

Wilson crossed his arms. "And why's that?"

"Because there's no chaos," I said, gesturing at the ground around the body. "As I said, control. No torn-up grass. No stains on his hands or knees. He didn't see it coming."

Dante frowned. "Could've been jumped."

"Maybe," I conceded. "But you fight back if you're jumped. Even getting stabbed in the kidney, adrenaline would give you a couple of seconds to do something."

I pointed at Barry's arms. "He went down like his body turned off. He was calm when he got stabbed. Relaxed. Guided to the ground." I glanced at Mia. "Science and facts."

"Fascinating," Mia murmured, rolling her eyes.

I looked back at the door. "He was heading inside. Which means the killer was likely heading inside with him."

Wilson's eyes narrowed. "So, you're saying he knew them."

"I'm saying he didn't fear them," I corrected. "Didn't see them as a threat. Someone he saw every day."

Then I turned toward the crowd.

That's where the truth always was, if you knew what you were looking for. Bodies were honest, sure—but people were chatty. Even when they weren't talking.

I scanned faces the way I used to scan waiting rooms. Same energy. Same desperation. Different consequences.

There were the obvious ones: the grief tourists with their phones held chest-high trying to film a dead man. The neighbours pretending they were here out of concern instead of curiosity. The couple whispering turning it into a dinner table conversation.

Then there were the useful ones: the people who weren't performing. The people who'd gone quiet because they were actually scared. The ones whose eyes kept moving—not to the body—but to the cops, waiting for an answer.

And then I saw him.

Not front row or shoved up against the tape. He'd picked the driveway fence line—close enough to see the front door, far enough to pretend he wasn't desperate to.

Hands in his pockets. Shoulders set. Expression tight in a way that wasn't grief and wasn't shock, but resentment.

I took one step toward him, then stopped and glanced back at Barry. Something about the way Barry's right hand lay bothered me. The fingers were half-curled as if he'd been holding onto something.

Except his palm was empty.

No phone. No wallet. No keys.

People didn't walk from their car to their front door without keys. Not unless they wanted to stand outside looking stupid.

Barry hadn't looked stupid. Barry had looked normal. Confident. Mid-routine.

I walked back and crouched just enough to see his hand properly without getting too close, and there it was: a faint red line across the skin, like something had been pressed into it hard for half a second. A thin imprint.

A keyring.

I glanced back to the crowd, my eyes not landing on the man right away, to avoid spooking him. I straightened and walked over to the driveway, eyes still scanning the others before meeting his gaze.

I walked toward him. "Hey," I called casually. "Quick question."

He didn't answer right away. Just stared at me with eyes that had already decided I was a problem.

"You live on this street?"

His jaw tightened. "Across," he said shortly.

"Neighbour," I said, giving him a nod. "Lucky you."

His gaze slipped past me to the body, then away again too fast. He didn't want to look too long, because looking meant feeling, and feeling meant cracking.

I nodded once. "Hold your hands out."

"What?" he frowned.

I lifted my own hands, palms up, showing that I was only demonstrating a harmless little exercise. "Just—hands. For just a second."

His shoulders tightened. "Why?"

"Because I'm a psychic," I said flatly.

His face twisted. Confusion and irritation colliding. "You're not—"

"I know," I agreed. "But it's all part of the fun."

A few heads nearby turned toward us. Wilson's attention snapped to me. Mia watched from behind the others, expression unreadable and mildly entertained.

I kept my tone light and friendly. "Humour me. Unless you're worried I'm going to see something you don't want me to."

"I don't have to do anything you say," he spat.

"That's true. But here's the thing—you're either an innocent neighbour who's furious at the world, or you're the guy who walked Barry to his front steps and put a knife in his back."

His eyes flashed.

"Try not to react," I added, as if that was helpful. "It ruins the magic."

He swallowed hard.

"Come on. Hands out," I instructed again, and he finally obliged. "Good, good."

I studied his palms briefly. No blood. Nothing out of the ordinary. At least not on his hands.

Swiftly, I gently grabbed his wrists, placing my two fingers over his pulse. He tried to pull away, but I didn't let him.

"Quick question. Did you go for a walk last night?" I kept my eyes locked on his.

"What—no," he said quickly.

Lie.

"Did you hear anything last night?"

"No!"

Lie.

"Really? No dog barking? No tyres screeching?" I pressed before I landed one more. "No car alarm?"

His eyebrows raised for a split second.

"There was a car alarm briefly," a voice came from further down the police line. "Stopped pretty quick."

"I would imagine," I said, not turning to see who spoke.

"Let go—" the man started, but I spoke over him.

"See… when someone walks from their car to their front door, they usually hold their keys. And the body is a very reactive thing. It likes to tense up when it's in shock."

His face went still.

"Getting stabbed in the kidney can cause a bit of shock," I said, removing my hands from the man and mimicking my hand clenching.

"I'm gonna say he hit the little alarm button on the remote. You grabbed it to shut it off, but before you could put it back, neighbours started stirring."

"You don't know what you're talking about," he said, but his voice had gone thin around the edges.

"Maybe I don't. But you do have blood on your shoe."

His eyes snapped down, and mine followed, landing on a tiny speck of blood on his shoelace.

"Why wouldn't you change them?" I asked with a small shrug.

His eyes met mine again, and his nostrils flared. "He deserved it."

There it was. The truth.

People didn't say 'deserved' unless they'd been building a story in their head for months.

I didn't even have to guess which story, because he practically shoved it into the air between us.

"You know what he did?" the man hissed, voice rising. "You know what he signed off on? The construction. The zoning. The pipes—my kids were drinking dirt for weeks. Got sick. And he—he kept smiling like it was fine."

I let him talk. Not because I cared about his speech, but because anger made people careless. Angry people loved to perform. It meant I didn't have to come up with any more evidence.

"He ruined my house," he said, and his eyes shone with something ugly. "He ruined—"

"Yeah," I interrupted softly. "I get it. It's still murder."

His face tightened.

Then he looked to the street and turned and bolted.

"Oh, he's a runner," I said, and the order to chase was called.

Wilson moved faster than I thought he could, barking orders as officers surged forward. The crowd erupted—phones lifting higher, bodies shifting, excitement spilling out of them.

The neighbour slammed through a gap between two onlookers, almost knocking someone over, and disappeared into the street.

Dante stared at me, both impressed and thinking I was unbearable.

"Are you happy now?" he hissed as I wandered back toward him.

"Ecstatic."

Mia stepped closer, gaze still on the chase. "You're good," she said, and the words were almost a compliment until you heard the edge underneath them.

"I know," I said without looking at her. "It's a curse."

She smiled, keeping her eyes trained on me.

Wilson returned not five minutes later, breathing hard, and anger radiating off him. Behind him, the neighbour was being hauled back toward a cruiser, face twisted, and wrists already being cuffed.

Wilson stared at me. "Two minutes," he said slowly. "And you turn it into a damn parade."

"Still hit the two-minute mark. And, you're welcome."

"I didn't say thank you."

"You're thinking it, though."

Wilson's eyes narrowed. "Get him out."

Dante grabbed my arm before anyone else could and hauled me toward the side of a patrol car.

"Are you trying to get me fired?" he snapped the second we were out of immediate earshot.

"I'm not trying. I can if you'd like."

"Red."

"What?" I asked, and now my humour had a crack in it, thin enough that I felt the real thing under it. The real thing was sharp.

Dante's face was tight. "What do you want?"

I stared at him. "I need you to find out what's happening with a case being handled by a local force," I said quietly.

Dante blinked. "Why? What case?"

"Lakeside Park. Young guy was killed."

"Lakeside?" Dante asked, and I gave him a small nod. "That'd be the precinct near Bellwood."

"You know the guys there?" I pressed, and Dante shrugged, his eyes searching mine.

"Can't say I've really worked with them. But this guy who died. This happened three nights ago, yeah?"

My stomach twisted, slow and sick.

"Yeah. You know about it?"

"Casey Edwards. File came through the NBI. I glanced at it. Was marked as suicide. It got filed."

"Why would a suicide go through NBI?" I pressed.

"I… I don't know." Dante's eyes sharpened. "How do you know about Casey?"

The name stuck to the forefront of my mind. His face. The blood. The sound of four shots ringing in my ears.

It wasn't a suicide.

I held Dante's gaze as the words left my mouth.

"Because I was there."

2

3 DAYS EARLIER—THURSDAY MORNING

Lakeside Park sat in the kind of spot city planners love because it lets them pretend they've fixed a problem without fixing it.

Not quite East Side. Not quite West Side. Just north enough to feel expensive on a brochure and close enough to the strip that, at night, it stopped feeling like a park and started feeling like a place people went when they didn't want to be seen.

At one in the morning, it was the perfect place to get away with just about anything.

The drive up had taken just under thirty minutes. The streets thinned out the further north I went. The houses got bigger, the fences got higher, and the hedges seemed endless.

But then the hedges stopped. The streetlights buzzed. And Lakeside appeared, half swallowed by trees.

The car park was mostly empty. One sedan tucked into a corner. A couple of bins overflowing with takeaway cups and receipts. The lights overhead never fully committed to staying on—flicker, hum, flicker— like they were negotiating with the darkness instead of fighting it.

I killed the engine. The silence inside the car wasn't peaceful. It was grating.

I'd been doing a lot of sitting lately. A lot of quiet, watching the clock change numbers and pretending that counted as progress.

When I'd been a doctor, time had meant something. Minutes were blood. Seconds were air. People yelled my name down hallways like it was the answer to something. I used to move through chaos with ease. I lived in it.

Then I lost my licence. I'd gone against the hospital board—a transplant that shouldn't have happened, a patient who shouldn't have, statistically, lived. Except he did. He was alive. He was thriving. Which was, apparently, the wrong kind of outcome.

Regardless, it was an outcome that stripped me of the ability to do something I was good at.

I tried to tell myself it was fine. That there were other ways to be useful. That I didn't need patients or a white coat to justify my existence.

Then Dante had dragged me into the NBI as a consultant, and I'd thought, there it is. A new way to be useful. A new way to keep the part of my brain that likes puzzles fed.

For a while, it worked. It worked too well.

I'd gotten used to being needed again. Used to people looking at me like I wasn't just a guy with a bad reputation and a history they didn't want to discuss.

Then last year happened.

One plan that went too far. One almost-dead agent because I'd believed I was smarter than the person I was chasing. They didn't say I was banned. They didn't make a big announcement. They just stopped calling. Which was worse, in a way. They could have at least kicked me out properly. Instead, they let me exist in limbo. Not fired. Just sidelined.

Replaced.

At least I got to keep my consultant badge.

I got out of the car and shut the door quietly. The air outside hit me like a slap. Cold and damp. It carried the smell of lake water and wet earth.

My breath fogged in front of me. I shoved my hands into my jacket pockets and started toward the path.

The entrance sign was half-lit and chipped at the bottom. Someone had tried to scratch a name into it once and given up halfway through. A council plaque near the gate declared the area "a treasured community space."

The path itself was wide, concrete, curving around the lake in lazy sweeps. Lamp posts sat at uneven intervals. Some worked. Some didn't. One buzzed loud enough to make me grind my teeth.

I walked without a goal. That was the point. To be moving without needing to arrive anywhere.

Home had felt too still.

Claire and the boys were asleep when I left. They always were at that hour. Claire had fallen asleep with some medical journal on her lap, glasses slightly crooked, a pen still in her hand like she'd been determined to out-stubborn fatigue and lost.

Miles had been starfished across his bed, one leg hanging off the edge, sheets twisted into a knot. Alex had insisted he wasn't tired—eyes bright, voice too loud—and then collapsed on the couch mid-sentence like someone had pulled his plug.

I'd carried him to bed and stood in the doorway, watching his chest rise and fall.

Sometimes I still did that. Watched them breathe. My body didn't trust the world to keep them safe unless I physically witnessed it happening. Claire used to call it sweet. I knew what it really was.

Fear.

The house itself had been quiet in that soft, domestic way. The kind people crave. The kind of quiet that was supposed to mean you'd done something right with your life.

And I had. Technically. A wife. Two kids. A decent house that didn't have bullet holes in the fence. A neighbourhood where the worst crime was someone's dog barking too loud in the middle of the night.

I'd built a life that didn't smell like the West Side. I'd gotten out.

And still—some nights—it didn't feel like mine. It felt like something I was borrowing. Like I was waiting for someone to knock on the door and tell me there had been a mistake.

Because the West Side had a way of clinging to you. It lived in your reflexes. In how you watched corners. In how you listened for tone changes in conversation. In how you never fully relaxed when you were alone in the dark.

Dante had never tried to get out.

Maybe that was the difference between us. Maybe he'd been smarter. Maybe he'd accepted what we were and decided there was no point pretending we could be something else.

Or maybe it was because he didn't have kids sleeping down the hall.

I walked further along the curve of the lake, letting the cold chew through my jacket.

The water was a dark smear to my right, still and heavy. No ripples. No reflections. Just black.

A bench sat near the edge of the path, empty, damp, and slightly crooked. Another bench further down had graffiti on the backrest— something angry and half illiterate. A bin leaned at an angle, lid missing, and contents scattered in a small fan across the concrete.

I told myself I was just here to walk. To breathe air and let my mind run until it had nothing else to think of, so I could finally sleep.

And then my mind settled on the NBI. I missed the work. I missed the adrenaline. I missed having something to focus on that wasn't bills and groceries, and the slow creeping awareness that I didn't know what I was meant to be if I wasn't solving something.

Being a husband and a father was good. It was the best thing I'd ever done. But the days could get quiet. Claire at work. The boys at school.

My phone sat heavy in my pocket, wanting to be used. Wanting me to call someone. Dante, probably. Or someone at the bureau who still remembered my name.

I didn't.

Pride is a stupid thing, but it's persistent. Besides, if they wanted me, they'd call. That was how it worked now. I didn't get to show up uninvited and pretend I belonged. I'd learned that lesson. Loudly.

The wind shifted, and the light buzz behind me cut out, plunging the path into a deeper shade of dark. Ahead, the curve of the path disappeared behind trees. Past that, another streetlight cast a pale pool of yellow across the concrete.

Something moved in that pool of light.

I slowed without meaning to.

A person stood near a bench up ahead. Hood up. Hands moving, faint and sharp like they were talking to someone. Except that the rest of the path was empty. And the darkness around them looked too thick to trust.

I stopped walking and watched. Trying to decide whether it was my business.

My body, unfortunately, had never been good at letting things not be my business.

The guy under the streetlight didn't look drunk—that was the first thing my brain offered up. He wasn't swaying or sloppy. His feet were planted but not relaxed—more like he'd glued himself there to stop himself from doing something stupid. His hands kept coming up, palms angled outward, then dropping back down, then up again. A calming motion. A bargaining motion.

He was talking, too. Mouth moving. Head tipping slightly as if he were listening for a response. Except there wasn't anyone there. Not that I saw, anyway.

The light created this hard little circle on the path and everything outside it turned into shadow. Trees, bushes, the lake. All of it blended together into one dark mass that could hide a person easily.

I stayed still and watched him for longer than I meant to. I told myself he was on a phone call. Bluetooth. That it was a bad breakup. A dramatic argument with someone over any number of things.

Then he flinched at something in the darkness to his left.

His shoulders tightened. His hands came up higher this time; elbows bent like he was trying to show he didn't have anything. He was trying to show he wasn't a threat.

My skin went cold.

The park suddenly felt different. Too quiet. Too many places for someone to stand and not be seen. I shifted my weight without thinking, eyes scanning the tree line and the bushes and the curve of the path behind him. Nothing moved.

And then the night tore open.

The first shot cracked through the park, loud enough that it felt physical. The sound ricocheted off the trees and came back as a harsh echo.

A muzzle flash flared from the darkness—bright and brief—and in that burst of light I saw a silhouette. An arm extended. A stance braced. A shape that existed for half a second and then vanished back into shadow.

The second shot followed so quickly that my brain didn't get time to finish processing the first.

Then a third.

Then a fourth.

The guy under the light jolted like something had yanked his strings. His knees buckled. He hit the pavement hard, shoulders slamming down first, legs folding awkwardly underneath him.

My body didn't move. My eyes swept the park, frantic. Trying to find the silhouette again. But there was nothing. Just the smell of gunpowder filling the air and the sound of my own breathing going too fast.

Then I heard it. Running.

Footsteps pounding away through the dark, uneven and messy. Not a clean sprint on concrete. More like someone cutting across whatever ground they could find—over tree roots and rocks, limping through it.

And then instinct took over.

I ran.

Fast and clumsy and driven by that stupid part of my brain that still believed if I got there in time, I could fix it. The distance between us disappeared too quickly. The streetlight above the bench threw everything into ugly clarity as I dropped beside him.

Young. Hoodie. Eyes open, wide and shining. He couldn't understand why the world had just done this to him. Blood soaked through his clothes in spreading patches, dark and fast. One stain near his upper chest. Another lower. Another blooming along his side.

Only three of the shots had hit him.

My hands moved before I thought. Pressure, pressure, pressure. "Hey." My voice came too calm for what it was. "Stay with me. Stay with me." His mouth opened, a thin gasp slipping out. He tried to speak, but it came out wet and broken.

I leaned closer, eyes darting over him in quick, clinical snapshots. Airway. Breathing. Colour. Chest movement. Breathing was there. Barely. Too fast. Too shallow. His body already knew what was coming.

I didn't go for compressions. They would just pump the blood out faster. Turn minutes into seconds. I needed pressure. I needed time. I needed an ambulance in about ten seconds.

My phone was in my pocket, suddenly feeling like it weighed more than a brick. I dug it out with shaking fingers and hit emergency with my thumb while my other hand stayed planted on the worst of the bleeding.

The kid's eyes met mine, panicked and begging.

"I'm here," I said, even though that didn't mean anything. "I've got you."

"Emergency services—"

"I need an ambulance now," I cut in. My voice didn't sound like mine. "Lakeside Park. Near the tree line at the bench with the working light. Multiple gunshot wounds."

The operator started asking questions like the script mattered more than the body under my hands.

I answered anyway. Location. Description. Was I safe.

I shoved my jacket open with my wrist, tore the fabric of my shirt up, and pressed it hard against one of the wounds as a makeshift pad. Blood soaked through almost immediately, warm and slick, turning the cloth useless in seconds.

My stomach rolled. I pressed harder.

"Hey," I said again to the kid. "Look at me. Stay awake."

His eyes tried. They found my face and clung to it like a lifeline. His hand twitched, fingers reaching weakly, then catching the sleeve of my jacket. He held on like it was the only thing stopping him from sliding away.

"Can you tell me your name?"

His lips moved. I leaned in. "What?"

A whisper scraped out, too faint to properly catch. I got the shape of a sound, not the word. The kind of thing you miss once and regret forever.

"I'm sorry," I said, even though I didn't know what I was apologising for. For being late. For being here. For not seeing the shooter. For the fact that my hands weren't enough.

His breathing hitched. A wet rattle caught in his throat, and my spine went cold. I'd heard that sound in emergency rooms. In ambulances. In rooms where the walls were bright and the floor was clean, and the blood didn't soak into grass.

Out here, it sounded worse. The world didn't care if it was dignified.

The operator was still talking, telling me help was on the way, telling me to keep pressure, telling me to stay with him.

I didn't respond. I didn't have spare air for it. I kept my eyes on the kid's face. On the rapid blinking. On the way, his gaze started to drift.

"No. No, don't do that. Come on. Stay with me."

In the distance, a siren finally cut through the night. Faint at first. Then closer.

Red and blue light flashed between the trees in brief pulses.

I didn't move. I didn't look away. I kept my hands where they were, pressing hard enough that my wrists ached, holding onto the only thing I could control.

"Help's coming," I told him, even as his grip on my sleeve loosened by a fraction. "Just—hold on."

Footsteps soon hit the path fast and heavy. Two paramedics ran into the pool of light. Their faces were focused, calm in the way you had to be when everything in front of you was loud.

"What've we got?" one of them asked, already dropping to his knees on the other side of the kid.

"Bullet wounds. Three. Chest and abdomen. He was conscious a minute ago."

The paramedic's eyes flicked over my hands. The blood. The soaked fabric I'd pressed against the wound.

"Alright. Sir, I need you to shift back. On my count."

"I can keep pressure," I said.

"I know," he replied, not unkind. "But I need space. We've got it."

The second paramedic leaned in. "Three wounds?"

"Yeah, yeah. Three," I confirmed.

"Okay."

On their count, I shifted, and they moved with practiced coordination. One replaced my hands with gauze and direct pressure, firm and immediate. The other cut fabric away with trauma shears, exposing skin in quick strips.

I shifted back onto my heels, hands hovering uselessly before I forced them to drop to my thighs. My palms were slick. My hands painted red. There were smears on my wrists, on my sleeves, and on the front of my shirt. Warmth already cooling.

The kid's eyes found mine once, unfocused now. His mouth opened as if he wanted to say something again.

Nothing came out.

His breathing made a wet sound. One paramedic swore under his breath and pressed harder while the other fitted an oxygen mask over the kid's face.

A police officer arrived behind them, slowing as he reached the light and took in the scene. He raised his radio immediately.

His voice droned, unclear and unfocused in my mind. I knew what he was doing. Relaying the scene. Setting a perimeter. Organising other officers.

Routine.

More officers arrived. One went past us with his torch sweeping low, the beam cutting across grass and the edge of the water. Another stopped at the bench, looking at the kid, at the blood, then away again quickly as if looking too long would make it personal.

The paramedics worked through their steps, exchanging words in short bursts that carried more urgency than volume. The first paramedic checked the kid's pulse again, then looked up at his partner. The look passed between them in half a second. I saw it anyway. I'd seen it hundreds of times.

They didn't stop.

The kid's hand, the one that had been gripping my sleeve, now lay still on the ground, loose. I stared at that hand too long.

The paramedic pressed his fingers to the kid's neck again and then shook his head once.

The first paramedic sat back slightly, shoulders rising once with a breath he'd been holding. More words flowed between them into the night.

The kid's eyes were still open. That was the only thing I could focus on. I swallowed and forced myself to look away before my brain started cataloguing. Fixating. Turning the last two minutes into a list of mistakes and maybes.

I stood up slowly. My knees complained. My sleeves stuck to my forearms. A different officer approached me. Older. Hair cropped short. He stopped at a safe distance, gaze landing on my hands.

"Sir," he said, "are you injured?"

"No."

"You touch him?"

"Yes. I tried to stop the bleeding."

"Okay." His eyes moved up to my face. "Name?"

I gave it.

He asked for my address. My phone number. My date of birth. I answered automatically.

"What were you doing out here at this hour?"

"Walking."

"Came alone?"

"Yes."

"Any drugs? Alcohol?"

"No."

He studied me longer than necessary, then nodded as if he'd decided I wasn't his problem.

"What did you see?"

I exhaled through my nose and forced myself back to the moment. "The victim was standing under the light. He was talking. I couldn't see who he was talking to. Then four shots. A muzzle flash in the dark. The outline of an arm. That's it."

"You see the shooter's face?"

"No."

"Height? Build?"

"No."

"What about clothes?"

"Nothing."

He wrote as I spoke, pen scratching across paper. He didn't look up much.

"Did you know the victim?"

"No."

The officer's eyes flicked toward the body again. Toward the paramedics pulling a sheet up. Toward the other officers spreading out along the path. "Alright. We may need you to do a formal statement."

"Okay."

"Alright. We'll be in touch."

"Shouldn't I come to the station now?"

He shook his head. "No. Not tonight, I mean. We've taken your details. You're covered in blood. Go home and clean yourself up."

My stomach rolled again, this time for a different reason.

"Okay," I said slowly. "And you'll call?"

"Yes," he said, almost impatiently. As if the answer was obvious. "If we need anything else."

Not when. If.

I watched him, trying to work out if he realised how that sounded. He didn't seem bothered. He shifted his weight and glanced toward one of the other officers, who was talking into his radio near the tree line.

Routine kept going.

I stood there for a moment, my gaze drifting to the young man lying lifeless on the ground. The blood was still slowly spreading further away from him.

I swallowed and looked away. "Alright," I said, mostly to myself.

The officer gave a small nod and stepped past me, already turning his attention back to the scene.

I started walking toward the car park. My hands were still wet. The cold air had started to tack the blood into the creases of my fingers. My sleeves stuck to my forearms when I moved. I kept my gaze forward and my shoulders level, like that could stop anyone from calling me back.

No one did.

The lamp behind me buzzed again. The path ahead was darker. The park felt longer on the way back. When I reached the car park, my car sat where I'd left it, too clean for what my clothes looked like now.

I unlocked my door. The click sounded too loud. As I got in, the scene played in my mind again. They hadn't taken me to the station.

That was the part I got stuck on.

A dead body. Me covered in blood. A dark park. A shooter I couldn't describe. And they'd let me walk away with a "we'll be in touch."

It didn't feel right.

I got into the driver's seat and sat there. Hands hovering near the wheel. I didn't want to touch anything. I touched it anyway and started the engine. As I pulled out of the car park, the flashing lights behind me stayed between the trees. The sirens were off now. The park was still busy but contained. Managed.

I drove toward home with the thin unease that someone would call me tomorrow and tell me where to show up. Because they said they would.

And for a little while, I believed them.

3

PRESENT DAY—SUNDAY NIGHT

The back terrace wasn't fancy, but it was mine. Timber boards, a barbecue that hadn't seen action in months, and a railing that looked out over a yard the boys treated like a war zone.

Inside, Miles laughed while Alex's sharper voice negotiated the rules of a game he'd probably just invented. Claire's tone cut through it all every so often, calm and firm.

I stayed out here because I didn't want that noise to stop.

And I didn't want them to know.

Dante stood near the railing with his hands in his jacket pockets, shoulders slightly hunched against the afternoon air.

He looked at me. Really looked.

"You're telling me you stood there," he said, "covered in blood, at one in the morning, and they let you walk."

"They took my details. They asked the questions. Routine." I shrugged. "Then they let me walk."

Dante's mouth tightened. He nodded like he'd already decided how much he hated that.

"And no one called."

"Not the next day. Not the day after." I kept my voice even. It took effort. "Nothing."

Dante dragged a hand over his face. "Alright. Look… crimes near the strip can be… messy."

I waited.

"Bellwood's the closest precinct on the East Side," he continued. "West would be Canden. When something happens in that band between them, both sides start juggling the problem. Jurisdiction arguments and paperwork delays. Everyone's trying not to own it. Sometimes the NBI gets dragged in just to sort the mess out."

"Well, that explains why the file ends up in your system. It doesn't explain why it's marked a suicide. They have a witness. A statement. Someone who is taking their own life doesn't shoot themselves three times in the chest and gut."

Dante didn't answer straight away. He stared out at the yard. "I glanced at what came through," he said finally. "It was thin. Bare bones. Like someone wanted it closed."

My stomach did a slow turn. "You're saying someone wrote 'suicide' and moved on."

"I'm saying that's what the file says," he corrected. "I'm not saying it makes sense."

"It doesn't." The words came out sharper than I meant. I forced the edge back down. "He was talking to someone. He flinched at the dark like he could see them. I saw it. He was begging for his life."

Dante's eyes flicked to me. "But you didn't see the shooter."

"I saw enough to know someone else was there. Muzzle flash showed me someone was there."

He exhaled slowly through his nose. "Okay."

That one word carried too much.

'Fine, you're right'

'This is going to be a problem'

'*I don't want you anywhere near this*'

I leaned my elbows on the railing. "So, what now?"

Dante shifted his weight, and for a moment, he looked like he was sixteen again, standing on a West Side corner trying to decide whether to walk away from trouble or step into it.

"Now… you'll have to return the favour at some point. I'll look into it. Quietly. I'll pull the intake notes, see who logged it, who signed off on the classification. If it got tagged for NBI review, there'll be a reason on paper."

He paused.

"It could be clerical," Dante said, though it sounded like he didn't believe it. "Paperwork gets mixed up. Mistakes. It happens."

"And if not?" I asked. "If the reason is 'we don't care'?"

Dante's expression flattened. "Then I guess we'll dig more."

I nodded once. "That's why I called you."

"I know." His voice softened, just a fraction. "Just do me a favour and wait. Don't go poking around Bellwood or Canden."

I gave him a look. He gave one back, the kind that used to work on me when we were kids and the stakes were smaller.

"Look," he started with a sigh. "You push your luck with the bureau, whatever. The strip is different. The West is. It's not the same as when you were there. If they see you as a problem, they'll get rid of the problem."

"Or ignore it. They let me walk out of a park covered in someone else's blood."

Dante's jaw flexed. "Exactly."

From inside the house, Alex let out a triumphant whoop—some small victory. Claire's laugh followed, warm and real.

Dante heard it too. His gaze shifted toward the sliding door. "How's Claire?"

"She's fine," I said automatically.

He raised his hand and shook his head. "Red."

I looked away, out at the yard. "I think she sees that I hate being stuck at home all the time. When they're all here, it's good. But…"

"You're bored," Dante cut in, and I shrugged.

"It's too quiet."

"Well, let's hope it stays that way," Dante said, pushing off the railing. "I'll call you. As soon as I have something. *If* I have something."

"When," I corrected, and Dante grimaced.

"Just don't do anything stupid before I call."

"That doesn't sound like me."

"Red."

"I'll behave," I said, raising my hands in defence.

Dante looked unconvinced, but he let it go. He moved toward the side gate that led around to the driveway and left, the latch clicking softly behind him, and once he was gone, the terrace felt too open.

I stood there with my hands on the railing, staring at the yard like I'd find an answer in the trampled grass and plastic toys. The boys' laughter carried through the screen door. Claire's voice rose and fell with the easy patience of someone who'd done this a thousand times and still liked it.

I inhaled, let it out, and went back inside.

Warm air hit me first. Not heat—just the lived-in temperature of a house with people in it. The smell of the lunch the boys had earlier hung faintly in the background. Clean laundry. A hint of dish soap. The normal things, stacked on top of each other until they made a kind of safety.

Miles was on the living room rug with a blanket draped over his back like a cape, holding a foam sword in one hand and a plastic dinosaur in the other. Alex stood on the couch cushions, one foot on the armrest, and wearing the serious face of someone mid-campaign.

Claire was at the kitchen island, elbows braced, watching them with a mug of tea and the faintest smile. Her long blonde hair was pulled up in a loose knot, and she had one of my old hoodies on. It swallowed her hands.

She looked up when I came in. "You two done conspiring out

there?"

"For all you know," I started, moving to Claire and wrapping my arms around her waist. "We were planning a surprise for you."

"Were you?"

"We were not."

Alex whipped his head toward me. "Dad! Miles is cheating."

Miles gasped like he'd been accused of a war crime. "I'm not cheating. I'm doing magic."

Claire lifted her eyebrows. "Hear that, Honey? Magic."

"It's not cheating if it's magic," Miles insisted, cape flapping as he turned in a circle to demonstrate it.

I unwrapped my arms for Claire and walked over and nudged Alex's ankle. "No standing on the furniture."

He started to argue, then stopped when he saw my face. He did a quick recalculation and chose compliance, getting down from the lounge.

Claire watched the exchange and gave a gentle roll of her eyes, followed by a smile.

"Alright," I said, clapping my hands softly. "What's the crisis?"

"Miles is changing the rules as we play," Alex said, pointing harshly at Miles. "He says he can summon ghosts to help him fight."

Miles nodded hard. "I can."

Claire's mouth twitched. "Can you?"

"I can," Miles repeated, and then he leaned in conspiratorially. "I can talk to them."

"You can talk to dead people?" I questioned, and a small chuckle came from Claire.

Alex's eyes went narrow. "No, he can't."

"Yes, I can," Miles insisted. "Dad can do it, too!"

"That's not real," Alex said, spinning to face me.

"Wonder where he heard that from," Claire muttered into her coffee.

"It is!" Miles argued, and I raised my hands to offer some form of mediation.

"Alright, alright. Let's keep it down."

Alex crossed his arms. "If you can. Prove it."

This was what I'd missed in the quiet stretches: the way their brains chased games, the way Claire's presence held everything in place, the way I was pulled into the moment.

"Fine," I said, relishing the moment. "You want me to prove it? I'll prove it. I'll give you a real psychic."

Alex's face lit up with immediate suspicion. "You're not allowed to cheat."

"I would never cheat," I said, fake hurt lacing my voice. "How dare you."

Miles bounced on the spot. "He won't! He's like a psychic detective doctor."

"That's a mouthful."

"It's true!" Miles insisted.

I kept my eyes on Alex. "Alright. Here's the deal. You're going to hide something in the living room."

Alex's eyes sharpened. "What thing?"

I quickly scanned the room, searching for something reasonable for

Alex to hide. Plenty of toys were strewn across the floor and on the coffee table that had yet to be put away, and my gaze fell on a small, blue toy car that was flipped on its roof next to the television remote.

I walked over to it and picked it up, presenting it to the room like I were at a magic show. "This. Small. Easy to hide. Hard to find if you're not as good as I am."

Alex grabbed it. "Okay."

Miles hopped up and down. "Can I hide it?"

"No," Alex said immediately. "You'll mess it up."

Miles made a wounded sound and then slumped down on the couch.

I crouched in front of Alex until we were eye level. "Some ground rules."

Alex nodded once. Serious.

"You hide it somewhere in this room. It can't be on you."

Alex rolled his eyes. "I know."

"Not in the kitchen, either," I added, and Alex nodded.

"And then you'll read my mind, or a ghost will tell you?" His voice was sceptical, which means we had raised him right.

"No," I said quietly, so Miles wouldn't hear. "That's not real. You're going to tell me."

"How?" Alex asked, his voice matching mine.

"That's a secret."

I stood up straight. "Alright. Everyone, close their eyes. Alex, go hide it."

Miles clapped his hands over his eyes immediately.

Claire turned her back and started rinsing something at the sink, but

I knew she'd be watching in the reflection of the window. She wasn't subtle. She didn't need to be.

I raised my hand and covered my eyes, too, also turning around so Alex wouldn't accuse me of peeking.

After a minute, Alex announced, "Done!"

I turned back around and lowered my hands. Alex stood in the middle of the room with his hands behind his back and his face blank in the way kids think is convincing.

Miles dropped his hands from his eyes dramatically. "Okay! Find it! Find it!"

"Okay, okay, okay," I said, stretching my fingers like I needed to warm up. "First, I need contact."

Alex immediately leaned back. "No."

"That's how the game works. Spirits can be very picky," I added for Miles.

Claire made a quiet sound that might've been a laugh.

"Please don't teach them how to do these things," Claire warned, and I gave a little shrug.

"It's a very lucrative market," I said, shooting Claire a smile.

Alex sighed long and hard, then stepped forward and held out his hands. I took his wrists lightly, two fingers over his pulse, and took the weight of his arms.

"So, just relax," I instructed. "Let your arms be nice and loose."

Alex nodded, but tensed anyway.

"Okay." I lowered my voice into my best fake-mystic tone. "I'm getting... something."

Miles leaned forward, eyes bright and wide.

Alex smirked and stared at me as though we were in a staring contest he intended to win.

I watched him, not only his eyes but his mouth, his breathing, the tension in his shoulders. I shifted one step to the left, toward the hallway.

Alex's gaze flicked right, back toward the living room.

I shifted again, guiding him further into the living room. His arm flexed for the slightest moment away from the direction we were going.

I stopped.

I let one of my hands wander from his wrist and slowly glided in around the room, my gaze still steady on his face. Watching.

As my hand hovered in the direction of the bookshelf on the far wall, Alex's mouth twitched, and his eyes flickered toward it then back to me.

I took a slow step toward the bookshelf wall. Alex's pulse jumped as I guided him toward it.

"Are they telling you, Dad?" Miles asked, and I gave him a small smile.

"They're telling me a lot," I said softly, and Alex rolled his eyes.

"Nuh uh," he muttered, though he wasn't sure of himself.

As we came to a stop next to the bookshelf, I felt Alex flinch away from it again.

I kept one hand gently holding his wrist, while the other rested on one of the shelves. I let my eyes scan down the bookshelf. Neat rows, a few titles stacked horizontally, and a book on a lower shelf that didn't look to be sitting quite right.

Alex stared straight ahead, jaw tight.

I hummed as my hand drifted across the spines of the books, my gaze flicking back to Alex, watching his eyes jump to the same book I noticed.

"You know," I started, my hand still dramatically hovering over different books on the shelf. "When I was a doctor, I used to make trips down to the pediatric ward."

"Peda attic?" Miles questioned.

"Pediatric," Claire said slowly. "A place in a hospital where kids go when they're sick."

"I used to go and do tricks for them," I continued, my hand getting closer and closer to the jutted book. "Card tricks, mind reading… this."

Miles held his breath theatrically.

Alex's pulse jumped again.

"And that's how your mother and I met," I said, finally letting go of Alex's arm, my other hand resting on the jutted-out book.

Alex's breath hitched.

I pulled the book out just enough to peek behind it, and the toy car was wedged neatly behind it, flush against the wall.

I plucked it out and held it up.

Miles screamed, "No way!"

Alex's face fell. "What!"

"Magic, isn't it?" I said with a smile, handing the toy car to Alex, who stared in disbelief.

"Teach me!" Alex said quickly, and Miles joined in, too.

"And me!"

Claire leaned on the counter, smiling. "I, personally, want to hear more about how we met."

"No!" Miles yelled. "Do another one!"

"Me and your mother have to get started on dinner," I said, and Miles crossed his arms and huffed.

Alex groaned. "But—"

"No buts. Clean this mess up," Claire said.

I handed the car back to Alex and ruffled his hair. He tried to dodge, failed. "You heard your mother."

Both boys mumbled under their breath before slowly moving around the room and picking up their mess.

The rest of the night came and went. Alex and Miles began to wind down as tiredness started to take hold of them.

Claire and I stood in the kitchen waiting for both of them to be finished brushing their teeth so we could settle them in bed. Alex came out first, dragging his feet as he did. "I don't wanna go to bed," he mumbled, a pout sitting on his face.

"You need to get some rest," Claire said, moving across the kitchen toward the hall where Alex stood.

"But I'm not tired!" Alex groaned, doing his best to stifle a yawn.

"Clearly," I said, following Claire. "Come on, Bud, sleep is good for you."

Alex scrunched his face up but didn't argue. He turned and shuffled down the hall toward his bedroom.

I turned my head as we walked past Miles' room. The door was open, the light was on, but it was empty. I let a chuckle slip out. "Oh, no. Miles is missing," I said with an overdramatic tone.

Alex stopped and looked around, and another yawn escaped him. "Is he doing it again?"

Claire sighed through her nose, but a smile played on her lips.

I kept my face neutral. "Doing what again?"

"Are you going to help us find Miles, Alex?" Claire asked, trying to keep her tone serious but failing.

"This is dumb," Alex muttered, though he still stayed where he was.

I turned around and let my gaze fall on the cupboard across from the bathroom.

It was the same every night. A ritual I wasn't too sure where it came from, but it was something Miles insisted on doing. Right before bed, he hid. In the same place. The same cupboard. Every night.

We all played along.

I walked slowly back down the hall, Claire and Alex close behind me.

"Miles?" Claire called, her tone was light. "Where did you go?"

Silence.

I took another slow step, scanning the hallway as if I didn't know where he was hiding.

Alex rubbed his eyes and leaned his shoulder into the wall. "He's in the cupboard."

Claire shot him a look. "Alex."

"What? He is."

"We don't know that," Claire said, perfectly straight-faced.

I nodded. "Exactly. We don't know anything."

From within the cupboard, a tiny inhale tried to be quiet and failed.

Claire's mouth twitched. She turned her head away.

"Miles," she called again, louder. "Where could he be?"

Stillness.

Alex's eyes flicked to the cupboard door.

I stepped past it on purpose as though I'd missed it. "Alright," I said, my voice casual. "Guess we'll just go to bed. Such shame. Guess I won't be able to show him a card trick."

A muffled sound came from behind the cupboard. Half laugh, half outrage.

Claire folded her arms. "Yep. Can't show a trick to a missing boy."

I hummed in agreement, looking down the hallway toward their room. "I guess Alex will have to get two—"

The cupboard door jerked open. Miles burst out as if he'd been launched, hair sticking up on one side, face bright with victory. "You didn't find me!"

"It's Miles!" Claire announced, feigning surprise. "Where were you?"

"In there," he said, pointing at the cupboard, like no one had seem him come out.

Alex sighed. "Every night."

I crouched and tapped Miles' nose once. "You're getting sloppier."

Miles' eyes widened. "No, I'm not."

"You made a noise. We heard," Alex muttered.

"I didn't!"

"You did."

Miles stuck his tongue out.

Claire leaned down and kissed Miles' forehead. "Alright. We didn't find you. Happy?. Now time for bed."

Miles tried to bargain immediately. "Can I hide again?"

"No," Claire and Alex said at the exact same time.

I hid my smile. "Two against one. Bad luck."

Miles huffed, but he took Claire's hand and let her steer him toward his room. Alex trudged after them, already halfway asleep. Miles climbed into bed, then popped back up. "Dad."

"Yes."

He pointed at the cupboard down the hall. "Tomorrow I'm going to hide somewhere else."

Claire paused mid-tuck and gave me a look.

I kept my expression blank. "Somewhere else?"

Miles grinned. "Yep."

Alex groaned in the hallway. "Don't."

Claire pulled the blanket up to Miles' chin. "You can hide wherever you like tomorrow. Tonight, you're sleeping."

A quick card trick later, we were in Alex's room saying goodnight.

"I don't need a trick, Dad," he mumbled, his eyes already closed.

"No?" I asked, and he shook his head.

"Just teach me how to do the other one."

"Okay. But you need to be well rested for it."

Alex gave a small nod.

"Goodnight, baby," Claire said, kissing his forehead then moving out of the room.

"Night, pal," I whispered before following Claire into the hall, closing the door behind me.

"I'm pretty sure he fell asleep as he nodded at me," I said, and Claire let out a small laugh.

"And did you hear Miles?" Claire asked, moving her arm around me. "A new hiding spot."

"We both know he won't pick a new one."

Claire hummed as we moved further down the hall toward our bedroom. The door sat directly in front of us at the end of it. She flicked the light on and stepped inside first. I followed and shut the door behind us.

"Don't," she said, turning to face me and studying my face.

"I didn't say anything," I said, raising my eyebrows.

She pulled her hair tie out and shook her hair loose. "It's more what's going on in your head. You're tense. Your mind's working too hard."

"I'm fine."

Claire blinked slowly, walking over to me and hooking a finger into the front of my shirt, tugging gently. "Your mind is somewhere else, Ryan."

I exhaled through my nose. "It's nothing."

"It's not nothing," she corrected calmly. "It's just not something you want to bring into this room."

Sometimes I hated that she could read me so well.

I stepped closer, put my hands on her hips, and rested my forehead against hers. The simple contact narrowed the world down to just us.

"I'm not in trouble," I said quietly.

"I didn't say you were," Claire replied. Her voice softened on the next part. "But I know you. You're trying to distract yourself."

I gave a small, resigned shrug. "You know what it's about?"

"I know it has to do with the blood on your clothes a few nights ago."

I took a deep breath. "He was just a kid," I muttered, and I felt Claire nod against me.

"You don't have to," she said softly. "Not now. You had a good day. Let's leave it at that."

"Yeah."

"I mean, you broke into a crime scene," she added, pulling away and looking up at me. "But it was a good day."

"Dante told you."

She smiled. "He messaged asking me to keep you on a leash."

I watched her fold back the sheets on the bed until my phone vibrated in my pocket. Continuous.

I pulled it from my pocket and looked at the name on the screen. Dante.

Claire's head lifted. She didn't ask. She just watched.

I answered. "Yeah?"

"It came in as a shooting," Dante said. *"Unconfirmed assailant. Paramedics recorded multiple gunshot wounds. 'Witness present.' That's the first entry."*

My stomach tightened. "So, it was logged properly."

"At first," he said. *"Then it got reclassified. Not by Bellwood. Not by Canden. By us."*

I sat on the edge of the bed. Claire sat beside me, her hand settling on my thigh. "Reclassified as suicide."

"Yeah," Dante replied. *"And the report we've got is thin. Narrative stripped*

back. No follow-up notes. The witness section is empty."

"Empty how?"

"As in there's a line that says 'civilian witness contacted'—and nothing attached. No transcript. No statement."

"That doesn't make sense. I gave them everything."

"I know," Dante said, voice flat. *"But your details aren't in the system. No name. No number. No address. It's like you were never there."*

Silence stretched.

"There's an attending list," Dante continued. *"Two units, mixed names, gaps. But the change happened after the initial report. Not at the scene."*

"So, someone got to it later."

"Yeah," Dante said. *"Someone inside the NBI. It got pushed through to be closed. That's how it lands in our system without anyone actually working it."*

I stared at the wall. "Can you see who did it?"

"Not cleanly," he said. *"The action logs route through a shared credential. Somebody didn't want their name on it."*

"Convenient."

"Yeah," Dante said flatly. *"Very."*

Claire shifted beside me. I didn't look at her, but felt her attention, steady and sharp.

Dante's voice lowered. *"Red, I need you to not do anything stupid."*

Silence sat between us.

Then Dante added, *"Don't go to Bellwood asking questions. Not yet. Let me find the person behind the change first."*

I breathed in, slow, and let it out. "Okay," I lied.

Dante heard it anyway. *"Red."*

"I said okay."

Dante sighed. *"Just… let me know if you're going to be an idiot."*

"I can't promise that," I said honestly, and Dante cursed under his breath.

"I gotta go. I'll let you know if I find anything else."

The call ended.

Down the hall, the boys slept as if the world were simple.

But it was far from it.

4

The house was quiet.

Not weekend-quiet, where silence was just a pause between arguments about snacks and someone crashing a toy car into a wall. This was Monday quiet. The kind that meant everyone has somewhere else to be.

Claire had left for work first. Shower, coffee, keys, and a quick kiss that tasted like toothpaste. Then I took the boys to school—bags, shoes, and a last-minute scramble for whatever they'd forgotten twice already. When I got back home and the door closed behind me, the house settled. Quiet.

I stood in the kitchen with a mug in my hands and realised I'd been holding it long enough that it had gone cold. I hadn't taken a sip.

My phone sat on the bench beside the sink. Face-up, waiting. The rational part of my brain kept repeating Dante's warning.

Wait.

Let him work. Let him find the name behind the reclassification before I put my own hands on anything. That part was right often enough that I listened to it in courtrooms and patient rooms. But it had never been the part that decided what I did in moments like this.

I tapped the screen once. No new notifications. I checked anyway, because the action mattered more than the result. It was something to do with my hands.

Claire would be doing her rounds by now. The boys would be in class. Somewhere there'd be a whiteboard, a teacher talking, a kid passing a note, Miles' attention drifting like it always did when he got bored. All of it continuing without me, without this thing that had latched onto my head and refused to let go.

Three nights ago, I'd walked into this house with blood on my clothes. Claire hadn't asked questions right away. She never did. She gave me space and then, later, looked at me in that way that said she already knew the shape of the truth.

I'd told her enough. Not details. Not the wet sound, the copper smell, or the way the kid's eyes stayed open. Just the outline.

And then, the next day, I'd waited for a call that never came.

That part didn't sit right. It still didn't. Not because cops always do the right thing—they don't—but because the system likes paper. It likes names and numbers and signatures. It likes having someone to point at later if a question gets asked.

They took my details. I gave them everything. Now Dante was telling me my name wasn't even in the file. That wasn't carelessness. That was effort.

I set the mug down on the bench. I stared at the phone again, then forced myself to look away. I wasn't anxious. Not in the way Claire would call me out on. My chest wasn't tight. My breathing was normal. I wasn't spiralling. I was focused. But right now, there wasn't anything I could focus on.

I walked to the sink and ran the tap, tipping my untouched drink down the sink.

A witness doesn't vanish by accident.

If someone inside the NBI had touched that file, they'd done it for a reason. And whatever that reason was, it had started before Dante ever opened his mouth. Before I even knew the kid's name.

My phone buzzed once as I shut the tap off. It was Dante.

Nothing yet. Give me today.

I stared at it. That message didn't mean Dante hadn't looked. It meant he'd looked and hit resistance. The kind you don't get from honest delays. The kind that came with missing witness details and a suicide label slapped over three gunshot wounds.

Okay was all I sent back. A small lie.

I went back to the sink, grabbed my mug, dried it, and put it away. As though completing small tasks could keep the rest of my brain from running.

It didn't.

I tried the couch for five minutes. Tried the kitchen again. Tried the back terrace, where the sun hit the boards in a thin sheet, and the backyard sat empty except for a couple of plastic toys abandoned in the grass. The yard looked wrong without the boys in it. Too tidy. Too still.

That was when I stopped pretending I was going to wait. Grabbing my keys, I left peace behind me.

The drive to Lakeside Park took a little longer than it did at night. Traffic existed now. People in sensible cars, in work clothes, moving with purpose. A delivery van pulled out in front of me. Someone jogged along the footpath, headphones in, face blank with determination.

As the park came into view, I noticed how different it looked during the day. A neat green space framed by low fencing and council signage, the sort of place locals came to get some fresh air. Dog walkers. Parents with prams. Retirees with coffee cups and slow conversations.

The car park had cars in it now. A line of them, not full but getting close.

The lights above the lot weren't flickering. In daylight, they looked harmless. Switched off and waiting for darkness.

I parked in the far corner. Away from anyone else. Starting into the open and watching day-to-day life unfold before me.

I shut the engine off. The quiet inside the car was immediate.

I let my mind roll. Thinking of that night. The gunshots. Casey's face. The gaps that came after. The missing parts. The fact that the system had been scrubbed clean around me like I'd never knelt on that path with blood soaking through my shirt.

Someone had decided my presence was inconvenient. That didn't happen by accident. I got out and walked toward the entrance. The council plaque declaring it a treasured community space looked even more smug in daylight. Fresh stickers on the gate—dog owners reminded to pick up after their pets, people reminded to keep to the path, a faded missing cat flyer.

Normal.

The path curved around the lake in the same lazy sweep. The water was a dull blue-grey now, rippled by wind and small movement. Ducks skated across it. A man sat at the edge of the water on one of the benches, tossing something out toward them.

I stayed on the path and let my eyes adjust to seeing this place without darkness.

It didn't help. The memory of that night overlaid everything anyway.

The working streetlight. The bench. The kid's hoodie. The way his hands had come up like surrender. The muzzle flashes—brief, bright, and gone.

I walked with my hands in my pockets, shoulders easy, and pace normal. Not hurried.

As I came around the bend, the bench appeared. Same one. Same placement. Same scuffed timber slats. In daylight, it looked stupidly ordinary.

A woman sat on it now with a takeaway coffee, scrolling her phone. A small dog lay at her feet, leash slack, eyes half closed. When she glanced up at me, her look slid off my face without snagging. I was just another man walking the loop.

I kept going past her by a few metres, then slowed, turned my head, and let my feet carry me to the spot where the lamp's light would have landed at night. There was no marker. No stain. No tape. Nothing to suggest the concrete had held someone's blood three days ago.

That bothered me more than it should have. Not because I wanted a shrine. Because the absence felt like the whole point. Scrubbed clean so the world could move on.

I stopped where I thought he'd fallen and closed my eyes. I had to work with what I had.

That night, the victim had been under the light. The shooter had been in the darkness to his left, off the path, in the tree line. I turned until I was oriented the same way. Lake behind me. Path stretching to my right. Trees thick in front of me, with bushland that ran deeper than it looked. In daylight, it still provided cover. Too many trunks. Too much low scrub. Too many sightlines that broke cleanly at ten metres.

I walked a slow half-circle, tracking angles. Where would the shooter stand to get three hits and still remain unseen to someone on the path? The line of sight wouldn't have been perfect. He'd missed one shot.

That mattered.

People who knew how to shoot didn't usually miss from that range unless they were firing through cover or moving. So, the shooter had either been obstructed, rushed, or they didn't know how to shoot.

I looked at the ground where the tree line started. The grass gave way to old leaves, then low scrub. I stepped off the concrete and into the shade, careful with my footing on the uneven ground.

No tape. No cones. No obvious markers left behind. It looked like nothing had happened here.

Except my brain kept putting the body back on the path.

I moved deeper, a few metres at a time, stopping to look back toward the lamppost and the bench. I held my hands up in front of me, thumbs angled, using them as rough guides for distance and direction.

From here, the shooter would've had the victim slightly angled. The first shot could've been the cleanest—surprise, a stable stance, a target that didn't move yet. After that, panic. The victim jerks, drops, turns, and the angle gets worse. The shooter adjusts.

But he has to be quick.

I shifted left, then right, searching for the best angle through the trunks. There were a few. None of them were perfect. If he'd taken a step or two, he could've had a better line of sight. But moving made more variables. Instability. More chances to miss.

I took another slow half-circle and stopped, listening, because it was quiet enough that I could. Birds. Distant traffic. A jogger's footsteps were somewhere behind me on the main path.

No voices close enough to care about me, which was useful.

I crouched near a patch of dirt and leaves. If there had been shell casings, they'd be long gone. Cops would've taken them. Bagged them and put them into evidence. Still, I looked.

I scanned the ground for anything that didn't belong: disturbed leaves, snapped twigs, or an indentation where someone had planted a foot and shifted weight. The sort of detail you only find if you know where to look and have enough time to be annoying about it.

And I had the time.

Which is why I saw it. A small cluster of broken branches at shin height. It didn't mean it was anything. It could've been an animal moving through the brush. A kid moving to retrieve a ball. The police looking for evidence. But maybe it could've been the shooter escaping.

I followed the trace of movement. The bushland thickened quickly.

I moved in a line that made the most sense, even after I couldn't see clear signs of movement. Away from the open path, and into cover that would break sightlines fast.

Every ten metres, I stopped and looked back.

I could no longer see the lamp post, and the bench had disappeared behind the trees. The main path and the people using it were no longer in sight. The shooter hadn't needed to run far to become invisible. Even in daylight.

The ground sloped slightly, then levelled. I caught another sign of movement: a narrow scuff in the dirt where someone had cut a corner instead of staying on whatever faint track existed. It was off the beaten path. It was a decision made. Someone who knew where it would lead.

I followed it.

It wasn't long before the trees opened up near a service fence. It was an old chain link, partially hidden by vines. A gap near the bottom had been forced wider at some point, enough for most people to fit through. The ground around it was worn, and the dirt compacted. A human-made shortcut.

I ducked through it.

On the other side, the ground changed under my shoes. Fewer leaves and dirt, more compacted gravel and old concrete. A service lane ran along the park boundary, tight and half-shadowed even in daylight. The kind of lane built for bins, deliveries, and people who didn't want to be seen from the street.

I walked along the fence slowly, eyes moving, not just forward but up and down the lane. Rear doors. Roller shutters. Fire exits with flaking paint. A faded "No Parking" sign bolted to brick. The gap in the fence behind me wasn't the only access point; I spotted another section further down where the vines had been cut back, and the wire sagged, as if someone had tested it more than once.

The ground around both spots was worn. Not fresh or obvious—just used. Dirt was packed down where shoes had passed through in the same path repeatedly.

I stopped as I reached an alleyway that connected to the service lane. A straight shot to the main road of The Strip.

I got a strange sense of familiarity. I had been here before when I was younger. Not in the exact same spot, but close by.

I stared down the alley, my eyes tracing the walls and above the rusted doors that led down it. There were a few cameras. Some angled toward a loading bay. Others looking at the dumpsters lining the walls. I had a feeling that most of them didn't work and were only for decoration. Those of them that did work wouldn't be helpful.

Something I had learned when I was a kid running through The Strip is if you knew what you were doing and where you were going, staying unseen wasn't difficult. It was designed to be that way. No matter if you were heading East or West.

I began walking down the alleyway, leaving the service lane behind me. I stopped near one of the back doors and looked for cameras. I kept moving, letting my pace match the rhythm of someone who belonged here. No hovering. No obvious scanning. Just walking and taking in details.

Halfway down the alley, the sound of traffic became clearer as I closed in on the main street. It wasn't a roar. It was more a constant shuffle of engines, tyres over patched asphalt, and the occasional horn that felt like someone trying to remind the world they existed.

I slowed before I reached the mouth of the alley and took a second to listen.

Footsteps. A distant conversation. A metal shutter being pulled down somewhere. No sirens. No urgency. Just life moving forward.

I stepped out onto the sidewalk.

The Strip looked like it always had, which was the point. Businesses packed close, a few tired apartment buildings tucked above them, and side roads that peeled off toward housing at either end. It was maintained, to an extent. Pieces of both the East side and the West side snaked their way in. A constant battle for how it should look. Neither won.

Neutral territory meant nobody took full responsibility for it.

I started walking, not fast, not hesitant. If someone watched me, I wanted them to see a guy out for a walk. If someone else watched me, I wanted them to get bored quickly.

I kept my attention on the details that mattered. Lines of sight. Exits. Places someone could stop without being noticed. Places someone could leave quickly.

I tracked the alley I'd come out of and then looked along The Strip in both directions.

The shooter didn't need to run down an alley and onto The Strip. They could have stayed along the service lane, walked along the fence and circled back around on the East Side.

Or they could have ran across the main road and off into the West side.

Unfortunately, their final destination mattered. It would change how I look and what I was looking for. There was no easy way to find that information out, though.

I couldn't even be certain I had followed the same path the shooter took through the trees. It was an old trail that many others would have used.

I could only go off assumptions and logic. Logically, that path made the most sense. It was quick, easy, and out of sight. Even if I had run past Casey's body and into the tree line, I would have lost the shooter almost instantly.

So, I had no evidence. But I did have probability. That was still something.

I walked a block and then crossed at the corner, more out of instinct than need. The pattern of my movement mattered less than the way I was building the map in my head. Park. Fence gap. Service lane. Alley. Strip. Side roads. Back lots. Each point gave the shooter a choice.

Each choice left a trail for me that was harder to follow.

I kept walking, letting my gaze travel over signs, doorways, and windows. A small takeout place. A laundromat. A rundown barbershop. A pawn shop with a sun-faded display. The sort of businesses that did fine in neutral zones because people paid cash and didn't ask questions.

I stopped at a set of traffic lights and glanced across to the other side of the road. Pedestrians wandered across the street without waiting for the lights to allow them. The traffic was light enough to allow them. It always was.

I glanced down the street, taking in the surroundings I used to know so well, until they landed on a sign that looked like it had recently been redone.

'Mamma's'

I felt something tug in my chest, like an old memory trying to snag my attention.

It looked almost the same as it did when I was younger, and Dante and I would start and end our days tucked away in the back of the café. We didn't go there because it was good food, only because it was cheap and out of the way.

And because it was one place you could sit with your back to the door and not have to worry too much.

I sighed, pulling my phone out and looking at the last text Dante had sent. There was nothing new. No new information or guidelines on where to go. Or that's what I thought, until the phone started ringing in my hand and Dante's name filled the screen.

"I was thinking about you," I said, checking the street before crossing.

"Please tell me you have pants on," Dante said, his humour falling flat.

"I'd have to start charging you if I answer that." I reached the other side of the road, and my gaze found Mamma's again. "What have you got?"

"I've got your house in front of me, but no you," Dante said, his voice steady, but I could hear the annoyance.

"I'm out for a walk." I shrugged. "Why are you at my house?"

"I'd rather not talk about things that would get me fired from the NBI while at the NBI," Dante pointed out. *"Please don't tell me you're being stupid."*

"I'm not being stupid," I assured, slipping to the alley beside Mamma's and resting against the wall.

"Where are you?" Dante asked with a sigh. *"I'd rather do this in person."*

"Remember Mamma's?"

"You're at The Strip?" Dante questioned, and I could almost feel him cursing at the sky. *"Red, that's you being stupid."*

"I've just been looking."

"You're looking usually turns into touching."

A pause.

"Mamma's, yeah?" Dante asked, and I hummed.

"They changed the sign," I pointed out.

"They change it every few years." I heard the engine of Dante's car kick over. *"Give me forty."*

"I'll be waiting," I said before hanging up and shoving my phone back into my pocket.

I stayed in the alley after the call, letting the noise of The Strip settle back into its usual rhythm—tyres over patched asphalt, a half-laugh from someone smoking near a doorway, and the distant clack of a shutter coming down.

I pushed off the wall and moved back onto the main road, rounding the corners and walking into Mamma's, letting the bell announce me like I belonged here.

And that's all I needed; to act like I belonged. It would help me blend in better than any lie would. I glanced around the café. It was the same in all the ways that mattered. Cramped tables, scuffed floors, and the kind of lighting that made everyone look a little tired.

I walked to a booth at the back of the café and slid in. A waitress followed me over and poured me a coffee before shuffling away again. I held the mug in my hands and let the heat spread through them as I let everything I'd seen on the way here play back in my mind again.

There had to be something there. And I was going to pull it into the light.

5

Mamma's had never tried to be charming. It was a rectangle of tired tables, a counter that had seen too many elbows, and a floor that had absorbed too many spills.

I sat in the back booth with my shoulders loose. The mug sat between my hands. The heat was real, which was already an improvement on my morning, and I let it soak into my fingers without taking a sip.

People didn't look twice at a man alone in a café on The Strip. Not unless he gave them a reason. The Strip wasn't the kind of place where someone lingered over a flat white for the love of it. It got people who wanted cheap, quick, or quiet. Sometimes all three.

I watched the front door without staring at it. The counter, the staff, the small, repeating patterns that made the room predictable. The waitress drifted between tables like she'd done this for years and stopped caring a long time ago. Two men by the window spoke with their heads close together, hands visible, their voices low enough that it wasn't conversation so much as negotiation. A woman near the middle table scrolled her phone with her back to the wall, a takeaway cup untouched, eyes flicking up each time the bell rang.

A 'HELP WANTED' poster fluttered each time the door opened as though announcing it was there and hoping someone would answer the call.

I rolled the mug between my palms and tried not to think about the park. That didn't work. The memory was there under everything.

Three nights ago, there had been a kid under a lamp post and blood in my hands. Now there was a mug and a booth and the faint smell of grease. The contrast didn't settle very well in my brain.

Dante had said to wait. He had said he had found nothing yet, and it had been the kind of nothing that meant a door had been closed in his face.

So, I was doing what I could do: walking paths, mapping exits, and trying to find the pieces that were taken away.

The bell rang again.

I didn't turn my head. I didn't need to. The room shifted slightly. It wasn't dramatic. It never was. It was the way the air changed when someone walked in who carried tension like a weapon. Conversations didn't stop, but they dipped. The waitress didn't stiffen, but she glanced up. The woman with her back to the wall paused her scrolling.

Dante crossed the café in a straight line, hands empty, pace normal, eyes moving without looking like they were moving. He didn't wear the bureau on his sleeve, but it sat on him anyway—cleaner haircut than the Strip deserved, posture that came from being told where to stand for too many years.

He was the only person I knew who could fit seamlessly into both the East and West sides. He coexisted out of necessity, and there was a certain amount of respect that earned him.

He slid into the booth opposite me and placed his hands on the table.

"You look like shit," he said, waving to the waitress. "It's the lighting." I gestured to the dim lights above us. "You know me--usually a solid ten."

Dante hummed as the waitress came over and poured him a coffee before vanishing as quickly as she had come. His eyes flicked to my hands. To my face. To the space behind me. He didn't bother hiding it. Dante had never been good at pretending he wasn't watching.

"What're you trying to figure out there, big guy?" I asked, taking a small sip of my stone-cold coffee. The forty minutes had not been kind to it.

"How much of an idiot you've been."

I gave him a look.

He gave one back. The same one he'd been giving me since we were kids, and one of us had done something stupid, and the other one had to decide whether to be loyal or sensible. Dante liked to pretend he'd grown out of that. He hadn't. Neither had I.

We also never chose to be sensible.

"Before I tell you anything," he said quietly, "I hate you."

"That's… fair," I said with a small nod. "Pray tell, though."

"It's been a stressful few days. And I know it's only going to get worse."

"You're welcome."

"Red," Dante warned, and I let a small smile slip through.

"I know. But this is the right thing to do. Whatever's happened…"

"We need to look into."

We sat with that. The booth was too small for the amount of history in it. The vinyl seat creaked under Dante's weight like it didn't approve.

"I'm surprised you were able to make it out here," I said, breaking the silence.

"Yeah, I'm meant to be looking into something else," Dante admitted, taking a sip of his coffee. "This is just a detour."

"Let's make the detour quick then."

Dante nodded, leaning back in the seat.

"I haven't found anything," he started, a quick exhale escaping him. "Not any more than what I already told you."

"Right," I muttered, my voice staying steady. "You wanted to talk. So, you must've hit something."

Dante's jaw tightened. "I hit a wall. A real one."

"You weren't kidding when you said you had nothing."

"This is a different kind of nothing." He lowered his voice. "I can see the file exists. I can see the label. I can see certain entry headers. But the deeper layers? The audit trail? It's like someone put it behind a wall."

I frowned. "So, it wasn't a metaphor."

"It's restricted access," he clarified, his voice tinged with irritation. "Not normal case restrictions. Not 'only the assigned team can open this'. This is… someone burying it."

"That shouldn't be possible, right?" I asked, and felt my mouth tighten around the words. "Not without a reason logged."

"That's what I thought."

Dante paused, taking another sip of coffee and letting his mug hover. "I tried three routes. Standard intake path, internal search, and cross-referencing through incident logs. Every time, I can get to the same point and then it stops. Denied access."

"Meaning someone decided you don't have permission."

"Meaning someone decided a lot of people don't have permission," he corrected, and he tapped one finger against his mug like he wanted it to be someone's throat. "And that decision didn't come from a computer."

I didn't let myself react. Not outwardly. Inside, it settled into place with an uncomfortable kind of neatness. "Okay. So, you can't access it."

"I can access parts. I can access enough to know it's been cut. That's the problem."

I lifted my eyebrows.

Dante leaned forward slightly, elbows close, taking up less space. It made him look calmer than he was. "The file has seams. Places where something used to exist. Fields that should be populated. Metadata that references attachments that aren't there."

"Like the witness statement," I offered, and Dante nodded, his eyes holding mine.

"And like the narrative section. There are headings. There are timestamps. There are markers for edits. But the content is empty or replaced by a summary line that says nothing."

"Administratively closed," I said, and watched his face.

He nodded once. "Yeah. That part I can see. The pathway. The handoff. The label change. But not who."

"Because shared credentials."

Dante's mouth flattened. "Because shared credentials."

Shared credentials were a sin. Shared credentials were what people used when they wanted plausible deniability and enough distance to claim it was a mistake. It was the equivalent of wiping fingerprints off a knife but leaving the blood on it.

"So, someone inside the NBI did it," I said, keeping my voice low and steady.

"Someone inside the building, or someone with access or a way to get around it. And here's the other part..." He hesitated, just long enough that I knew he didn't like saying it. "If I push harder, it pings. Like a flag. A crimson one. Someone gets a report. Someone asks why I'm digging into a suicide that was never assigned, and that's been closed off."

I let that sit. "The more you dig, the more likely the cave collapses."

"And I've already dug pretty far," Dante pointed out. "And you're starting to knock on the support beams."

He said it like a joke, but his eyes didn't match it.

"So, we get some more support beams," I said with a shrug, but Dante shook his head.

"Or we dig somewhere else."

He let out a slow breath through his nose, and I watched him carefully. The shift in his eyes. The twitch at the side of his mouth. The rolling of his thumb against his mug. He was keeping something from me. Not lying. Just not telling.

My expression stayed flat. "Secrets make you age, you know."

"Don't read me, Red." He fell silent for a minute, then sighed. "I can't give you a neat file. I can't give you a name on the action log. I can't even give you half the entries without triggering something."

"But you do have something," I said quietly. "So, what do you have?"

Dante's eyes lifted. He held mine briefly, then nodded once.

Decision made.

He reached into his jacket carefully. He pulled out a small, folded piece of paper—creased twice and soft at the edges. It had been folded with care and precision. Most likely out of anxiety and stress.

He slid it across the table, face down. I didn't touch it straight away. "If this is a love note, my wife is going to be very upset."

"This is what I have," Dante said flatly. "And don't flip it like you're in a movie."

I flipped it like I was in a movie.

It was a note. Quick block letters, tight spacing. Not his usual handwriting—he'd always been neater than this—but it was his. I'd seen him scribble under pressure enough times to recognise it.

"What is this?"

"A place to dig," Dante said. "I can't pull the full case file, but some fields bleed into other systems. Peripheral stuff. Stuff I can find outside of the system."

My eyes tracked the first line.

Casey Edwards

Under it, an address. West Side. Not vague West Side either—an actual street, an actual number. Something you could put into a map and drive to.

I felt my stomach tighten. "You're sure?"

Dante's jaw flexed. "I'm pretty sure."

I looked up. "How'd you get it?"

Dante leaned in slightly. "One thing I can access without raising anything, is arrest records. Casey has one."

"Which had an address attached to it."

"I then ran the address through some utility checks that aren't part of our system."

"Utility checks?" I asked, folding the paper again.

"Bunch of different utilities run through a property," Dante explained, rolling his shoulders slightly. "Admin departments verify residency using those utilities as well as council rates and other stuff. I can access that without raising any flags."

"And you did that."

"I did enough to confirm the address wasn't a ghost. That Casey's name is still attached to it."

I stared at the folded paper again. Casey Edwards. West Side address.

The kid's face flickered in my head for half a second. Hoodie. Blood. The way his eyes had tried to tell me something I couldn't read. I forced the image down. Now wasn't the time to be reliving the memory.

"What was the arrest for?"

"Possession," Dante said quickly. "Picked up on the East Side. North, near Hartsville. No charges."

"No charges?" I pushed, and Dante shrugged.

"Slap on the wrist."

"West Side kid gets caught with drugs, and he gets shuffled back home. Who processed him?"

"I didn't look," Dante admitted. "Wasn't something I thought was important."

"It's probably not."

Silence settled between us again. The café moved around us; quiet but steady. Dante shifted and pulled his phone out before running his hand down his face.

"I need to go. Techs are at a scene, and I gotta head there."

"Big one?" I asked, letting my eyes study his face again.

"Not sure. Body's already been taken. Case just got handed to us."

I nodded and waited for Dante to get up. He didn't.

"Old age stopping your legs from working?" I joked, though Dante's face hardened.

"I gave you the address knowing what you're going to do," he said slowly, stowing his phone away. "But you need to be smart, Red."

"Always am," I assured him, but he shook his head.

"You haven't been there for a long time. And they're gonna remember you. The way you left."

"I'll keep a low profile."

"I know there's no point in me telling you to wait. To let me do it."

"Dante," I said, leaning back in my seat. "I can't just sit on my hands. Besides, they're your neighbours. I doubt they're going to take kindly to you snooping around."

"Yeah, they're my neighbours," Dante confirmed. "Means they'll be lenient if they catch me snooping. You? Not so much."

I held his gaze.

"I remember the streets," I said quietly. "I can get out quick if it comes to it."

"It's not the same as it was, Red," Dante warned, looking out the window. "It's more on edge these days. I stay out of it and keep to myself, and even I can feel it."

"In and out. That's all I'm doing." I paused, my gaze following Dante's. "You know I'll see more than you."

"You know, it's comments like that which make you hard to get along with."

I shrugged and looked back at Dante.

We sat in the quiet, letting the café move around us. The two men near the window were still talking hurriedly. The staff moved sluggishly, doing not much of anything. And the woman on her phone got up from her booth and headed to the counter.

Dante broke the silence. "Nothing stupid," he said, sliding out of the booth and standing up. "In and out."

"When have I ever done anything stupid?" I asked, following his actions and standing.

"We'll be here for the rest of our lives." Dante huffed and watched as I placed money down on the table. "I'll be at a scene. Lots of ears around me. Don't call unless you really need me."

"Aye-aye," I said, giving a small salute, and he rolled his eyes without returning the salute.

"Text me when you're home."

"I'll send you a flirty pic, how's that?"

"Can't wait," he said, and then he was already moving. No lingering. No goodbyes. The bell rang as he pushed through the door, and the café swallowed the gap he left behind.

I stayed standing, looking around the café one more time. Memories trying to stick to me like glue. I shook them off and headed to the exit.

Outside, the Strip hit me with heat and exhaust. The traffic wasn't heavy, but it never fully stopped. The slow shuffle of cars and people.

The note was still pressed into my hand. The name and address were planted firmly in my mind, waiting for me to act on it. I shoved the piece of paper into my pocket and kept walking. Heading back the way I came. My eyes tracing all the same things as before. Nothing was different.

I slipped back down the same alley, my pace remaining steady. The Strip fell away behind me in fragments—sounds muted by brick, daylight narrowed by fences and loading bays. Once I hit the service lane, I turned down it and walked along the fence. My eyes landed on a man leaning against a wall to my right, cigarette in his mouth, eyes following me. I gave him a small nod. He returned it.

Courtesy. Respect. A currency once you hit The Strip and the West.

I kept walking until I found the gap in the chain link again. Vines, wire, worn dirt at the base. The park on the other side looked almost polite in the sun. I moved back through the trees, my eyes scanning the ground. New footprints were packed into the dirt. More snapped branches around ankle height. I exhaled slowly through my nose.

When I hit the main path in the park, I saw it was busier than it was before. More people with their dogs, more people out for a walk. I kept looking ahead and wound my way around the path to the parking lot, sliding into my car once I reached it. I kicked the engine over, then pulled the piece of paper out again, reading the address.

I knew the suburb. It wasn't too far away from where I had lived when I was younger. I folded it again and tossed it into the cup holder, then pulled out of the parking lot. The road out of the park was slow— families, dog walkers, people taking their time like the world wasn't capable of snapping in half in a single night. I kept my speed steady and my eyes moving.

It wasn't long before I found myself turning onto The Strip, and I drove along it, taking it in from a different angle. My car rolled past Mamma's then I came to a stop a red light, my indicator on to turn left.

The light changed. I turned and I almost felt the change instantly. There was no sign. No barrier. No indication that things were different, but they were. The asphalt changed first. Then the buildings. Then the faces on the footpaths. I was over the line. Into the West.

6

The asphalt was patched in uneven squares, though the potholes still outnumbered the repairs. Streetlights leaned a fraction too far in directions they shouldn't. Power lines drooped low enough that they made the sky feel smaller. I rolled through the streets, swerving to miss what potholes I could. Ignoring the looks from other drivers on the road who were no doubt thinking my car was too nice to be on this side of town.

My eyes drifted to the sidewalks and side streets, taking in the people who made the world around them seem lived-in. Men on milk crates near a corner store. Two people passing a small bag of something between each other with no urgency. A kid too young to be leaning with a cigarette pinched between two fingers like he'd done it a hundred times already.

No one out here tried to hide anything.

That wasn't the part that made my jaw tighten. That part was familiar. I'd grown up with it. I'd watched it become normal because it was normal for us. What got me was how much of it there was. It was common when I was a kid, but it was still hidden. Now, it was out in the open.

My mind tinged with how Dante felt about it. Not that he had a choice in the matter. He may have been an agent at the NBI, but this was his home. The fewer waves he made, the better.

Leaving it to the local police was the only real option.

My car continued to roll through the neighbourhood. Boarded-up shopfronts with open signs still glowing behind the plywood. Metal shutters were half down, as if the businesses had decided to keep working but refused to look hopeful while doing it. A butcher with faded lettering, a barber with a cracked pole that still turned, and a small grocery with a security screen that had been repaired so many times it looked like a patchwork quilt.

The West had always been rough around the edges, but it hadn't always looked like the edges were all that was left. I kept my hands loose on the wheel, eyes moving. Not darting. Not panicked. Just collecting. Taking in what information I could.

The address Dante had given me sat in the cup holder, bouncing slightly as I drove over the uneven road. I didn't need to look at it again. I'd read it enough already, and it had carved itself into the map in my head as the old streets I used to roam flooded back into my mind.

A few turns. A stretch of road with a pothole I remembered, only bigger now. A corner where the fence was curled over in half with barbed wire wrapped around it. I took it all in without letting my face change.

Then I saw him.

Same lean. Same cigarette. Same posture that looked casual until you noticed the way his weight was set—ready to move if he needed to. He wasn't right up on the curb, but he didn't have to be. He was close enough for me to see him clearly, even in the shadow of the building he sheltered under.

His eyes tracked my car as I passed. Not curiosity. Recognition.

My stomach tightened around nothing. It could've been a coincidence. The Strip bled into the West. People drifted between them all day. He could've just been one of those who drifted. But I had seen him in the service lane. I'd clocked the way he watched me there And now he was here.

That wasn't a coincidence.

The smart move was to keep driving, then turn around and go back to the East side. Back home. Pretend I hadn't crossed a line I'd spent years convincing myself I'd left behind.

The smart move was also the one I wasn't here to make. I kept going.

The house was on a quieter street that still wasn't quiet. It was the kind where the noise didn't disappear, it just became background: a TV behind thin walls, music from a car parked with its windows down, a distant argument that didn't need an audience.

I slowed as I approached and did one pass. A slow roll. Casual. Eyes straight. My peripheral vision was doing all the work. The house wasn't a house in the way the East would call it one. It was a single-storey place with an old veranda and paint that had given up years ago. The front yard was more dirt than grass, and the fence that ran around it was full of holes and incomplete. A car sat out front on blocks. All four wheels were long gone.

There was movement inside the house. Shadows shifting behind curtains that weren't quite closed. A silhouette crossed the front room and then disappeared.

I kept going to the end of the block and turned around. I did a second pass. Slower. A kid on a bike watched me with open suspicion before rolling past me.

My eyes flickered to a few different people loitering around between houses and down a laneway. My skin prickled, and my stomach twisted. I was being watched. The way they held themselves and positioned—they were waiting for something, or someone, to tell them to move.

I must've been the trigger.

I swallowed, and continued with what I came here to do.

I parked two houses down and killed the engine. The silence inside my car arrived too quickly. I forced my breathing to stay even as I watched the street behind me in the rearview mirror.

Nothing obvious. The same people I saw before, shifting. But no one rushing out, no immediate confrontation. Just the usual West Side rhythm: people existing in the open, watching everything because they had to. I shifted my gaze to the house. Front door shut. Curtains still. Then a flicker again—someone peering, maybe, or just moving through the room.

If Casey lived here, someone else lived here now, too, or lived here with him. Family. Friends. Someone. Maybe someone who had information. Someone who might know why he'd been at Lakeside Park last Wednesday.

I forced myself to wait another minute, then got out.

Closing the car door quietly, I walked toward the house without rushing. The trick was to look like you had a reason to be there, even if your reason was only in your head. No one paid attention to you unless you gave them a reason to.

My eyes stayed forward, but my awareness widened.

A car idling at the corner. Two men near it, pretending they weren't watching. A figure at the far end of the street stepping out from behind a fence and angling their body to track my movement. And then, across the street, a flash of a cigarette and that same lean.

He'd followed me.

His face had a ring of familiarity to it. Maybe someone I used to know when I was younger. But age had taken any resemblance I could hold on to.

I felt the urge to turn back. To take the hint. To leave before this became a problem I couldn't talk my way out of.

Then I remembered the kid's eyes. The way they'd stayed open. The fear. The question that sat in them.

'Why?

I kept walking. Up close, the house looked worse. A crack running down the wall near the window. What was remaining of the fence sagged with parts almost along the ground. The front steps were worn smooth in the middle where too many feet had stepped in the same place.

I stopped at the gate, not touching it yet. Just listening.

From inside, low voices. Not clear enough to catch words. Then there was movement. Someone pacing or just moving from room to room. I leaned slightly, eyes flicking to the mailbox. No name. Or the name had been stripped off long ago.

I stepped back. And that was when I heard boots on gravel behind me. Not running. Not trying to surprise me. Deliberate. A warning that the encounter was happening whether I wanted it or not.

I turned slowly.

There were men behind me—more than a couple, less than a crowd. Enough to make the street feel smaller. They fanned out with casual purpose.

Angelo stood at the front.

For a second, my brain tried to overlay him with the last version I'd known. Eighteen. A little scrawny with too much confidence, and a grin that always looked one step away from a fistfight. That version didn't fit anymore.

This Angelo was thicker around the shoulders, older in the eyes, and scarred in places that told you the West didn't do mercy. His hair was cut close. His jaw was set like a lock. The grin was gone.

He looked at me like I was a debt he'd never agreed to forgive. "Well," he said slowly. "Ryan fucking Red."

His voice was calm though it carried an edge like a razor that could slice through anything in its way. I let my hands hang loose at my sides.

My palms open in a way that told everyone I wasn't planning on doing anything stupid.

"Angelo," I said, forcing a smile. "It's good to see you."

He didn't respond right away. He tilted his head, his eyes scanning my clothes, my car, and how I was holding myself.

Then he smiled. No warmth. No humour. "Climbed down from your throne to visit some old friends?" Angelo's voice mixed with the gravel and settled like a memory in my mind.

The men behind him shifted, small and practised. Reminding me the numbers weren't in my favour.

"Just passing through, really," I said, my voice steady, though I didn't feel it.

"With a pit stop in The Strip. Stephen was meant to be your warning." Angelo gestured his head subtly to the man who had followed me from service lane.

As the name hit my ears, his face focused in my mind. I did remember Stephen. He'd been someone who had skulked in the background when I was a kid. Always lurking around my parents and Angelo's father.

He would have to be in his seventies now, and it showed. "Well," I said carefully. "Stephen is hard to pick out of a crowd these days."

"Maybe your memory just isn't what it used to be." Angelo shifted, taking a step forward.

I didn't move.

"Because if it was," Angelo continued. "You'd know better than to come back here."

"I'm just—" I started, but Angelo cut me off.

"Being somewhere you don't belong."

My heart beat unevenly as I kept my eyes trained on Angelo. He was calm on the outside. But beneath it, he was angry. I could see it in his eyes. How they scanned over me. How his jaw set, and his shoulders squared. It wasn't aggressive, but it was settling under the surface.

"Look, I'll be out of your hair soon," I said, raising my hands defensively. "Trust me, I have a family to get home to."

"Family," Angelo echoed, and a few of the guys behind him snorted.

Angelo lifted a hand and the sound stopped. He hadn't needed to raise his voice. That was new. Old Angelo would've enjoyed the performance. This one didn't waste energy on it.

"You got kids?" Angelo asked, though I knew it wasn't a real question. "They gonna be con artists, too?"

The words hit heavier than they should. Bearing down on me like an anchor.

"I don't do that anymore," I said quietly, and Angelo let out a single bark-like laugh.

"Yeah?" he turned slightly to face the men behind him. "If y'all don't remember Red here, he used to be a practiced bullshitter."

A laugh rippled around me and my jaw tensed before I forced myself to relax. Angelo turned back to me.

"From, what, thirteen?" Angelo continued. "He used to wander over to the East. Rich suburbs. Broken families. Widows. Anyone who was desperate enough. They'd pay a fortune for you to lie to them."

"Just did what Mum and Dad taught me," I mumbled, my eyes not leaving Angelo.

"They also teach you to abandon your family?" Angelo questioned, taking another step closer. "All that money. Could've made a difference around here but you just… left."

I didn't respond. I didn't know how. I had tried to leave the West behind me, but pieces of it always clung like dirt under my fingernails.

Angelo watched me sit in the silence. "Nothing to say?" he asked quietly. "That must be a first."

"What do you want me to say?" I asked, and Angelo exhaled hard.

He glanced once, quickly, down my body, then back to my face. "New clothes. Fresh haircut. Clean skin. That says a lot."

"It says I have a job. Well, had. And soap."

Angelo's mouth pulled into something that wasn't a smile.

His guys shifted again, tiny movements. Impatience building. I kept my gaze on Angelo's face. His expression was controlled, but he wasn't calm. He was holding something down with both hands.

I tried to find a seam I could pull that wasn't going to tear us open.

"How's the old man?" I asked, trying to lean on a sliver of connection Angelo may still have to me.

Angelo didn't blink. "Dead," he said shortly. "Why do you think I'm the one standing here?"

The words hit like a door slamming.

The street blurred with memory. Angelo's father leaning against a fence, arms crossed, watching us like we were all strays he'd decided to feed anyway. A man who didn't smile much but always seemed to know exactly what you were thinking before you did.

He also had taught me a thing or two. I pushed the thought down. "I didn't know."

Angelo shrugged as if it didn't matter what I knew. "Of course you didn't, You were busy forgetting where you came from."

I breathed in slowly through my nose. Let it out just as slow. "I'm not here to start something. I don't want trouble."

Angelo's eyes narrowed, and his voice dropped. "Trouble's already here. That's what you bring, Red."

I shifted my weight, careful to keep my body language open. No sudden turns. No reach for the car keys I didn't have in my hand. No glances toward exits that would look like fear.

Angelo took another step closer. Close enough now that the space between us felt deliberate. "You know what I remember? I remember you coming back from the East with that stupid little smirk. Like you'd cracked a code no one else knew existed."

I didn't answer.

Angelo didn't need me to.

"You'd sit there," he continued, tilting his head, voice calm, "and you'd tell us all about the woman with the dead husband and the man with the guilt and the kid who 'had a good aura'." He scoffed. "You remember that shit you used to say?"

I clenched my jaw before I could stop it. "We all did things we needed to do, Angie," I said softly.

"You lost the right to call me that." He was bearing down on me now. "When you abandoned us, for what? Med school?"

"It was survival," I pointed out, and his expression sharpened.

"Yeah. Survival for you."

He leaned in a fraction more. "And what about us? What about Dante? What about me? What about the people who had your back while you went East and lied to strangers for cash?"

I took a slow breath and held his eyes. "I didn't ask you to have my back."

Angelo's laugh was short and ugly. "No. You didn't ask. You just took. Same as always."

He turned his head slightly. "Red here didn't just leave. He cleaned out every dollar he'd stacked. Every cent. Saved it all up and hid it from everyone. Then he walked."

The men behind him murmured, some nodding like they'd heard it or been there. Others just watched me.

Angelo looked back at me. "At least Dante didn't abandon his family. Yeah, he works with scum, but he's still here."

I swallowed. "You're right." I let the words sit. "And I can't take that back. So, if you want me gone. I'll go."

"Go," Angelo said without hesitation. "Before I change my mind."

I nodded once. "Okay, but before I do go, just humour me once." Angelo's eyes narrowed. "Do you know Casey Edwards?"

Angelo didn't answer. Not with his words. But his eyes flickered, his weight shifted, and twitch ran along his jaw.

"That's a yes," I muttered quietly.

"Don't read me, Red," Angelo warned.

The warning had a familiar shape. It was the same anger he used to carry when we were teenagers, and I'd call his bluff in front of a crowd.

I lifted my hands slightly, palms open. "I'm just asking."

Angelo stared at me, then his gaze slid toward the house beside us. "What do you want with Casey?" he asked, curiosity getting the better of him.

I didn't hesitate. Hesitation was a lie in this neighbourhood. "He's dead," I said, and Angelo looked to the ground.

If I hadn't seen it, I wouldn't have believed it, but there was sadness etched onto his face. It wasn't dramatic. It wasn't a collapse. It was a small, involuntary slackness at the corners of his mouth. A heaviness that made his shoulders settle for half a beat like the weight had been added all at once.

He turned slightly to the man on his right. "Head inside. Tell Blaze."

My eyes followed the man he sent as he walked toward Casey's house. I wanted to ask who Blaze was, but before I could, Angelo spoke again. Louder and more commanding.

"Spread!"

Without complaint or hesitation, the group that had surrounded us dispersed, each going a different direction, leaving Angelo and myself alone. The street didn't feel safer with them gone. It felt watched. The whole block had grown eyes.

Angelo kept his gaze down for another second. Then he looked back up at me, expression hard again like he'd rebuilt the wall. "Casey's dead?" he asked, clearly still processing the information.

I nodded. "Shot."

"Fuck."

"You didn't know he was missing?" I questioned, and Angelo shot me a glare.

"Had no reason to think he was," he answered after a moment. "Did he come through your hospital?"

I scanned his face. He was trying to read me like I did him. Figure out how I knew about Casey and what happened.

"No, I don't do that anymore," I said slowly. "He got shot in front of me."

"Where?"

"Lakeside Park." I paused. "Do you know why he was there?"

Angelo didn't answer. He didn't have to. His face already told me.

Yes.

"Why are you asking about it?" Angelo asked, and my jaw tightened.

"Because no one else is," I said simply. "File's been altered."

"You work for the cops, too, now?" Angelo scoffed.

"Something like that," I muttered, my eyes glancing to his fists, which were in tight balls. Angelo's eyes followed mine, and he relaxed his fists instantly.

A loud bang came from Casey's house, and the sound of glass shattering rang out.

"We'll handle it," Angelo said when the sound died. "You can go back to the East and pretend like this never happened."

"I can't do that," I said, and Angelo raised his hand.

"I don't care what you can and can't do. Casey was our family. Not your problem."

There was a beat where the street seemed to pause. Somewhere down the block, music thumped from a car with the windows down. A dog barked once and then stopped.

"You need to leave," Angelo said, though his voice was different, not hateful, just pressuring.

"Angie, I can help find who did this," I said, and Angelo scoffed.

"I know who did this."

The words sat between us, and Angelo let my eyes run over his face. He let his expression tell me the truth. He didn't know. But he did have a name.

"We aren't the only group in the West anymore, Red." Angelo's voice was low and controlled, and let what he said sit heavily in my stomach. That complicated things. If it were gang-related and this was the first move, it would escalate quickly and uncontrollably.

"We'll handle it," Angelo repeated, the gesture toward my car. "Get out, Red."

I stared, letting the information roll over in my mind, before giving him a small nod. "It was good to see you, Angie."

He grunted at me, and I turned away from him, slowly moving toward my car. I kept my rhythm calm and deliberate. Fast movements meant fear, and fear meant bringing action you couldn't run from.

"And, Red?" Angelo called after me. I didn't turn. "Stay the fuck out of the West."

I let Angelo's words follow me, and I slid into my car and closed the door. I still felt his eyes on me as I kicked the engine over and pulled away from the curb. I drove past Angelo and down the street, our conversation sitting in the backseat. It replayed over and over. The words, his face, the way he held himself.

Then the night it happened. Casey. How he acted before he was shot. How he looked as he bled out.

And then there was the file. The lack of information. The tampering.

Each piece looked like it was for a different puzzle. I just needed to find a way to connect them. As I reached the lights to turn onto The Strip, the street behind me filled the rearview. I couldn't let it go. I couldn't scrub myself clean of the case and move on.

And I couldn't scrub the West Side off me either.

7

The house was quiet, and the silence settled in with the darkness as if it belonged there.

It wasn't the empty-house quiet I'd had yesterday. This was the lived-in version—walls still holding the day's noise like a memory, little traces of the boys lingering in the corners. A jumper draped over the back of a chair. A stray toy was abandoned near the hallway. The faint smell of dinner clinging to the air.

The boys were asleep down the hall, and Claire had done the rounds twice as if she didn't trust them to stay asleep without supervision. I sat at the kitchen table with the piece of paper Dante had given me open beside my elbow, its edges a little wrinkled from being handled too much. The only light came from the lamp tucked in the corner, dim enough that it made the room feel smaller and more private.

Claire leaned against the counter with her arms crossed. She looked ready for bed, and the way she held herself made that obvious, but she stayed put anyway.

"You're trapped again," Claire said softly.

"How's that?" I asked, my eyes resting on hers and taking in their warmth.

"You're trying to force yourself to be calm and keep your breathing normal when your brain is running a hundred miles an hour."

Her words sat between us, and I nodded.

"I'm just thinking," I said quietly, and Claire let out a soft laugh.

"You're thinking about yesterday."

"Yeah."

My time in the West Side sat pretty at the front of my mind. Every part of it rolling on top of itself, trying to piece itself together. Nothing had clicked into place.

"You don't have a lot to work with, Ryan," Claire reminded me, trying to find the words to pull me out of my head. "Basically scraps."

"Scraps are still something I can use to fill in the gaps," I said, and Claire hummed.

We sat in the quiet, and then Claire pushed off the counter, crossing the room to stand beside me. Her hand found my shoulder and gripped it gently. She leaned down and kissed the top of my head.

"Are you filling in the gaps?" she asked, pulling out the seat next to me and sliding into it, her hand moving to mine, lacing our fingers together.

"Nothing fits cleanly," I admitted, and Claire's fingers tightened around mine.

"Is what I know everything?"

I nodded. I never hid anything from Claire. I couldn't if I wanted to. She was the one person who was able to read me as well as I read others.

"Well, you can't go poking back around in the West," she pointed out. "So, what do you do?"

I didn't answer. I let my eyes wander down to our hands, feeling her warmth and letting myself lean into it.

"Or should I say, what don't you do?" Claire questioned, and I smirked half-heartedly.

"Don't go in the West," I repeated, looking back at her. "Not yet, anyway."

"Guessing I won't be able to talk you out of it completely?"

"For a few days you will."

Silence fell again, then Claire let out a sigh.

"There's something else on your mind," she said softly, her eyes tracing my face. "You're carrying something else."

"I'm…" I trailed off, trying to find the right words to say. "I thought I'd gotten out."

Claire didn't say anything. She waited, watching me and letting her hand tighten around mine. It was grounding.

"I thought it was the right thing. To get out. But being back there felt… I don't know… I could still see myself there."

"You can't erase your past," Claire said, her thumb grazing the back of my hand. "You can't scrub it off you. Every choice led you here. With us. Would you consider that the right choice?"

I fought a smile, and hummed agreement. "I would."

"This young man… Casey," Claire started, leaning in slightly and lowering her voice. "I know you'll make the right choices to figure out who did this and why. That's what you do. Just don't get stuck in here." Claire reached up and placed her hand on my cheek.

"I would never," I muttered, and Claire rolled her eyes at the lie.

"No, of course." She scoffed. "You never used to do it when you didn't know what was wrong with a patient."

I let out a soft laugh.

Claire watched me with that look she got when she'd landed the point and didn't need to twist the knife. She kept her hand on my cheek a second longer, then slid it down to my jaw, thumb brushing the faint stubble.

"You're stubborn," she asked softly. "That's why you always find the answer."

"Sometimes I just find it too late."

Claire exhaled. "Do you hear yourself?"

"I do," I mumbled. "I just don't always listen."

"Really? I thought you loved the sound of your own voice," she said with a chuckle.

I turned my hand over on the table and let my fingers curl around hers properly. "You're not wrong."

"I'm never wrong," Claire said, then smirked when my eyebrows lifted and repeated. "I'm never wrong."

"Okay, okay," I said, letting the weight lift for a moment.

It felt nice. The room settled. The familiar quiet pressed in around us, softening the edges of everything I didn't want to think about.

Then my eyes fell onto the piece of paper again. Casey's name stared back at me.

Claire's eyes followed mine, then came back up to me. "You're doing it again."

"Doing what?" I looked back at Claire.

"Staring at it like it's going to start talking."

"It'd be helpful."

Claire snorted. "What do you think it would say?"

"Maybe it'd tell me something I missed that night."

"You don't miss things," Claire pointed out, and I shrugged.

"Maybe if I was closer. I could've seen something else."

"If you were closer… there could've been two victims that night."

The words sat heavily at the table with us.

"I'm surprised Angelo didn't try make me the second victim yesterday."

"Don't joke about that," Claire said sternly.

"Sorry. It's just… he's right to be angry."

"You two were close."

"A long time ago."

"Do you think he had anything to do with it?" Claire asked, trying to dig my brain out of the past.

I shook my head. "No. He didn't know."

"That gives you something," Claire said quietly.

"What's that?"

"One less person to look into."

I let out a thin breath that was almost a laugh.

"Honestly, I'm not even sure if we have people to look into to begin with."

Claire's gaze drifted to the paper beside my elbow—Casey's name and address sitting their harmlessly—then back to me. She didn't argue. She didn't need to. She'd seen me circle a problem like this before, turning it over until something finally caught.

A knock came at the front door, steady and unhurried. In the quiet house, it carried, but it didn't feel alarming. Claire headed for the hall at an easy pace, as though midnight visits were a regular occurrence.

Another knock followed.

I stood and trailed after her, keeping my steps light for the boys' sake. Claire reached the door, opened it, and Dante was there on the porch with his jacket half-zipped, shoulders slightly tucked against the cool air. He looked worn out.

"Dante, hi," Claire said, surprised but not alarmed.

"Hey, Claire," Dante said, then nodded at me. "Red."

"If I knew you were coming, I would've left you some dinner," Claire said, stepping back to let him in.

"It's fine," Dante said, moving inside. "I'm not here for long."

He took the invitation and stepped over the threshold.

"Whoa," I said, looking him over. "You look like shit."

Dante's mouth twitched. "Thanks."

"Just returning the favour," I said with a shrug.

Claire gave me a look that said, 'don't start,' then turned back to

Dante. "Do you want a tea?"

"Coffee, please," Dante said without hesitation.

"It's almost midnight," Claire pointed out, and Dante waved the words off as though they meant nothing to him.

"I'll need it. I'm to the NBI after this."

That made my posture tighten without asking permission. "You didn't come from there?"

"Nah," Dante said, and he ran a hand over his face. "Spent all day door-knocking, then tonight was looking at labs and working with techs."

"Big case?"

"The NBI thinks it's going to be," Dante said. He glanced toward the hall, lowered his voice automatically, and added, "And honestly, I think I agree."

Claire's expression shifted from sleepy to sharp. She gestured him toward the kitchen. "Come in. Sit. I'll make you that coffee."

Dante followed us through, the same as he'd done a hundred times before. Claire moved around the kitchen with quiet competence, the kind that didn't clatter or announce itself.

Dante sat at the table opposite me. His gaze flicked to the paper beside me. When Claire set the coffee in front of him, he wrapped his hands around the mug and inhaled like the smell alone could keep him upright. He took a sip, then another, and his eyes finally lifted to mine.

"Whole scene was staged," Dante said, as though the conversation had never stopped. "Like whoever did it wanted it to be a performance."

"That bad?" I asked

Dante's jaw tightened. "They painted a number on the bedroom door in the victim's blood."

Claire went still by the counter. "Jesus," she breathed.

"What number?" I asked tentatively.

"One. My guess, it was to tell us how many bodies were inside." Dante watched my face to see if I agreed with him. "I wouldn't be surprised if they ended up calling you in for this one."

I frowned. "Why? The psychic can't handle a little blood?"

Claire's eyes narrowed at me, warning, but Dante didn't rise to it. He looked too tired for my shit.

"Oh, no," Dante said flatly. "She's on it, too. But the wounds. The cuts. Precise and surgical." He paused, then added, "They might want your opinion."

"Is that why you dropped by?" I asked. "For the warning?"

"One of the reasons," Dante said. He leaned forward slightly, elbows near the table edge, voice dropping another notch. "If they do call you in, you're going to need to be careful and keep your mouth shut."

I lifted my brows.

"I always do," I said, and I gave him my most innocent face. "When have I ever spoken out of turn?"

Claire turned her head slowly toward me, expression unimpressed.

"Let's not play that game," she said dryly.

Dante made a sound that might've been a laugh if he'd had the energy to commit. Then his face reset, all business. "Casey's file got flagged."

The words hit with a thud, heavy and wrong.

"What?" I asked. "How?"

"I don't know. I haven't touched it since the other day. Something happened with it sometime today."

"How do you know?" I asked. "Wilson call you?"

Dante shook his head. "No. Stephanie sent me a message."

Claire's brow furrowed. "Stephanie?"

I looked at Dante, then at Claire. "Isn't that Theresa's PA?"

"Yeah. Something has triggered that went above Wilson."

My mind started moving before I could stop it. Casey's file getting flagged meant something had changed. Again. Or someone had looked. Again. "You think someone else is looking into it?"

"Or whoever altered it the first time has tried to clean it up some more and caused it to flag."

Claire's arms crossed over her chest, tension showing across her face. "Why would they risk that?"

I stared at the paper. Casey's name stared back. "Unless they know it's being looked into."

Dante nodded. "Whatever it is, if they call you in, Red, you need to keep your head down."

"When have I ever—" I started.

Claire cut me off with a look sharp enough to draw blood. "Come on, Ryan."

I exhaled through my nose and lifted a hand in surrender. "Yeah, alright. Fair."

Dante watched that exchange and took another sip of his coffee. "Did you learn anything yesterday?" he asked. "You never called."

I leaned back in my chair. "Yeah, sorry about that. I was too busy washing my underwear."

"That bad?" Dante asked, and his tone suggested he already knew the answer.

"I was followed the moment I set foot in The Strip."

Dante's eyes narrowed. "Unlike you not to notice."

"I did notice."

"You just didn't care."

I lifted one shoulder. "What can I say? I live for danger."

Dante's mouth twitched again, this time with actual humour scraping through. "You hid behind me every time we used to do a bust."

"Not important," I said quickly.

Dante leaned forward, back to business. "What happened?"

"Angelo came to say hi."

Dante's expression went tight in a way that made it clear he knew exactly what that meant. "Geez. And how'd that go?"

"Well," I said, keeping my voice steady, "he did not pull me into a 'welcome home' hug."

"I could imagine. Did you at least get anything from it?"

"He knew Casey."

Dante's eyes sharpened. "How well?"

"Like family, apparently. And the look on his face when I told him Casey died makes me believe that."

"He didn't know Casey died?"

"No. Then he told someone to go and let Blaze know."

Dante blinked once. "Blaze?"

"Yeah. I don't know. Not a name I remember. I was kind of hoping you'd met him."

Dante snorted quietly. "I tend to keep to myself out there, Red. They don't really want an NBI agent mingling at their barbeques."

"Considering they seem pretty open about all the illegal crap they're doing, that doesn't surprise me," I said. I felt Claire's eyes on me, but I kept going anyway. "I know you said it was different now but—"

"I know," Dante said, cutting in before I could work myself into a rant. "But waving my badge will make things worse, and the local cops are…" He paused, searching for the right word. "I don't know."

"Scared?" Claire proposed.

"Or a part of the gang," I said, and I hated how easily the words came. "Either of them."

Dante's eyebrows lifted. "You know about that?" he asked carefully.

I looked at him. "Since when did the West split?"

Dante's gaze flicked down, then back up to meet mine. "Since Angelo's dad was killed. You remember Sterling?"

"Vernon?"

"That's the one. Decided to take things into his own hands one day. Not sure how no one else was killed."

"Until now."

Dante shook his head. "I don't think this is related."

"Why?"

He leaned back, eyes tired but steady. "Why now?" he said. "It's been nine years since it happened. It's been calm. They each have their own turf. The West keeps running." He gestured vaguely, as if the whole machine of it was too big to fit in the room. "Why risk that? And why

Casey?"

I spread my hands in front of me, palms open. "There are too many reasons to list."

Claire's eyes moved between us. "Could Casey have been on both sides?"

The question hung there. Quiet. Dangerous.

"There's a motive," I muttered.

"Barely," Dante said with a huff.

"We don't have much else, Dante. We have nothing, actually."

"But you don't believe it."

I held his gaze. "No," I admitted. "But it could be a start."

Claire leaned in slightly. "Lay it out."

I tapped the edge of the paper with my fingertip. "If Casey was working both sides of the West and someone found out, that's reason to kill him."

"But Angelo didn't know," Dante added.

"Which wouldn't make sense if it were gang-related."

Claire's brow furrowed. "Why?"

"If you wanted to make someone hurt, you wouldn't keep it a secret," I pointed out. "You'd make sure everyone knew."

Dante's gaze drifted as he thought. "Unless it's deeper than just a gang thing."

"Unless it's someone within the same family," I said, and the words tasted sour as soon as they left my mouth.

Dante's attention snapped back. "You said Casey looked like he knew whoever shot him."

"Doesn't narrow it down. Especially if he did work both sides."

"No," Dante agreed, "but it does give us a name."

I didn't blink. "Blaze."

Dante nodded. "Angelo made a point for someone to tell him Casey was dead. Why him specifically?"

"He was closer to Casey than the others. Or at least that's how it looked."

Claire's voice went tight. "Okay. So, what does this mean?" She glanced at me, then at Dante. "You are going back in there?"

"No," Dante said immediately. "He isn't."

"I—" I started, but Dante didn't let me finish.

"I will see what I can find out," Dante said, voice firm.

I stared at him. "That's just as bad of an idea."

"It'll have to do. You just need to give me some time." He lifted his coffee slightly. "Especially with this other case going on."

Claire's fingers curled around the edge of the counter. "What about the file? How would this Blaze guy have anything to do with that?"

Dante's expression tightened. "There are some smart and resourceful people in the West. It wouldn't surprise me if they found a way to get into the system."

"They'd have no reason to," I said.

"That we know of," Dante pointed out.

His phone buzzed on the table; the sudden sound sharp in the quiet kitchen. Dante looked down at it, and his whole posture shifted. He stood, pushing the chair back carefully so it wouldn't scrape too loudly.

"Look, I gotta go," Dante murmured. "Just sit on your hands, Red.

At least until I know what flagged the case."

I tilted my head. "You think I'll make it worse?"

"I have no doubt," Dante said, and the fact he said it like a certainty made it worse than if he'd yelled it.

Claire walked him to the door while I followed a step behind.

"Thank you for the coffee, Claire," Dante said at the entryway.

"Anytime."

Dante nodded at both of us, then slipped back into the night like he belonged to it. The door clicked shut, and the house rushed to fill the space he'd left behind.

Claire turned toward me slowly. "You have that look on your face."

"What look is that?" I asked, already knowing.

"A disagreeing look."

I exhaled and rubbed a hand over my mouth. My mind was already pulling at threads Dante had left on the table.

"I think there's something else going on that we aren't seeing."

Claire stepped closer. Her voice softened, but her eyes didn't. "Just promise me something. Don't do anything stupid."

I looked at her, at the tired line in her expression and the way she still stood between me and the worst parts of myself without even thinking about it. Unfortunately, I couldn't promise her that.

Because I was probably going to do something stupid.

8

The week slid by in that way days do when you're pretending not to count them.

Routine took over. Breakfast plates. School bags. One missing shoe that became everyone's problem. Claire's reminders were delivered with the same calm precision she used at work, even when she was still half asleep. The boys were loud, sticky, and impossibly certain the world existed to be climbed upon and argued with.

And underneath all of it, the case kept tapping me on the shoulder like a kid who'd learned they got attention by being annoying.

It wasn't constant. It didn't need to be. It showed up in the gaps. While I was brushing my teeth, I'd catch myself thinking about Angelo's face, the way it had gone rigid when he heard Casey was dead. While I was tying a shoelace, I'd remember Dante saying the file got flagged, and the word flagged would turn over in my mind like a stone I couldn't put down. While I was washing my hands, I'd feel the blood on them, refusing to wash off.

Normal life, and then the other thing.

Seeping through, trying to belong.

By Saturday, the house had that particular afternoon glow—sunlight cutting through the living room and turning dust into something almost pretty. The boys were in the middle of a game that wasn't really a game so much as an argument with props. Miles had donned a blanket for a cape again. A few pillows and cushions had become 'the base.' And Alex was holding a foam sword.

Claire was on the couch, one leg folded under her, the other stretched out like she didn't have the energy to commit to comfort properly. She'd done a night shift on Friday and hadn't really slept since. You could see it in the softer edge of her focus.

She was awake like a phone on one percent battery—technically functional, but any second now you're going to watch it turn off.

I was on the floor with the boys because I'd made the mistake of sitting down and they'd taken that as a binding contract.

"Dad. You have to guard the base," Alex pointed out.

"I am guarding the base," I said, gesturing loosely around me.

"No," Alex corrected immediately, "you're just sitting."

I looked down at my hands. "I'm holding the position."

"But I can easily get to the base and destroy it," he said, waving his foam sword in my direction.

Claire made a small sound that might've been a laugh if she had more energy. It came out quiet and tired, but still fond.

My phone buzzed in my pocket. The vibration was small. The effect wasn't. It had been loud enough for the boys to hear it and come to attention.

"Who is it?" Alex asked, a frown forming on his face.

"Uh, the King," I said slowly. "Maybe he wants to surrender."

That got a groan from both of them, dramatic and rehearsed.

"That's not how the game works," Miles whined, and Alex nodded in agreement.

I pulled the phone out and checked the screen as it continued to vibrate in my hand.

Wilson.

I stood, stretching my legs as I did, and feeling them ache. "I, uh, laid traps all in front of the base," I told the boys. "So, you gotta dodge them."

"No!" Miles yelled. "He's smarter than we thought."

Claire let out a small chuckle as I mouthed an 'ouch'.

I stepped into the hallway where the house got quieter, the living room noise muffled behind me.

I answered after a short sigh. "Hello."

"Red," Wilson said.

His voice sounded the same as it always did. Controlled and steady. No emotion I could grab onto.

"To what do I owe the pleasure?"

"I need you to come in," Wilson said.

I glanced at the family photos on the wall—sticky little faces and crooked smiles. "Is this social?" I asked. "Am I being asked out for lunch?"

"Thirty minutes," Wilson said shortly. Then the call ended. No goodbye. No courtesy.

I stared at the screen, then let my arm drop. When I stepped back into the living room, Claire was already watching me. She didn't ask who it was. She didn't need to. The look on my face had probably done the announcing for me.

"Was that the call?" Claire asked.

"Going out on a limb, yeah. It was."

Claire's shoulders lifted and fell in a small exhale like she'd been holding her breath without realising it. "Go."

I glanced at her, then at the boys. Miles had now taken off the cape and was trying to use it to whip Alex, who was doing his best to fend it off.

"You're off the night shift," I said, keeping my voice light because the alternative would make this too real. "You need sleep."

She held my gaze. "I'll manage."

"The boys will eat you alive."

"Ryan," Claire warned, and her tone cut to the bone.

I held my hands in surrender. "Okay… okay."

Claire pushed herself up from the couch, moving like her body was made of lead, but her mind refused to let that win. She crossed to me and melted into my arms. "Remember what Dante said," she said quietly.

I gave her a small nod. "It'll be somewhere in my mind… for sure."

Claire pulled away, and her expression softened, just a fraction. She reached up and touched my jaw with her fingertips, grounding me in the way she always did.

"I love you."

"I love you," Claire echoed.

Behind her, Miles yelled, "Mum, Alex is cheating!"

Claire didn't even turn her head. "No one is cheating," she called back, and somehow it sounded like a medical order.

I went to the hallway drawer and pulled it open. It was a mess of ordinary things—spare keys, pens, batteries, a tape measure, a little pile of coins that never got spent. My consultant badge sat underneath all of it, buried on purpose, the lettering 'NBI' catching the light as I lifted it out. I grabbed my keys, closed the drawer, and paused at the living room doorway.

"Be good," I told the boys.

They both looked at me like they had never been anything other than good.

"We are good," Miles stated, offended.

Claire gave me a look over her shoulder that translated easily: 'go before they make you stay.'

So, I did.

Outside, the afternoon was bright and busy. The street had kids on bikes and someone mowing a lawn, the smell of cut grass floating over as if the world was determined to stay normal. I got into the car and sat for a moment before starting it; my badge resting neatly on the passenger seat.

The drive was quiet in the way Saturday afternoons always were. People going to sport or heading to shops. Parents with strollers and iced coffees. A traffic light held me long enough to watch a dog hang its head out a window, tongue lolling, living its best life without any concept of murder investigations.

Lucky bastard.

I arrived at NBI with the sun starting to fall low and the afternoon struggling to pretend it wasn't slowly tipping toward evening.

From the outside, the place looked the same—glass, concrete, and sharp angles that made you feel like you were trespassing even when you weren't. It wasn't built to welcome anyone. It was built to remind you who held authority.

The gate line crawled forward one car at a time. People in sedans and government-issued SUVs, windows up, faces forward, all of them wearing that expression that said I belong here, or I've learned how to look like I belong here. I had neither. I had a badge and a desire to be somewhere else.

The booth window opened as I rolled up to it.

Tom, the security guard, leaned out, and his face changed so fast it was almost funny. Surprise first. Then a grin that didn't quite make it to his eyes. "Holy shit. Red?"

"Hey, Tom," I muttered, trying to return his grin.

"It's been a while." He looked over my face and nodded at nothing. "Thought you were never coming back."

"And yet, here I am."

Tom's gaze dropped to the passenger seat where my badge sat, then back up to my face.

I grabbed it and held it up for the cameras to see. "Still allowed inside. For now."

Tom snorted. "Head on through."

The gate lifted, and I drove in.

The parking lot was packed, with almost every space filled. I found a spot on the far edge and killed the engine. Heat rolled in through the open door the second I stepped out, the kind that clung to your skin. I locked the car and started toward the building.

There was always a moment at places like this where you could feel the transition. Outside was ordinary: sun, cars, a faint smell of exhaust, someone laughing somewhere. Inside was a different world. Climate-controlled. Polished. Quiet in a way that wasn't peaceful, just regulated. The lobby swallowed sound. Shoes on tile. Low voices. A muted beep every time someone got cleared.

I flashed my badge at the first checkpoint, and the guard barely looked at my face before waving me toward the detectors. The machine didn't care who I was. It cared what I carried. That was the closest thing to fairness the building offered.

I kept moving.

The elevator was slow. I stepped in with two agents I didn't recognise. They both looked at me, then looked away fast. The doors opened on Wilson's floor, and the air changed again—it felt more urgent. The hallway smelled like old coffee and forgotten food. Somewhere, a phone rang and got answered on the first ring.

I walked past the small kitchenette—stainless steel sink, dirty dishes, and a sad bowl of individually wrapped mints no one wanted.

The bullpen opened up ahead: rows of desks, partitions, monitors, and the low hum of everyone pretending they weren't exhausted. Most people didn't look up. Their eyes stayed on screens. Their hands stayed on keyboards. Their shoulders stayed tight. Some did glance over, and their faces shifted into something displeased, like my presence was a smell they didn't want in their office.

Most of the faces I knew. People I had worked with before. They didn't matter. They had written me off. With one exception. A younger guy—I remember him starting a week before my incident a year ago. He looked up as I passed, hesitated, then offered a small wave. His smile was quick, polite, and a little uncertain. I nodded back once. I wasn't going to ruin his politeness. It was a delicate thing in this office.

Dante's desk sat off to the side, cluttered in the way his mind worked—organised chaos. He stood as I came level with him, moving like he'd been watching for me.

"You got the call," he stated, leaning on his partition.

"I did. Kinda thought you'd be at the scene, though."

"I was." Dante lowered his voice. "We're heading back now, actually. Just had to deal with some paperwork."

"What is it?"

Dante brought his voice even lower, the way everyone did in the bullpen even when no one was listening. "Looks like the same person from earlier this week."

That got my attention. "The staged scene?"

Dante nodded. "Same style. Same kind of precision. Same… theatrical bullshit."

"That would explain the call."

Dante's gaze held mine. "You should head in. And remember what I said."

I exhaled. "I know."

"You don't," Dante said, and it wasn't a joke.

I gave him a look. "You sound like Claire."

"Good. Then maybe you'll listen. Or do I need to take my shirt off for that?"

I shrugged. "I won't say it wouldn't help."

Dante rolled his eyes and clapped me on the shoulder. "I'll see you out there."

He stepped back from his desk and motioned with two fingers. A few people peeled away immediately—a man with a tablet, a woman with her hair twisted tight at the back of her head, and another agent who moved as though he was permanently bracing for impact. Their names played in the back of my mind, but I swatted them away.

They didn't say anything. They didn't need to. Dante was the kind of person people followed without thinking about it. Dante and his small crew headed out and soon vanished from sight.

I stood there, my eyes landed on the younger agent who was staring at me, though I quickly looked away as our eyes met. I shook my head, then turned toward Wilson's office. His door was shut. Which made sense. If you wanted privacy, you got an office. If you wanted power, you kept the door closed.

I knocked once, and Wilson's voice came almost immediately. "Come in."

I pushed through the door and closed it behind me, looking out the window beside it to see the bullpen. Wilson could see out. No one could see in.

Wilson sat behind his desk as if he'd been assembled there. Not relaxed or tense. Placed. He looked up at me.

"Oh, captain, my captain," I said with a salute.

"Have a seat." Wilson gestured to the seat across from him.

"Usually, I would stand on the desk after that," I pointed out.

Wilson didn't blink. He didn't even give me the courtesy of pretending I'd made a joke.

"Okay," I mouthed, and sat down.

Wilson watched me. He was trying to get a read on me.

"Saw you with Dante out there," Wilson stated after a moment. "He let you know what happened?"

"A murder may have been mentioned, yeah."

Wilson's mouth moved, but not enough to be called a smile.

"I want you to head out there," he said shortly. "Take a look at the scene. The team will debrief you and give you what you need. Then, when the bodies are being examined, I want you there."

"Bodies?" I asked, raising my eyebrows. "Plural?"

"Two victims."

I let Wilson's words hang in the air, clinging to the dust particles.

I sighed. "I mean…" I leaned back slightly, "this is all very sudden. What if I have things planned?"

Wilson's eyes stayed steady. "What?" he asked. "Like a trip to visit old friends?"

The words sat between us and didn't move.

I kept my expression blank because I didn't know how much he knew. Clearly, it was something, and that could have also been a testament to how much he was involved in.

"I'm just saying," I said slowly, "I feel undervalued as a consultant."

"Maybe that's because you don't act like one." Wilson's words were sharper now. The shift on his face lingered on disappointment when I hadn't reacted the way he wanted.

I tilted my head. "I can sense you're still a little upset about what happened last year."

Wilson's voice now went colder without getting louder. "Two agents almost died because you thought you knew better."

"And yet, no one did die," I pointed out. "And we caught the bad guy, did we not? I would call that a win."

"You need to learn restraint," Wilson insisted. "And responsibility." He paused. "That is why you will be going with a consultant who has both."

"I don't think—" I started.

"Mia is already working this case," Wilson cut in. "Think of it as… shadowing her."

Shadowing. Like I was an intern. Like she was better than me.

"I really have better things to do," I voiced with a shrug.

Wilson's gaze sharpened a fraction, and his voice changed—not angry, not threatening. But mild. Which was worse.

"Sometimes… the best thing you can do is listen to those around you. You start looking at things that shouldn't be looked at, and pulling threads, things tend to unravel quickly. And you don't want to be falling with those threads around your neck."

Wilson paused, his eyes tracing my face.

"You work what we tell you to, then you go home. Got it?"

I felt the shift immediately, like my body had recognised danger before my brain had caught up. This wasn't about the serial killer. That isn't why he called me in. This was Wilson repositioning me like a piece on a board, moving me where he wanted my attention.

Because he didn't want it somewhere else.

I kept my expression smooth. I kept my hands still. Whatever he was looking for on my face, he wouldn't find it.

I still didn't answer.

Wilson leaned back slightly, as if we were having a normal conversation. "You're good at what you do, Red. I'd hate to see it all go to waste."

I nodded slowly, letting the moment stretch just long enough to feel like I was deciding. "Alrighty then," I said, slapping my hands onto my knees. "Where is the circus act?"

Wilson stood, and I followed suit. "This way."

We walked together out of his office and back through the bullpen. Heads stayed down. Screens stayed bright.

Wilson led me down a corridor I hadn't walked in a long time, past doors with frosted glass and small nameplates, and into a separate room.

Mia was already there.

The room was colder than the corridor outside it, and I attributed it to the company it held. It was a large briefing room. A large board ran along one wall, already crowded with photographs, printouts, and timeline markers. The table beneath it was littered with files spread open as if the case had been physically poured out and left to dry.

Crime scene photos. Evidence logs. A couple of maps. And a stack of papers I would never look at, even if I did work the case. The chairs and tables facing it all remained empty.

Mia stood near the board with her arms folded, posture easy and controlled. She didn't look up right away. She was studying the photos with the same expression Claire wore when she was reading discharge notes—focused, detached, and quietly judging whoever had created the mess.

Wilson stopped at the threshold as if he didn't want to contaminate the room further. "I'll leave you two alone. I want you at the scene in no longer than thirty minutes."

His eyes landed on me when he said it. Then he was gone, the door closing behind him with a soft click.

Mia's gaze stayed on the board. "I did hear that I was babysitting today."

"Yeah," I muttered, looking around. "That would make sense. Clowns do usually entertain children."

Mia finally turned her head toward me, slow and deliberate. Her eyes were sharp, and the kind of calm she carried wasn't comfort. It was control.

"You calling yourself a child?" she asked, and I shrugged. "Look, I'm not here to catch the crap coming out of your mouth."

"And what are you here for exactly?" I probed, stepping closer to the table, scanning the spread.

Photos of a bedroom. Blood. Tape markers. The bodies.

"I'm getting a sense of the scene before I head there," Mia said calmly. "The bodies won't be there, so this is my chance to see them."

I glanced at her. "You didn't go on the initial call?"

Mia's mouth tightened, but she corrected herself almost instantly. "I'm not fond of seeing dead bodies."

I let my eyebrows lift. "Says the one who apparently speaks to the dead."

Mia didn't flinch, which told me she'd heard worse from better people. "I see them the way they were when they were happiest," she said quietly. "Not mutilated."

I made a small gesture toward the photos. "But seeing them in pictures is a-okay?"

"I still don't enjoy it. No."

There was something odd about the way she said it. Not defensive. Not performative. Just a matter-of-fact like she'd decided where her limits were and didn't intend to apologise for them.

I looked back to the board. It wasn't the blood that bothered me. It was the arrangement. The intention. The way the scene had been built to be read.

The same person as Dante's first scene. The same precision. The same idea of an audience.

Theatrical.

"So," I murmured, "what're we reading here? What's the vibe?"

Mia's eyes shifted from the photos to me, and her focus changed. It sharpened.

"You're very arrogant," she said bluntly.

I stared at her, then nodded. "Thank you."

"And sure of yourself," Mia continued. "You think your intelligence should be the only required factor to place yourself above others. You need it to be. Because below it all there's a scared little boy who's afraid he isn't good enough."

Silence dropped into the room.

Even the air-conditioning seemed to hesitate as though it wasn't sure it was allowed to keep running. I blinked once. Slowly. Then I let out a quiet breath through my nose and looked at her like she'd just done a party trick.

"Wow," I breathed. "I'm shaken. You read that in a psychology book somewhere, or was that just freestyle?"

Mia held my gaze without blinking. "You're more transparent than you think."

There it was. That tone. The one that wanted me to believe she had some special access to the inside of my skull. I'd met people like her before. I used to be one. Not psychic. Just people who were good at reading others.

I didn't give her the satisfaction of reacting. I let my eyes drift back to the photos instead, because the photos were honest. The only things that were in this room.

A bedroom. A bed stripped to the frame. Evidence markers like punctuation. Blood in arcs and smears.

"Well," I said, keeping my voice light, "this has been fun. At least the crime scene is going to feel like a delight in comparison."

I turned and headed for the door. Mia followed. Unfortunately.

We moved back down the corridor, then into the bullpen. The room barely acknowledged us. People stayed glued to screens, phones, and folders.

The elevator ride down was quiet. Mia stood beside me without touching the wall, hands loosely clasped in front of her. I stared at the numbers above the doors as they ticked down and tried not to think about Wilson's voice. Threads that shouldn't be pulled.

By the time we hit the main floor, I'd managed to put my face back into something neutral. I pushed through the last set of doors toward the exit—and heard heels behind me, crisp and controlled, the sound of someone who wanted to be noticed.

"Today has been full of surprises," Theresa said, loud enough for most people in the lobby to hear.

I stopped and turned. Theresa stood a few paces back, looking like she'd stepped out of a board meeting and into my day out of spite.

"You know, I would be surprised to hear your voice," I said slowly, "but the sound of your cloven hooves gave you away."

Theresa didn't react. If anything, her mouth tightened slightly like she was resisting the urge to smile. I glanced down at the heels she wore that announced her to everyone in the building. Clean and polished, but uneven. The left heel was slightly longer than the right. Compensating.

"Charming as always. I see Wilson made the call to drag you back in," Theresa said, eyes narrowing as she spoke.

"Well," I started, returning my gaze to hers, "what can I say? I'm the apple of his eye."

A young man beside her made a soft scoffing sound—small, dismissive, and practiced. He'd grown up scoffing at people for sport. My gaze shifted to him. He was around twenty, maybe a little older. Clean-cut. Comfortable. The kind of comfort that didn't come from confidence, but from knowing the world would move out of your way because someone important wanted it to.

I didn't like him on instinct, which was unfair, but my instincts had earned their arrogance. "I don't think we've met."

Theresa's hand moved slightly, a gesture that could've passed as an introduction if it wasn't so clearly possession. "This is my son," she introduced. "Bryce."

Bryce's eyes flicked over me. Not curious. Not impressed.

He offered his hand. I shook it. His grip was firm, trained, and just a touch too long. It was the kind of handshake that wanted you to remember it.

"Bryce," I repeated.

Behind Theresa, Stephanie stood half a step back, phone in one hand and a tablet in the other. She was watching everything without looking like she was watching. A knee brace hugged her leg under her skirt, and the way she shifted her weight told me it wasn't for decoration.

Theresa's gaze stayed on me.

"Anyway," I said, stepping back, "things to be, places to do, all of that stuff."

"Do try to avoid collateral damage, Red."

"Well, I know who's going to be there." I gestured loosely to Mia. "So, I can't promise anything."

Theresa's eyes narrowed a fraction, but she didn't reply. She didn't need to. She'd won just by existing in my path and reminding me who else was watching.

I turned with a fake smile and walked out of the building.

The sun hit like a slap. I took one breath and kept moving toward my car. Mia was still behind me, her heels tapping across the pavement.

"You just get along with everyone, don't you?"

I clicked my keys and glanced back at her "Of course, I'm a magnet for friendship."

Mia's expression didn't change, but her eyes tracked me.

I got into the car and shut the door, sealing myself into quiet.

My eyes stayed on the front of the building. Stephanie and Bryce walked out. I let my gaze follow them, feeling my gut tighten as the implication of Theresa being involved in Casey's case settled in my mind. Bryce peeled off in a different direction from Stephanie, and I rolled my eyes at the way he carried himself.

Just like his mother.

I exhaled through my nose, turned the key, and the engine caught. The sound filled my ears, and I tried to let it drown out the words Wilson had said, and as I pulled out of the parking lot, falling in line behind Mia's car, and let the Saturday traffic swallow me, my thoughts turned to one thing.

Whatever thread I was pulling, it was clearly tugging on something.

And I wasn't intending on stopping.

9

I kept a steady distance from Mia's car as we wound our way through traffic. She didn't hesitate at intersections--no double-checking, no drifting--just straight lines and clean turns like she'd memorised the route.

The drive was long. I had no idea why Wilson thought we could get there in thirty minutes. We pushed further east, then dipped south, the streets changing gradually as the houses got bigger and the gardens got tidier. More brick. More stone. Driveways wide enough to park three cars without blocking the footpath. The kind of neighbourhood people spent their entire life trying to afford to get into, but few actually did.

It took us a little over an hour before Mia turned down a street that was now blocked off end to end.

The perimeter spanned the entire road. Yellow tape crossed from a street sign to a tree, then again to the mirror of a patrol car. Police vehicles sat angled to funnel traffic away. An officer stood at one end of the tape with a clipboard, another at the opposite side, talking into a radio. A couple of neighbours lingered on their driveways pretending they weren't watching.

What surprised me was that there were no journalists or news vans around. They must have all got what they wanted and left after the bodies were removed.

Mia found a space close enough to be convenient without being in anyone's way. I parked a few metres behind her and cut the engine. Cool air wrapped around me as I opened the car door. The afternoon was on the cusp of turning into night, and you could feel it in the freeze The streetlamps gently illuminated the street, clashing with the harsh red and blue of the police cruisers.

I stepped out of my car and shut the door behind me, pocketing my keys, and falling into step beside Mia without saying anything. She didn't look over. She walked toward the police tape with purpose, badge already in hand.

The officer at the tape glanced at Mia's credentials, then at mine when I lifted it. His eyes didn't linger. He raised the tape and waved us through. Mia ducked under cleanly. I followed, bending just enough to clear it, keeping my eyes forward and my face neutral.

We walked down the middle of the road, away from the cluster of uniformed officers and toward the house that had pulled the whole street into orbit. A large place, pale exterior, neat garden beds, and a front porch wide enough to fit a small crowd. Two tech vans were parked nearby with their back doors open. People in gloves and shoe covers moved in and out with evidence cases. Someone carried a rolled-up light stand. Another person spoke quietly into a phone, back turned.

Mia broke the silence first. "I'm surprised you haven't made a joke yet," she observed, eyes on the house.

"And what would I joke about?" I asked, matching her pace.

"Me. Whether I feel anything. Your general distaste for me. Honestly, any number of things."

I kept my gaze ahead. "My distaste isn't for you," I told her. "It's for what you do. And how you do it."

Mia's posture didn't change. "What I *can* do and *what* I do represent me," she returned. "And I can't change that."

"You can. You just don't want to."

She didn't take the bait.

I watched a tech step onto the porch, pause to adjust shoe covers, then disappear inside. No bodies. Dante had said that much. Still, the street carried the weight of what had happened here. The neighbours didn't linger, at least not anymore. Those that had been outside when we arrived had wandered back inside.

I glanced sideways at Mia. "I'll admit you're smart. And you're no doubt you're good at what you do at the NBI. So, why would you want that hidden behind a lie? Why hide accomplishments behind it?"

Mia finally looked at me, brief and direct. "You're so narrow-minded. You refuse to see outside your own little box. You see what's in front of you, and you take it as the truth. Not even considering anything else."

"Oh," I said, letting it sit dry, "and that's what your powers told you?"

"That's what your file told me," Mia answered without missing a step. "What? You expected me not to look you up? I wanted to know who I was replacing. It was big shoes to fill. And an even bigger ego."

I let out a quiet breath. "Seems like you've got the ego part sorted."

Mia's expression stayed level. "You really have no respect for what I do, do you?"

"No. Because I used to do what you do. I know the tricks and the lies. And I know how vulnerable people can be."

Mia's eyes flicked forward again, scanning the scene.

"Especially after losing someone," I continued, keeping my voice low. "The hope that they want. You shouldn't bring those lies here. Not to people like that."

Mia slowed a fraction, not stopping, just adjusting her pace so she could answer without looking rushed. "I offer what I can because I have the ability to help people. No lies."

She held my gaze, then looked back to the house "Now, I don't know who you used to be or what you used to do. But we are not the same."

"Yeah. Well, I guess we'll find out."

We hit the front step together—Mia first, then me, half a stride behind.

Dante stood at the door with the three agents he'd brought along. They were lined up in that neat, professional way that always looked more like a barrier than a welcome. My eyes settled on Troy first. The face of one of the men I had almost got killed last time I worked a case with the team.

Dante's eyes flicked between me and Mia, then settled on me with the tired patience of a man who was regretting his day.

"Red," he greeted, then nodded to the three behind him. "You remember Brooke, Lavern, and Troy."

I took them in properly. Brooke's face was neutral in the way people got when they'd decided you were more trouble than you were worth. Lavern's eyes held that faint disgust that she never bothered to hide. Troy didn't bother with subtlety at all. He looked at me as though he wouldn't bother to help if I were on fire.

Which was fair.

"It's great to be back," I offered.

Nothing. Not even the courtesy of a blink that said they'd heard me.

Dante didn't react either. He dipped his chin at them and gestured—back to work. Brooke turned away immediately. Lavern shifted her attention to a tech looking through scene photos. Troy held my gaze a second longer, then moved past me.

Dante stepped a little closer, dropping his voice. "You going to be able to behave yourself?"

"Hey, I'm just here to shadow," I replied, letting my tone stay light. The word tasted like an insult.

Mia didn't wait for the rest of the conversation. She shook her head once, then walked past Dante and straight into the house.

Dante watched her go, then looked back at me. "Gonna take that as a no."

I stared after Mia's back. "Psychic. What a joke."

"No one has to like it or agree with it," Dante replied. His expression stayed flat, but there was a weariness underneath it. "But she helps close cases. Just like you."

"Yeah." I scoffed. "But I never had to throw a séance to do it."

Dante winced as if I'd stepped on his foot. "That was one time."

I blinked at him. "Seriously?"

Dante exhaled, then rubbed a hand down his face. "Can we just…"

He didn't finish the sentence. He didn't need to. The house behind him was quiet, and it had the kind of quiet that demanded you stop making jokes and start being useful.

Dante gestured toward the doorway. I lifted both hands in surrender and stepped inside.

The air changed as soon as I crossed the threshold—cooler, filtered, and carrying that faint mix of cleaning product and something older underneath it. The entryway was wide and neat. Shoes lined up on a rack by the wall, arranged carefully. A framed photo sat on a side table: a couple smiling somewhere sunny, arms around each other. The kind of picture you took when you were happy and didn't think the world could reach inside your home.

Techs were moving somewhere deeper in the house, quiet voices carrying down the hall. A camera shutter clicked once, sharp in the stillness. We moved through at a controlled pace. Mia had already disappeared into the house. Dante squeezed past me in the hallway, taking the lead and showing me where to go.

We turned into the living room. It was large, open plan, expensive furniture arranged in a way that suggested someone had paid for it to look effortless. A throw blanket folded perfectly over the arm of the couch. A bowl on the coffee table that held nothing but decoration. Framed photos on the wall—holidays, birthdays, a dog, the same couple again, always together. An open door stood in the far corner of the room.

I saw it immediately.

The number was there. Painted in blood on the door.

I stopped without meaning to. "I thought there were only two victims."

Dante didn't look at me yet. His attention stayed on the room. "There were."

We moved closer. Dante went in first, shoulder brushing the doorframe as he stepped through. I lingered outside; eyes fixed on the number. The blood had dried dark. It had texture. Not just a smear. A deliberate stroke.

"Both victims' blood was used," Dante noted from inside.

I stepped closer, still not crossing the threshold. "This the second scene laid out like this?"

"Yeah. That we know of."

I nodded once, letting my gaze travel over the door again. "That checks out," I murmured. "I'm gonna assume you've found all the murders so far. Unless there's a higher number somewhere else."

Dante's head turned toward me. "Why?"

"One victim at the first," I said, keeping my voice low. "Two here. And a three on the door." I pointed at it without touching. "It's a tally."

Dante stared at the number as if it might change if he stared long enough. "That's disconcerting."

"Yeah," I agreed. "That's one word for it."

I moved past him and into the room. The techs had stripped the bedroom down, but you could still feel what had happened. Evidence markers on the floor. Tape lines. The faint shine of dried blood on the floor and walls.

My eyes drifted round the room. Two side tables. Two sets of personal clutter, one neater than the other. A book left face down. A glass on a coaster. Clothes folded on a chair like someone intended to put them away later. Photos on the dresser—more of them smiling, arms around each other, the ordinary intimacy of a shared life captured in small frames.

Two people who lived together. And died together.

I kept my eyes on the details, letting them settle in my mind where they could do damage later.

"Can we have the room?" Dante asked, voice level.

No one moved.

Mia stood near the dresser with her arms folded, eyes on the far wall like she was waiting for the room to rearrange itself for her. Two techs hovered near the bed, gloves on, cameras hanging from their necks, looking between Dante and Mia like they'd rather be anywhere else.

Dante didn't repeat himself. He didn't need to. He just held the space until the moment tipped.

Mia's jaw tightened. Then she stepped toward the door without a word. The techs followed. The door clicked shut behind them, and the house noise dropped away.

Dante turned to me. "What happened?"

I kept my eyes on the dresser photos—two smiling faces in a frame. "Well, you weren't wrong about the case being flagged."

"That's why you're here."

I let out a thin breath. "Wilson made it pretty obvious I'm here so he has some control over what I'm doing. This case just happens to fit my scope."

Dante's gaze sharpened. "So, you think it's Wilson who altered the case?"

"All I know is he knows about it. And Theresa does. Stephanie wouldn't have sent that message if she didn't."

Dante leaned back a fraction as if he needed a little distance to think. "And how do they know you're looking into it?"

"My guess?" I glanced toward the door, then back to him. "They're keeping an eye on me. My name was on the initial report. They know I'm aware of it."

Dante's mouth tightened. "So, why bury it?"

"That's what we're gonna find out."

Dante watched me, weighing how far I'd already gone in my head. "You think someone in the NBI had something to do with it?"

"Maybe. Having a reason why would be a great next step."

A knock cut through the quiet. Dante didn't flinch. He just angled his head toward the door like he'd expected it. "Yeah?"

The door opened, and Mia stepped in without waiting for permission. Her eyes swept the room once—fast and practised—then landed on Dante. "Are you two done?" she asked. "I'd like to work."

Dante's expression didn't change, but the muscle in his jaw ticked.

I stepped toward the doorway, making room. "Oh, by all means," I murmured as I passed. "Commune."

Mia's eyes followed me, cool and unimpressed.

I stopped beside her, just close enough that she had to acknowledge me. "Make sure to tell the spirits I said hi."

Mia gave me a smile that had no warmth, and I walked out of the bedroom. Dante followed, shutting the door behind us gently.

"Can you at least try to get along?" he asked under his breath as we moved down the hall.

I glanced at him. "What do you mean? I try very hard to be likeable."

Dante made a small sound. "Right."

We moved back through the living room and down the hall until we stepped outside and onto the front lawn. The rest of Dante's team was scattered along with most of the techs. Equipment was being packed, and uniformed officers were moving along the edges of the scene. Brook and Lavern were on the porch talking quietly, and Troy was leaning against a tech's van with his arms crossed. His eyes still carried the same resentment as before.

Dante's phone rang. He checked the screen, and the shift in his face was immediate. Not panic. Something closer to wary recognition. "Yeah?"

I watched him listen. His posture stayed loose, but his eyes tightened, as if the voice on the other end had reached straight into his chest.

Dante didn't speak much. A couple of short responses. A pause. Then he pulled the phone away from his ear and held it out to me. "For you."

I frowned and took it. "Hello?"

There was a brief silence on the other end, then Angelo's voice came through low and steady. Though there was something else laced into it. Pain.

"Get to the West," he ordered. *"Now."*

My grip tightened around the phone. "What?"

He didn't answer the question. He gave me an address instead, and then the line went dead. I stared at the phone for half a second, then lowered it. Silence hung in the air around me.

Dante searched my face, and I glanced back to the house. Mia had reappeared, standing in the doorway. Arms crossed and eyes sharp. Troy's gaze locked onto me like he'd been waiting for another reason to hate me.

"I have to go," I said, loud enough for them to hear me.

"Of course you do," Mia remarked, voice dry.

I glanced at her. "Thought you were meant to be talking to ghosts?"

Mia's expression didn't shift. She tilted her head slightly, calm as ever. "Just came to ask Troy for assistance."

I looked back at Dante, lowering my voice and repeating, "I need to go."

Before Dante could answer, Troy pushed off the van.

"Good to know you haven't changed," he scolded. "Still doing whatever you want."

I turned toward him slowly. "Is there a problem?"

Troy's mouth twitched—close to a smile, but not there.

"Not at all. Just the same old shit."

Dante's voice came sharp and quiet. "Red."

I ignored him. I stepped closer to Troy, not crowding him, just enough that he had to either talk to me or back down. "Sorry," I replied, "do you not think you can handle this without me?"

Troy's jaw flexed.

Dante tried again. "Red."

I still didn't stop because Angelo's call had lit something in me, and I didn't have the patience for his grudge today.

I turned my voice up again. "Whoever did this," I announced, gesturing back toward the house, "is new. An amateur. Too showy for their own good." Techs paused. Brooke looked up. Lavern's head turned. Even one of the uniformed officers looked over.

"They dressed the scene up for presentation," I continued, voice steady, "and they paint a number on a door like it's art." I let my eyes sweep around me, catching faces. "My guess? They'll be sloppy. They'll make a mistake."

The street had gone still. Twenty-plus people, at least. All watching me now. I stared at Troy, letting the last part land clean. "If you can't catch someone as pathetic as that," I finished, "that's not my problem."

Dante leaned in close enough that only I heard him.

"Could've done that better."

I didn't look at him. "Yeah, well, why pull a thread when I can burn the whole sweater."

Dante exhaled.

Troy said nothing.

I gave a small, sarcastic smile, then turned on my heel and walked down the street. Dante stayed beside me, matching my pace, trying not to look like he was escorting me out of a scene.

"What did he want?"

"Me to go to him."

Dante's eyes narrowed. "Why?"

I shot him a look. "Funnily enough, he wasn't that chatty."

Dante hesitated. "You need me to come?"

"No. You deal with this." I paused, then added quietly, "I'm sorry about the fallout that may come with it."

Dante's mouth tightened. "Yeah, I'm not gonna be thrilled with what Wilson will say."

I stopped at the police tape at the end of the street and looked over at him as he stopped beside me, giving him the closest thing I could manage to an apologetic smile.

Dante nodded once, deciding to take what he could get. "Don't die."

"Don't get fired," I shot back. His mouth twitched, but he didn't smile.

I ducked under the tape and headed for my car, keys already in my hand. The street was still quiet again behind me, though I knew it wouldn't stay that way once I was out of earshot.

Angelo's voice stayed in my head, threaded with pain, and I knew I couldn't ignore it.

10

The drive out of the East didn't feel long at first. Just traffic lights and lane changes, Saturday night in its usual rhythm—cars drifting, people heading out and home. Then the city started letting go. Streets opened up. Suburbs thinned. The sky darkened and my body started complaining. I looked at the time and realised it had been an hour.

I let out a small sigh and continued to follow the streets. The address Angelo had given me sat on my phone screen, telling me which turns to take. The car hummed along as I drove. The road rolled under me, and every few minutes I checked the time again as if doing so would get me to my destination any faster.

It didn't. There was still another hour to go.

Unfortunately, my mind didn't stay on the driving for long. It folded over the day in neat, irritating loops. Wilson, in his office, calm, sharp and deliberate. He hadn't raised his voice. He didn't need to. He'd said the kind of things that sounded general if you weren't listening properly. The kind of warning you could pretend wasn't a warning at all. Work what you're told. Don't wander. Don't pull at anything you're not meant to touch.

Then Theresa showing up like she'd been waiting in the lobby with a stopwatch. Clean and in command. It felt as though they had planned for me to be ambushed. A reminder. Or a threat.

Then the West shoved its way into the same mental space, slipping in between the cracks. Two gangs. A split. Sterling on one side. Angelo on the other. Casey dead in the middle. Maybe it was gang-related. Maybe it wasn't. Maybe it was both. The problem was that there were too many variables and no clear direction to follow. Every time I tried to lay it out, something came and kicked all of the pieces.

And then the question I'd been avoiding finally took centre stage, because it was the one that mattered. Why would Angelo call me into the West?

Not Dante. Not one of his own people. Me.

I tightened my grip on the steering wheel and kept driving. The streetlights started showing up less frequently as I got closer to The Strip, letting the darkness creep in closer. Most things were still open. It was still functioning. People still wandered the street. But it was even less inviting now. Still neutral. It just felt less so.

I turned in and clocked Stephen almost instantly.

He was near the corner that gave him a good view both ways. He leaned back against the wall as if he belonged there. One hand was in his pocket, the other pinching a cigarette. He watched my car approach and recognition hit him. He didn't move or react. He just watched as if he'd been told I was coming.

Crossing into the West was quieter. Less movement. Less noise. Less people trying to convince you everything was fine. But there were still people.

On the footpaths. On corners. Sitting on steps. Standing in doorways with their arms folded. Small groups with their heads together. Eyes tracking my car. Last time, the looks had been hard. Territorial. Letting me know I wasn't wanted.

This time was different. Cautious. Tight. Eyes that didn't linger too long. People who looked away quickly. It felt like an echo of fear. A shift in the air.

I didn't like it.

I followed the map's directions deeper. A couple more turns. A few streets that got narrower and darker. Houses that looked tired. Fences that leaned as if they'd given up. Windows covered with boards or curtains that never opened. I turned onto the street Angelo had given me, a suburb or two away from Casey's house, and slowed. It was quiet.

Too quiet.

Streetlamps flickered overhead, light stuttering across the road. I pulled into the curb and parked on the opposite side of the street of the address I would soon be walking into.

I killed the engine and let the silence settle around the car. No music. No voices. No yelling. Just distant traffic and the hum of suburbia that kept doing its thing. I sat there, hand still on the keys, and scanned around me.

Nothing moved.

I got out, shut the door quietly, and pocketed my keys. The night air had settled completely now, letting the chill run under my collar and sit freshly on my skin. I looked up at the streetlamps again. The darkness between them swallowed everything the light didn't touch.

I crossed the street slowly. Eyes peeled. Head up. Hands empty. I wasn't a fighter. I didn't have a weapon. If this was a trap, I'd turned up with nothing but the habit to say things that made things worse.

Dante's offer to come circled in my mind. I'd said no because I was very good at making decisions that looked brave and felt stupid later. A tinge of regret kept in, but I pushed it away. My shoes hit the footpath. I kept moving, staying aware of the windows, the doorways, and the gaps between cars. The shadows didn't shift. The street stayed quiet.

That worried me.

The house Angelo had told me was worse up close. The porch sagged, and the steps were cracked and snapped in places, with wood splintering at the edges. The railing wobbled when I touched it, and paint peeled off the door in long strips that curled at the ends.

I climbed the steps carefully, putting my weight where the wood looked least offended by it, and raised my hand to knock. The door opened before my knuckles hit it. Angelo stood in the doorway, filling most of it.

"What? No hug?" I asked because I was never good at being quiet.

Angelo didn't answer. His eyes stayed on me, and I read him the way

I always did, because it was easier than asking questions. Pain sat in his face. Heavy and immediate. The tired in his eyes gave him away.

He stepped aside without a word. I moved past him into the house, and the door clicked shut behind me. The air inside was stale. Dust and old carpet. Something faint underneath that my brain recognised and didn't want to name.

Angelo walked into the open-plan living area and moved to the side, giving me a clear view.

A body lay sprawled on the carpet. Blood pooled underneath, dark and wide. I stopped. Two bullet wounds to the chest, clean and precise.

And then my eyes lifted, because dead bodies didn't appear on their own. Angelo stood a few steps away, watching me, his face set hard around whatever he was trying not to say.

I didn't speak straight away. Not because I was shocked. I'd seen bodies. I'd seen worse. But there was a difference between a taped-off crime scene with uniformed officers and techs, and an empty house in the West with Angelo standing in the shadows watching.

I turned back to the body. The blood had been sitting for a while. It had spread into the carpet and then started to set, darker at the centre and tacky around the edges. The man on the floor lay on his back, one arm angled out, the other bent awkwardly, palm half-open. He had fallen where he stood. Not running.

I let my eyes continue to go over the body, assessing it. Then I did the same to Angelo. He wasn't pacing. He wasn't looking away. He stood near the edge of the living area with his shoulders squared, arms crossed, and his face set hard around something he was containing.

I exhaled slowly. "Who is he?" I asked, keeping my voice level.

Angelo's eyes dropped to the body and came back to me. "Blaze."

I looked back down at him. Blaze. Someone who had mattered before. Now dead as well. "Why'd you call me?"

Angelo's jaw tightened. "To talk."

I let out a short breath. "About this? About Casey? I thought you knew who did it. That you didn't need me."

"I was wrong," Angelo returned, calm but not soft. "Which I'm guessing you already knew."

I didn't deny it. He didn't need me to. "Is this you asking for my help?"

Angelo's mouth pulled tight. "Maybe it's me who's helping you."

I bit the inside of my cheek., neither of us moved. The house stayed quiet around us.

Angelo looked down at Blaze again. His tone was different. Careful and deliberate. "Is there anything that could've saved him?"

"Other than not being shot?" I shot back automatically.

Angelo didn't react and kept his expression flat. "Could we have kept him alive?" Angelo rephrased the question.

I exhaled, then moved closer to Blaze and crouched, keeping my balance steady. The blood smell was stronger down here. I studied the shirt first—dark fabric, soaked through around the entry points. I pinched the fabric lightly between two fingers and lifted just enough to see the edges of the wounds without shifting his body. Clean. Precise. No ragged tearing. Slight burns on the fabric of the shirt. The shooter had been standing close, making it almost impossible to miss.

One shot sat high, just left of centre. The other was lower on the right. If they tracked the way they looked, the first would've punched straight through the heart. The second would've collapsed a lung.

"He would've died almost instantly," I muttered, glancing up at Angelo. "The first one would've done it."

Angelo nodded once. No relief. No satisfaction. Just a grim kind of confirmation.

"When did you find him?" I asked.

"Just before I called. Not long after the gunshots."

"You heard them?"

"A lot of people did. Neighbours came running."

"They see anything?"

Angelo shook his head. "No. They heard someone running. A couple went after them but got nothing."

I looked back at Blaze, taking in the position again. No sign of struggle. No sign of surprise. He was looking at the killer as they pulled the trigger.

Just like Casey.

I scanned the floor for casings and saw none. Which either meant the gun was a revolver or someone had already picked them up. "Casings?"

"None," Angelo answered flatly, and I nodded.

I paused, then I sighed. "This is the same person."

Angelo's brow furrowed. "Yeah, I'm assuming."

"I'm not."

He shifted his weight.

"You thought it was the other gang at first, yeah?" I questioned, and Angelo shrugged.

"That was the thought," Angelo admitted.

"It crossed my mind as well after you said it."

Angelo's gaze slid past me, somewhere into the room, then snapped back. "It doesn't make sense after this."

"Why after this?"

"Blaze wasn't a player. Not really."

I rose to a half-stand and turned toward him. "What was he to Casey?"

Angelo hesitated for a fraction, then answered anyway.

"They were together. Blaze is from The Strip. Moved in with Casey when they got serious."

I glanced around again, letting the room make its point.

"This isn't Casey's house," I noted.

Angelo's mouth tightened. "This isn't anyone's house."

I let that sit. "Okay. So, you don't think he'd be a target if it was gang related?"

"No one would know him. He kept to himself."

My eyes drifted back to Blaze. "Alright… then what was Casey to you?" I asked. "To the gang? Other than just family."

Angelo didn't posture. He didn't puff up. He just answered. "He was a runner."

"Drugs?"

"Cash," Angelo corrected.

"For?"

"A lot of people."

I pinched the bridge of my nose. "Is this your idea of help?" I asked, letting the bite show.

Angelo met it without flinching. "He ran money between both sides of the West, and into the East."

My head tilted. "You're going to have to explain a little bit better to me what's going on, Angie."

Angelo snapped before the last syllable even finished. "Don't fucking call me that, Red. I'm not in the mood."

I lifted a hand slowly—not apologising, just acknowledging the boundary. "What money?" I asked. "If the West is split, why is there cash flow between the two, and what's going to the East?"

Angelo exhaled, controlled on purpose "The West runs on bribes and understanding, Red. Sterling's group keep to themselves, and we keep to ourselves." His gaze hardened. "Come on, Red, why do you think no cops are here?"

Too many questions slammed into my head at once. I reigned in my focus into one. "You're paying cops off?"

Angelo nodded. "Since before you left. I didn't know it until I was a bit older."

He paused. "It's complicated. Now more than before."

I was only half listening, because things had started shifting into place whether I wanted them to or not. Wilson's tone. Theresa's timing. Casey's file being altered. The fact that it had been touched inside the system at all.

"The running to the East?" I asked, forcing myself back to him.

Angelo's eyes narrowed slightly. "What do you want me to say, Red?"

"I want you to say it plainly."

Angelo gave a short, humourless scoff. "Plainly. Plainly is someone killed Casey and then decided they needed to kill his partner as well."

"If there's money involved, that's motive."

"Motive," Angelo echoed, as if the word irritated him.

I clenched my jaw. "Maybe if you didn't throw me out last time, this wouldn't have happened."

Angelo's stare sharpened fast. "Want to rephrase that?"

I didn't. "Maybe he knew something. He wasn't killed for nothing, Angelo."

"And you would've figured it out?" Angelo challenged.

"I would've had something to work with," I shot back.

Silence.

I looked back down at Blaze, staying crouched for another second, eyes on the dried edge of the blood pool, then I stood. My knees complained. My patience did, too.

Angelo watched me the whole time, expression locked in place.

"You give money to the other gang?" I asked, keeping my voice low.

Angelo shook his head once. "They give us money. For the bribes."

I stared at him. "So, you're telling me Sterling's crew pays you so you can pay cops."

"More or less."

I turned that over in my head and hated how quickly it slotted into something that made sense. Not good sense. Practical sense. The sort of thing the world ran on when you stripped off the nice labels.

"Casey went to get it," I said, thinking out loud, "then he handed it out, and went East."

Angelo didn't interrupt. He didn't correct me. He just let me build it because he wanted me to arrive at the same conclusion without him having to drag me there.

My jaw tightened. "Where was the money going in the East?" I asked, the flatness in my voice already telling Angelo I already knew the answer.

Angelo's eyes didn't move. "Gotta keep the bureau out somehow."

The air shifted. I wanted to ask for a list of names, but I already had one building in my head.

"Fuck.". I took a slow breath through my nose, forced the thought to stay tidy enough to hold. "The file."

Angelo's brow creased. "What file?"

"Casey's," I clarified, then lifted my eyes to his. "That's why they're burying it."

Angelo nodded as though he already knew who 'they' were.

Which would make sense. I was almost positive the list of names in my head matched the one he had. I looked at Blaze again and didn't really see him. I saw numbers in a system. The way paperwork could disappear when the right person decided it should. The way a death could turn into a footnote if it threatened the wrong people.

I forced myself back into the room. "What was Casey doing last Wednesday?" I asked. "Why was he out?"

Angelo's eyes dipped for half a second, then came back up. "He… that was a run."

"He didn't have anything with him," I pressed. "Come on, Angelo.

One in the morning. Lakeside."

Angelo exhaled, and it came out sharp. "He would've been finished by then. On his way back." Angelo's gaze flicked past me toward the front of the house, then back to my face. "This could be the NBI."

I blinked once. "What makes you say that?"

Angelo's jaw flexed. He walked two steps to the side and looked around the room as if the walls might answer for him. Then he looked at me again. "We're looking at a change."

"What kind of change?"

Angelo's laugh came out short and harsh. "Look at this place, Red. It was never paradise, but lately it's gotten worse." His eyes narrowed. "My father wanted to stop the payments before Sterling put a bullet in his head."

I didn't move. I didn't soften my face. I let the words hang there because they deserved space. "And you want to stop them, too," I said quietly.

"It's a discussion," Angelo answered, and his mouth twisted. "One that's been happening."

"That doesn't narrow it to the NBI," I pointed out.

"But it narrows it to people who don't want change," Angelo countered. "People who benefit."

He watched me as if he wanted to see whether I'd accept it. Whether I'd finally admit the East had been leaning on the West for longer than I wanted to believe.

"But it's something," Angelo continued. "Isn't that what you wanted?"

"I think you're wrong," I replied, keeping my voice calm and even.

Angelo's expression sharpened. "Nothing new."

"It just circles back to being any number of people."

I shifted my attention back to Blaze and then to the room itself. Angelo hadn't been lying when he said this wasn't anyone's house. It wasn't lived in. There was no furniture. No clutter. It had been empty until Blaze and whoever else had entered it.

"So, we narrow it down," I muttered. "Blaze came to meet someone here. I don't think it was by chance."

Angelo's gaze held mine.

"Whoever did this… knew him," I added, voice steady, "and they knew Casey as well."

Angelo didn't argue. He waited.

"This… this is personal," I finished.

Angelo's eyes flicked down toward Blaze, then back up. "Someone who knew both of them?"

"Maybe."

"Someone from Sterling's side?"

"I don't know."

"Someone from my side?" Angelo asked, and there was something raw under the question that he didn't bother covering.

"I don't know," I admitted.

Angelo scoffed. "You don't seem know a lot."

I gave him a look. "I can only assume, Angie."

Angelo's head snapped up. "Don't."

I held his gaze. "Fine. Sorry."

Silence settled again. It wasn't awkward. It was heavy. Angelo didn't do awkward. He did anger or nothing He broke it first. "The boys think whoever did it might have got their leg caught on the window when they ran."

I frowned. "Why? Blood?"

Angelo shook his head, already moving. "Nah. They said it sounded like they were limping. Maybe popped a knee on the way out."

I straightened fully and gestured loosely. "Show me."

Angelo led the way through the short hall at the back, through a doorway, and into a smaller room that smelled damp. It had the same stripped feeling as the rest of the place. Bare walls and a thin curtain that didn't cover the window properly.

The window was open. I stepped closer and looked at the frame. No obvious scrape marks. No fresh chips in the paint. No torn fabric caught on a nail.

Angelo stood off to the side and watched me work. He didn't hover. He didn't offer commentary. He trusted his own people, and he trusted himself. Trusting me was a new thing, and it looked uncomfortable on him.

I leaned out the window and looked down. The drop wasn't much. Someone could step out and be on the ground fast. The yard below was concrete. Flat. No uneven garden edge. No soft dirt to hide a bad landing.

That didn't match what I'd expected. My mind flicked back to the night Casey died. The sound of someone running. The uneven ground around the path and through the tree line. The way the steps had changed as they moved away.

I straightened and let my gaze travel once more over the concrete. I nodded. "Maybe they were already injured," I murmured.

Angelo's eyes narrowed. "From what? You think Blaze did something to them?"

I shook my head. "I don't know. But I don't think so."

Angelo huffed but didn't say anything.

I turned to look at him again. His face had tightened, and his eyes remained sharp, locked on me.

I stepped back from the window and sighed. My mind was going too fast. Each new bit of information folding in on itself, and I couldn't keep up. Anger and frustration fit neatly among it all.

"Call me if anything else happens," I finally said. I knew I had to take everything and sift through it somewhere else. I need it to make sense, and I couldn't do it here.

Angelo's expression didn't change. "Yeah?"

"Yeah," I confirmed.

I reached into my wallet and dug until I found it. The card was worn at the edges and slightly bent from being carried too long. Hospital branding. A relic from my old life. Same name and number. I held it out.

Angelo's eyes dropped to it, then lifted to me. "Thought you weren't a doctor anymore?"

I shrugged. "What can I say? I'm sentimental."

He took the card, glanced at it, then slipped it into his pocket without comment.

We walked back into the main room, moving around Blaze. Angelo stopped near the edge of the living area again, posture rigid, and gaze fixed on the body.

"What are you going to do?" he asked without looking at me.

"I… am going home," I said slowly.

Angelo's head turned toward me, sharp. "Home?"

"Yeah. Home. I want to be back in time to tuck my boys in."

Angelo didn't say anything, so I turned toward the front door. "Red."

I slowed but didn't turn. His hand closed around my arm. Not gentle. Not violent. A grip that meant he needed to be sure I was still there, still listening.

I turned my head slightly and looked at him. His eyes were glassy in a way he'd hate if he knew I'd noticed. His jaw was clenched hard enough to ache "You find this fucker," Angelo said, voice low, "you tell me."

I held his stare. "You'll be on the list."

Angelo's grip tightened. "I'll be the first one."

We stayed like that for a moment, the house quiet around us, Blaze on the carpet, blood set into the fibres, and the West pressing in on the windows.

Then Angelo's hand loosened. I stepped back. "Bye, Angelo…"

He didn't answer. He just stood there and watched as I headed out into the street.

I reached my car and slid inside. I just sat there, letting my hands rest on the wheel. The new information swirled in my head along with the unanswered questions.

Nothing told me why Casey was dead. Or why Blaze had to die. Only why it was being buried.

So, maybe it was time I stopped caring who saw me digging.

11

Mamma's smelled the same as it always had. Fresh coffee, stale pastries, and old fryer oil all clinging to the air, fighting for dominance. I sat in a booth near the window with a mug between my hands, sipping slow, letting the heat anchor me. It was mid-morning, but the Strip didn't do mornings politely. It didn't wake up so much as it stayed awake.

A few people were scattered through the café. Quiet. Phones down and eyes on cups. Shoulders turned away from everyone else. Everyone was minding their own business.

The Strip felt on edge. Not the usual kind either. Not the kind where it sat as a dividing line between two different worlds that bleed into it. This was heavier and thicker. Like the air had weight, and if you stopped moving, it would crush you.

Maybe the news of Casey's death had travelled properly now. Maybe he'd mattered more around here than anyone in the East wanted to believe. Or maybe it was Blaze. Maybe that one hit closer. Maybe that one changed something.

I looked out through the glass and took The Strip in properly. People moved along the footpath in small currents. Shops half-open, shutters rattling, and signage buzzing. A few teenagers loitered outside a corner store, heads together, occasionally looking around them as though waiting for someone to approach. A woman pushed a pram past without looking at anything. Pace steady and jaw set.

My mind hadn't stopped from the night before. I'd driven home with Angelo's words lodged under my ribs and Blaze on that carpet refusing to leave my head. Even when I turned the key in my own door, the West came in with me.

But I still followed the routine. Dinner. Games. Bed.

We found Miles quickly in the cupboard across from the bathroom. Tucked inside like a cat, with his knees tightly to his chest and his hands over his mouth, trying not to laugh or make a noise. Alex had groaned about it as always, despite the smile on his face.

"We found you," I'd muttered, leaning down.

He'd giggled and crawled out on all fours like a little goblin. I'd ruffled his hair as he insisted that he'd find a new spot tomorrow. Claire and I tucked them into bed after that. Same as always. As if routine would keep the world outside at bay.

As we'd settled back into the kitchen, Claire had propped herself against the counter, arms folded loosely, trying to look casual even though she was reading my face line by line. "What happened?" she'd asked.

I told her.

Her mouth had tightened when I got to the bribes. The money. The way the West ran and how the East enabled it. "Of course," she'd muttered, disgust and exhaustion carrying the words.

I hadn't slept much after that. Just stared at the ceiling and turned over Wilson, and Theresa, and the way the NBI moved when it wanted something buried. Now I was here, drinking my second cup of coffee, pretending I could force answers out of the air around me.

The coffee cooled faster than I drank it. The mug left a ring on the table, and I watched it darken as it dried, like a slow stain. The bell above the door chimed. My head lifted before I could stop it, and Dante walked in.

He scanned the room, taking in his surroundings, before his eyes landed on me, and he headed over, shrugging his jacket off as he slid into the booth across from me. We exchanged a small hello, and then we fell quiet. Letting the space settle. Letting the café noise wrap around us just enough to feel private.

A waitress drifted past with a pot of coffee and topped up our mugs. She didn't linger. She didn't look at us twice. She just moved on, and we sat there with steam rising between us.

"You or me first?" I finally asked.

Dante leaned back slightly, eyes fixed on my face. "Well, I still have a job."

I tipped my head. "And me?"

His mouth twitched, close to a smile, but not quite. "Did you have anything to start with?"

I lifted one shoulder and let it drop again because I didn't have an answer for that.

Dante took a sip of his coffee, set the mug down carefully, and then exhaled slowly.

"I will say, about thirteen of the twenty-six people who were still at the crime scene, put in some form of complaint about you."

A breath slipped out of me. "Hey, that'd almost be a new record. That's also too many people at a crime scene."

"I'm surprised Wilson hasn't called you, to be honest."

"He full of joy?" I asked, eyes narrowing.

Dante's gaze slid off to the side. "When I saw him this morning, it looked like the vein on his forehead was going to explode."

"I'd pay to see that." I lifted my mug in a tiny salute and took a sip.

Quiet settled again, but it wasn't comfortable. It was the kind that came right before you cut into something. Dante broke it first, voice lower. "So, what happened?"

I watched the street through the window for half a beat, then brought my eyes back to him.

"Blaze was killed."

Dante's jaw flexed once. "I heard. Word carries pretty quick."

"Glad to see that hasn't changed."

Dante's gaze held mine. "You find out who he was?"

"Casey's partner."

"You think it was a hate crime?" Dante kept his tone steady.

"Well, from what I'm piecing together, whoever killed both of them knew them." I let the words sit. Then tightened them. "At least well enough for Blaze to meet up with them."

Dante's eyes narrowed. "So, you're not going to rule it out?"

"I'm not ruling anything out yet."

Silence. Not awkward. Just heavy. Dante watched me like he was waiting for the part I'd been avoiding. I watched him back, weighing how much I could say without lighting his life on fire. I took another sip without tasting it.

"Casey ran money." My voice stayed low. "Bribes. Local cops and the NBI. The money is to keep the West as it is. Let them do what they want."

I watched Dante's face as it landed. There was the flicker. The pause. The small tightening around his eyes. The reaction was someone who didn't know about the money.

Honest.

That was good to know. He leaned back a fraction. "That's why the file's fucked."

"Yeah." I rolled my mug slightly between my palms. "There are talks to stop the money. Shift the West into something more… habitable."

"Could be a touchy thing for some people." Dante didn't sound amused.

He was listening, but his mind was still stuck on the bribes and the NBI. Mine was too. I'd woken up with it sitting in my chest like a stone. I just didn't want it steering the whole conversation.

"There would be a lot of people who benefit from the current situation who wouldn't want it to change," I mumbled.

Dante stared past my shoulder, eyes unfocused. Running names. Running angles. Trying to make the ugly version of the world line up with the real one. It was all the same either way.

I continued. "But… if you want to stop the change, why would you kill the guy running the money? And his partner?"

Dante leaned forward, elbows near the edge of the table. "You'd go for Angelo."

"The one trying to make the change." I set my jaw. "That's what they did to his dad."

Dante nodded slowly, pieces clicking into place. "That's why the split happened."

"But whoever killed Casey had to know about the runs." I kept my voice steady, even as my thoughts sped up. "Angelo said the night he died, he was doing one. So, whoever killed him knew where he'd be and at what time."

"That does fit into the NBI angle." Dante's fingers tapped once against the mug, then stopped.

"But would they know Casey well enough to know Blaze?" I asked. "And again, why kill Blaze?"

I shifted my mug slightly, watched the coffee swirl, and then continued. "Let's throw Wilson's name down," I began, keeping my voice low. "He takes the money. He's heard it might stop coming through. He kills Casey as a warning. A threat. Whatever." I paused, eyes flicking to the window and back. "What's the reason to kill Blaze as well?"

Dante leaned in a fraction, forearms resting near the edge of the table. "Maybe the personal connection is further than the money."

"I do like the idea of integrating Wilson," I admitted, even though it tasted wrong in my mouth.

Dante's expression tightened. "You're not going anywhere near Wilson. Or the NBI. Not until we… I don't know." The end of it dropped off, frustration replacing the rest. He didn't like that he didn't know. I didn't either, but I'd been living in that space longer.

I watched his face, looking at him spin everything in his mind. "You good?"

Dante exhaled through his nose. "I can't really lie to you, can I?"

"I can pretend I don't notice," I offered.

"Well, then, yeah. I'm fine."

I nodded, being the good friend I am. "Okay," I conceded, lifting my hands a little as if surrendering. "No NBI. Not yet. Won't hurt to have a list, though."

Dante gave a brief nod.

"Wilson. Theresa. David." I ticked them off in my head, but the names tasted sour on my tongue.

Dante's brow furrowed. "That's a straight line to the top. What about sideways? Other SSAs like Wilson?"

"Then the list starts getting pretty long," I replied, already picturing it: names stacked on names, each one with enough authority to make things disappear.

"One name is already too long."

I nodded because he wasn't wrong. "Stephanie." The name slipped out before I could talk myself out of it.

The brace flashed in my mind—white against dark clothes, the way it caught the light in the lobby. I hadn't been sure why I'd clocked it at the time. Now it had a place to sit.

Dante's eyes narrowed slightly. "You think?"

"The shooter has a limp," I said bluntly.

Dante shifted in the booth, as if the idea had snagged on something uncomfortable. "I guess she'd most likely know about it."

"I mean, she messaged you about the file." I watched his reaction carefully.

"That was a direct feedline from Theresa, though," Dante countered.

"Fair. But look," I said, and the edge crept in despite me trying to keep it calm, "I'd rather have a lot of suspects than no suspects."

Dante didn't argue. He just watched me. "Alright," he relented, shifting gears. "And what about Blaze?"

"What about him?"

"We're looking at people connected to Casey." Dante's voice stayed even, practical. "Surely we try to find someone who can link Blaze?"

"He was originally from The Strip," I pointed out. "He could know people from both sides."

"Or it's someone from here," Dante added, eyes flicking briefly toward the front of the café.

"We aren't narrowing it down," I muttered. My eyes drifted again, uninvited, and landed on the HELP WANTED flyer taped near the door. Edges curled. Black marker shouting for staff like the place was bleeding workers faster than it could replace them.

Then the thought slid into place. "What if we work the case normally?"

Dante's mouth twisted. "I can't access the file. Not fully."

"Not the actual file," I clarified, leaning forward slightly. "The field work. That flashy badge of yours isn't being paid off to stay out of The Strip."

Dante's face screwed up at my wording. "If Blaze was from here and met Casey here, surely people knew them," I continued before he could lecture me. "Friends or family. We door-knock. Ask around. Find a personal connection."

"I don't have time, Red." Dante's eyes held mine, apologetic and irritated at the same time.

"The other case," I guessed.

"Technically, the only case." Dante's tone went dry. "The one you're meant to be on, too."

"Yeah, well," I replied, jaw tightening, "we know why they want me there."

Dante's eyes flicked down to his mug, then back up. "I don't know what they're gonna want now."

I gave an acknowledged shrug. "What've they got you doing today?"

Dante let out a breath and rubbed his thumb along the handle of the mug. "I'm meant to be doing what you want me to do here, but over there."

"You're in for a long drive," I said with a forced laugh.

"Yeah." His mouth pulled into something close to a smile. "I get to take your favourite person as well."

"There's so many of them," I replied, rolling my eyes. "You'll have to be specific."

"Mia." Dante didn't hesitate.

"Ironically, should've seen that coming."

We both sort of laughed. Not properly. Not the kind that cleared anything out. Just a brief release so we didn't choke on everything else.

"You're gonna leave me here on my own," I complained, leaning back into the booth.

"I am." Dante's tone stayed flat, but his eyes softened a fraction.

My mind cycled through a few things—routes, names, risks, and the way The Strip watched you when you didn't belong. Then it landed on something solid.

"It's fine," I said, a decision forming as I spoke. "I think I have a plan."

Dante's eyebrows rose. "Do I want to know?"

"I'll get back to you on that." I tilted my head toward the door. "You should go. Wouldn't want her to sniff me out on you."

Dante huffed a laugh, but it didn't reach his eyes. Then his expression shifted, quieter. More serious. "Can you just do me a favour?"

"You ask that a lot."

"I feel I need to." Dante held my gaze, and there was something in it he didn't dress up with humour.

I shrugged as if I wasn't bracing for whatever he was about to say.

"Remember you have a family," Dante said plainly.

"You jealous?" I shot back automatically with a smirk.

Dante didn't take the bait. "Red. It's Sunday. You're here."

The words hit cleaner than I wanted them to. I nodded slowly, because he was right, and because I didn't have a good defence that didn't make me sound worse.

Dante slid out of the booth and stood, rolling his shoulders like he was putting the job back on. "Call me if anything happens." He adjusted his jacket as he spoke. "I'll keep you updated on my end."

"Roger, roger."

Dante's mouth twitched, and then he turned and headed out. The bell chimed again as the door swung shut behind him. I stayed there, hands still around my mug, letting Dante's words play in my head. I'd give myself an hour, then I'd go home.

I looked out the window again, and the plan I'd latched onto shifted into my main focus. If I were going to parade around The Strip, flaunting the neutrality of it, I was going to need someone to back me up. Someone who knew things and had eyes everywhere.

And then I saw him. Cigarette between his lips, leaning against a wall on the other side of the street. His eyes were already locked in my direction.

Stephen.

I downed my coffee, wiped my thumb over the rim of the mug, and slid out of the booth. I left money on the table without counting it twice, and headed for the door.

Outside, The Strip hit me with its usual mix of noise and movement. I crossed the street at an even pace, eyes up, hands free, and stopped in front of Stephen. His stare stayed locked on me.

"Nice day, isn't it?" I offered.

He didn't answer. Didn't blink. Just watched.

"Stephen, isn't it?" I tried again, keeping my tone light.

Nothing. I shifted my weight, letting a second pass. "I feel like there's some underlying hostility here."

Stephen's expression didn't change.

"Or you're deaf, which would put a damper on my plan."

A grunt came out of him, low and rough.

"That's something," I muttered under my breath.

I leaned against the wall beside him, close enough that he'd have to move if he wanted distance. He lit another cigarette with steady hands, the flame catching briefly against his face, and took a drag without looking away from the street.

"Look. Angelo and I have set aside our differences. Or at least I have. He still sort of looks like he'll eat my heart, but… all I want to do is find out who killed Casey and Blaze."

Stephen let out a thin exhale through his nose.

"Now, you seem to look like a guy that knows a few people," I continued, watching him. "Maybe you even knew Blaze before he moved out of The Strip. All I'm asking is for a tour guide that points me in the right direction."

His eyes shifted to me again, and I caught the pause. The considering. The part where he ran the risk through his head.

"One hour," I pressed, keeping my voice level. "That's all I want. Then you can go back to being the… busy man you were being."

"I don't like you." Stephen's voice was raspy and cracked.

"That is a common occurrence," I replied, letting it land without pushing.

We went quiet. Stephen stared ahead, jaw clenching. "But Angelo said to help if you asked." He paused. "You piss me off, though, I'll cut you," he warned, his eyes sharp.

"And if I charm you, you'll fall in love with me," I shot back, raising both hands a little, palms out.

Stephen moved his hand to his pocket, reaching for something. "Whoa, alright, alright," I cut in quickly, taking a half-step back. "Starting now, yeah?"

He scoffed, the sound sharp, and reset his posture as if he'd decided I wasn't worth the effort of proving a point.

"Cool." I nodded once, as if we'd just agreed on something normal. "Shall we?"

I gestured down the street, and Stephen's gaze followed it. He just stared, unmoving. Then, with a grunt that sounded like the hardest thing he'd ever done, he pushed off the wall and began walking.

And I fell in step right beside him.

12

We walked down The Strip without conversation.

Stephen stayed a half-step ahead, not hurrying, not slowing, just setting a pace that made it clear he wasn't escorting me so much as allowing me to follow. He didn't look back. He didn't need to. I kept close enough that anyone watching would read us as a unit, and far enough that I could still move if things went sideways.

The Strip pretended it was normal. Pretended that the sanctity and shine of the East had some semblance of matter here, and the deals and pain of the West didn't breach its borders.

I let my mind take it all in and tried to place Casey and Blaze in it. Two people walking on the same concrete, buying the same coffee, passing the same corner store, and standing outside the same places, making the same decisions.

Places I'd been when I was younger. The kind of familiarity that didn't come with nostalgia, just muscle memory. I remembered where to step around cracks in the pavement and which corners collected groups that didn't like being watched, and I remembered which doors never opened unless you were expected.

Some eyes lingered on me. Not hostile, exactly. More curious. Measuring. Trying to sort me into a category that made sense: East, West, cop, not-cop, problem, or passing through. A few faces flicked away as soon as mine lifted, and a few didn't.

I didn't recognise anyone. It was as though all the people I had once known had been cycled out and moved on, or age had taken away any features I could easily latch onto and connect to a memory.

Stephen kept his hands where they were easy to see. Just loose at his sides or tucked near his pockets without going in. Non-threatening, yet still in a position they could react quickly if needed. Every now and then his head shifted slightly, a glance that lasted half a second, and I started tracking what he was tracking—a man leaning in a doorway with his arms folded, a car idling too long at the curb, and a pair of teenagers that looked like they were pretending not to watch us.

Nothing immediate. But The Strip didn't do immediate. It did slow and patient.

Stephen turned without warning, cutting down an alley which held loading docks, garbage, and a few small shops which looked like they were no longer trading, though the movement behind the doors said otherwise.

A few steps later, he slowed. The place we stopped in front of was an older barbershop. The shutter was half-down, and bars covered the rest of the shop front. A sign peeked out from it all and said OPEN, and Stephen pulled on the door gently. Locked. He didn't rattle the handle. He raised his knuckles and knocked, firm and specific. Not a random knock. A pattern.

He waited. After a moment, there was movement behind the glass. Then the door opened. An older woman stood there, framed in the crack. She was short, and she held herself as if height had never mattered much. Her hair was grey and pulled back tight, and her eyes were sharp enough to cut. She looked past Stephen first, checking the street behind us, and then her gaze landed on me.

Stephen gave a brief nod. The woman returned it, and then she stepped back, letting us inside without a word.

The air in the barbershop hit me all at once—cleaner than I expected, but still heavy with the smell of hair product and what I could only describe as burnt hair. The floors were scuffed. The mirrors had chips and stains on them. Two barber chairs sat empty, black leather cracked at the edges, and a broom leaned in the corner.

No customers. That was the first thing that stood out. Not even a man pretending he wasn't listening in the chair while he got his neck cleaned up. No one waiting with a magazine they weren't reading. Just us, the woman, and the quiet. She didn't close the door straight away. She looked out again, then locked it behind us.

Then she turned, chin lifting slightly. "Who's getting the cut?" the woman asked.

Stephen's tone was steady. "No cut, Barb."

She glanced between the both of us. Not rude. Just assessing. Taking in my boots, my posture, the way I held my hands, and the way my eyes kept moving, taking everything in.

"Don't bring your shit into my shop, Steve," Barb warned.

Stephen tilted his head toward me without looking away from her. "Not mine. His."

I let out a small breath through my nose and stepped forward half a pace, because if I was going to be blamed for the shit, I might as well own it. "Barb, is it?"

Her expression didn't soften. "And what shit are you bringing in here?"

"No shit," I replied, keeping my voice easy even as her stare seemed to pierce me harder. "Just trying to find out a little about a guy named Blaze?"

Barb's face changed by a fraction. Not grief. Not shock. Something more like confirmation. "Good kid. Shame what happened."

"Kid?" I echoed before I could stop myself.

"He was only, what, twenty?" Barb added, eyes shifting briefly to Stephen like she expected him to correct her.

Stephen answered with a grunt.

The number landed wrong in my head. Blaze on the carpet had looked older than twenty. But death did that. It took youth and made it look like something else.

"Grew up around here," Barb continued. "Why do you wanna know?"

I opened my mouth, and my instincts tried to do what they always did—smooth the edges, shape the truth into something that sounded harmless—but Barb's stare didn't leave room for harmless.

"I'm just looking into—" I started.

"No. Nope. Not West Side shit in here." Barb cut me off before I could finish.

"This isn't West Side," I pushed back, because it wasn't, and because The Strip was supposed to be the one place you could breathe without choosing a side.

Barb didn't budge. "Sounds like it."

"Well, yeah, okay," I admitted. "It's kind of West Side."

"Jesus," Stephen muttered. He stepped in front of me, body angling slightly so Barb had to look at him instead. He dropped his voice lower, and for the first time since we'd left Mamma's, he sounded like he actually meant something. "We're doing this for Casey,"

I blinked once. That was the first real card he'd played.

"You knew Casey?" I asked, the question slipping out before I could filter it.

Barb made a sound that wasn't quite a laugh. "Everyone knew Casey."

"In what way?" I pressed.

Barb's gaze stayed on me, and I got the sense she didn't like being interrogated in her own shop.

But she answered. "He came from the East when he was, what, seven?" Barb said, thinking as she spoke. "By himself. Stuck around in The Strip for a few years. Moved on to the West."

I didn't move. My thoughts stalled, then started again. Seven years old. Alone. "He left the East alone?"

"Yeah," Barb confirmed.

The image didn't fit the Casey I'd built in my head. Runner. Gang-adjacent. Buried file. Now I was trying to imagine a seven-year-old walking into the Strip alone and deciding it was better than where he'd come from.

"Anyone know why?" I pressed.

Barb's eyes narrowed slightly. "I'm going to assume Blaze did."

My mind wandered, pulling threads whether I wanted it to or not. If Blaze had known the reason Casey left the East, that meant Blaze hadn't just been a boyfriend. He'd been trusted. That meant the killer wasn't just shooting a partner. They were cutting off someone who knew something.

Barb's voice dragged me back. "There was a woman who used to come visit sometimes when he was here," she added, careful like she didn't want to hand me too much.

"From where?"

"The East." Barb's tone sharpened. "Don't ask me about her, I don't know shit."

I turned my head slightly toward Stephen, because he'd dragged me here, and because he'd positioned himself as the person with the eyes and ears. "Mother?"

Stephen's lip curled. "The fuck would I know."

"Aren't you the eyes and ears?" I pushed because it was that or nothing. "Shouldn't you know something?"

Stephen's gaze snapped to me. His hand moved toward his pocket. "You want me to get my fucking knife out?"

The words weren't loud. They didn't need to be. The threat was in how casual he made it. I held both hands up, not high, just enough to show I'd heard him.

"I think I'm good. Next?"

Stephen cursed under his breath and shifted toward the door like he'd decided the barbershop had reached its usefulness.

That was my cue. "Thank you," I said, aiming it at Barb, and keeping my tone level.

Barb gave a courteous nod, minimal but real, and her eyes flicked past me to Stephen as if she was making sure he didn't do something stupid on the way out.

I followed Stephen out of the barbershop, and the door clicked behind us. "Is her name really Barb, or is it just because of the barber thing?" I asked, letting the humour sit on top of the annoyance.

Stephen glanced at me, eyes flat, then turned his head forward and kept walking. I shrugged and fell in behind him, hands loose at my sides, pace matching his. The Strip swallowed us again. Noise, movement, and that controlled tension sitting under it all, as if everyone was waiting for the next thing to go wrong and trying not to be the one standing closest when it did.

Barb's words kept repeating anyway. Casey had come from the East when he was seven. By himself. Stuck around in The Strip for a few years, then moved on to the West.

Seven.

I tried to picture it properly, not as a concept, but as a kid with too-big shoes and a stomach that knew hunger too well, walking into this place and deciding it was safer than wherever he'd been.

And then there was the woman. The East. Professional. Visiting sometimes. Maybe a mother, but maybe not. If she were his mother, why would she let him leave at a young age and only come to visit sometimes? Why not try to get him back to the East?

And if she wasn't his mother, who was she? What was she to Casey? She was clearly someone who looked like they belonged to the East enough that Barb could label her that quickly without needing to explain.

Stephen cut us across another street without signalling, and I followed. He moved as if he already had a map laid out in his head and he wasn't interested in explaining any of it to me.

We did a few more stops after that. Not the kind of stops that felt like leads. More like Stephen testing doors and testing people, seeing who would open and who would pretend they weren't home. We knocked, we waited, and we got nothing that landed clean. A door cracked open an inch, then closed again without a word. A woman called out from behind a curtain that she didn't know anyone, and a man sitting on a milk crate outside a shop stared at Stephen, stared at me, and then spat to the side like we'd wasted his time by existing near him.

Some conversations happened anyway, short, guarded, and mostly useless. A name here, a shrug there, and a whole lot of not-my-problem.

It wasn't Blaze that people remembered. Not properly. There were vague confirmations—'yeah, I knew him,' 'yeah, I saw him around,' 'good kid, quiet kid'—and then the topic slid back to Casey every time, like Casey had taken up space in this place in a way Blaze hadn't managed to.

Nothing about Blaze's family. Nothing about friends. Nothing about who he'd meet, and nothing about who he'd avoid. Nothing about the woman, either.

Every time I tried to angle the questions toward her, the answers dried up faster. People's eyes shifted away. Shoulders tightened. Someone muttered 'East' as if it was a reason not to talk, and someone else told Stephen to take me somewhere else.

Stephen didn't argue. He just kept walking, and I kept following, letting the lack of answers stack up in my head. By the time we had almost finished our small loop of The Strip, my patience had started to fray. The Strip hadn't given me anything I could bring back to Dante and call progress, and I didn't like that feeling.

Stephen slowed, then stopped, and I came to a halt beside him. "Last one," he said, voice rough. "Then your hour's up."

I looked at where we'd ended up and felt my eyebrows lift before I could stop them. The familiar front of Mamma's stared back at me, the window catching the daylight, the inside a dimmer rectangle behind the glass.

"Mamma's?"

Stephen nodded.

"Why didn't we start here?" I asked because it wasn't a bad question, and because his version of helping me had so far looked like a guided tour of disappointment.

"We going in or not?" Stephen asked, already shifting his weight toward the door.

"Yeah, yeah," I muttered, and followed him across.

The bell above the door chimed as we stepped inside, that same cheap sound that had felt louder earlier when Dante left, and the café smell hit me again—coffee, fryer oil, and whatever pastry had been sitting too long under plastic.

Stephen moved straight to the counter like he owned the floor plan. I stayed half a step behind him, eyes flicking through the room out of habit. A few people sat scattered as before, and a couple of them looked up as we came in, then looked away like they'd decided not to get involved in whatever this was.

The waitress from earlier came over, wiping her hands on her apron. She looked at Stephen first, then at me, and her eyes narrowed slightly. "You realise you left too much cash here?"

I leaned forward slightly and gave a small smile. "What? Oh, no, no. It's fine." She didn't smile back. She just studied me like she didn't trust generosity from strangers.

"He's here about Blaze and Casey, Lucy," Stephen said, the words blunt and direct.

Lucy's gaze snapped back to Stephen. "Oh?"

"Did you know them?" I asked.

"Most people here did."

"The Strip here, or Mamma's here?"

"Both," Lucy said, and then her face shifted slightly as if she'd decided that was enough and she'd already said too much. "I mean,

Casey came to Mamma's a lot. He was close with Rochelle."

The name landed with a small jolt, because it was the first thing all day that sounded like a person and not a label.

"And Rochelle… is she here today?" I asked, keeping my tone even.

Lucy's eyes flickered past my shoulder, landing briefly on the HELP WANTED poster near the door. The edges were still curled. The ink was still bold. The desperation in it hadn't faded.

"She died," Lucy said quietly. "Not long ago."

"Oh." I swallowed the immediate instinct to fill the silence with something clever. "I'm sorry."

Lucy nodded once, quick and tight. "Casey used to come grab her after a shift and run into the East together," Lucy continued, the words coming faster now that she'd started. "Always had someone to meet."

"Do you know who?"

Lucy shook her head. "I never asked. I always assumed it was that woman that came to visit." My spine straightened a fraction. There it was again. The woman. Not just Barb's memory. Someone else's as well.

"Do you know who she was?"

"No," Lucy said, firm. "Someone Casey knew, though. She was very professional. Very East Side."

I let that sit, eyes unfocused as I turned it over. Professional wasn't a description people on The Strip used unless they meant it, and 'East Side' wasn't just geography. It was a category.

Stephen pushed off the counter, the movement sharp like he was done with the conversation before it could get too comfortable. "Alright. Hour's up."

"Wait," I cut in, turning toward him.

Stephen didn't look at me. He just dipped his head slightly at Lucy, an acknowledgement without warmth, and headed for the door.

"Lucy," he said, and it sounded like a goodbye he didn't waste on anyone else.

Lucy nodded back, and her eyes shifted away, already disengaging.

I gave her another small smile. "Thank you."

Then I followed Stephen out. The bell chimed again as the door swung shut behind us. The sound was bright enough that it made a couple of people inside look up, and I felt their eyes track us through the window, curious but cautious. Outside, The Strip pressed in again.

"Do you not find that interesting?" I asked Stephen as we stepped away from the café.

Stephen kept walking. "Not my job to find things interesting."

"Come on," I said, picking up pace to match him. "I feel like we've connected here. You gotta give me some personality."

Stephen's face tightened. Displeasure.

"Alright, fine," I said, letting the humour drop away enough to sound serious. "How about some information? Surely you know something about this woman."

Stephen exhaled and kept his eyes on the street ahead. "Suit."

I blinked. "Suit?"

Stephen's shoulders lifted in a small shrug that meant nothing and everything at once. "Got fancier over time. But always a suit."

"You're really not that helpful at all."

Stephen responded with a grunt, the sound half acknowledgement and half warning. We made it another few steps before he spoke again, and when he did, his voice had changed slightly. Not softer. Just less dismissive.

"There was someone else."

I turned my head toward him. "When?"

"Since Casey first came. A kid."

My stomach tightened a fraction. "Do you know who they are? What they look like?"

Stephen shook his head once. "Always wore a hood up. Never really saw them."

A hood. A kid. Hanging around Casey since the beginning, which meant they'd been there when Casey was seven and alone, and they'd stayed close enough that Stephen noticed them even if he didn't know them.

"Did you see them recently?"

Stephen didn't answer straight away. He kept walking, eyes scanning the street as if he was checking whether anyone was close enough to hear. Then he gave a small nod. "Yeah. Maybe two weeks ago."

Two weeks. Just before Casey died.

My brain reached for the closest thing it could connect to that timeframe, and the image of Stephanie's knee brace flickered up whether I wanted it to or not. The limp. The uneven footsteps. The message to Dante.

I forced myself to keep my face neutral. "Did they have a knee brace?"

Stephen looked at me, and for a moment, his stare felt sharper. Then he shrugged. "Didn't see. They did seem to limp slightly, though."

The words hit and stayed.

My thoughts started moving faster, pieces shifting around, new shapes forming where there had been blanks. Limp wasn't a person, and it wasn't a name, but it was a direction, and right now I'd take any direction I could get.

Stephen turned away from me and started walking again.

"Bye," I called after him, long and drawn out.

He didn't respond. He just kept walking, pulling out another cigarette as he went, leaving me on the footpath with The Strip moving around me.

I stayed where I was, watching his back get smaller, and kept turning the pieces over until they pointed somewhere I could follow.

13

The drive home was strange.

Not because the roads had changed, or the traffic had decided to behave for once, but because my head wouldn't stay in the car. It kept slipping back to The Strip, to the barbershop, to Lucy's careful tone, and to Stephen's blunt little gift of information on the way out.

I kept one hand steady on the wheel and let the other hover near my phone on the passenger seat, the screen dark. I'd already sent Dante a quick message to call when he could. Nothing more.

Not over text.

The street my house sat on was quiet in that comfortable East-side way. Neighbours' lawns trimmed. Cars parked neatly. Porches that didn't sag and fences that didn't lean like they'd given up. The kind of place that made you forget the rest of the city existed unless you went looking for it.

I turned into my driveway, rolled to a stop, and shut the car off.

The silence after the engine died settled fast. I sat staring at the house. The tidy, clean garden and large glass windows catching the sun's rays. The house Claire and I had worked hard to afford, and the one we'd worked hard to keep feeling safe.

It looked exactly like it should.

That didn't mean anything.

My mind slid back to Casey. Seven years old. Walking out of the East alone and into The Strip. Barb had said it like it was a strange little detail in a life full of strange little details, but it wouldn't leave me alone.

Did he have a family?

Did they kick him out, or did he run? Did he lose them in a way no one talked about because it was easier to say he'd just left?

The mystery woman visiting him had to mean something. Not just that she existed, but that multiple people remembered her the same way. Professional and East side. The kind of person you noticed because she didn't belong, and because she didn't try to pretend she did.

Then there was the other kid. A kid who'd been around since the beginning, Stephen had said. Since Casey first came. How could no one know who they were? How could no one have seen their face? Were they always secretive, hood up, head down, moving through The Strip like fog?

They had clearly known Casey for most of his life. They were clearly close. Maybe they would have known Blaze. Maybe they would have thought he knew something he shouldn't.

My thoughts landed on Stephanie. The limp. The brace. She looked around the same age as Casey and Blaze. Early twenties. There wasn't motive, not yet, but there were connections. And they always had a way of making things messy.

Then my mind went to Theresa. I pictured her in a suit, because of course I did. She'd been clean, in command, and perfectly timed in Wilson's lobby like she'd been waiting for me to show my face. The idea of her being the mystery woman made a certain kind of sense if you squinted at it. East side. Professional. Connected to the bureau. Connected to the file.

But why would she be visiting Casey when he was a kid? Why would she bother? Past connections didn't make sense, not with what I knew. Not yet. Though if Theresa was the woman, it linked Stephanie even more, and my brain liked that because it connected the dots neatly.

The problem was that nothing about this case was neat. There were pieces missing. Too many pieces.

Dante's words slipped in amongst everything else. *It's Sunday. You're here.*

Claire wasn't at work. The boys weren't at school. The day was supposed to be slow. Normal. And I hadn't been home. I lifted my eyes to the windows and saw movement inside. A shadow crossing a room. A small figure darting past.

I let out a slow sigh, unlatched my seatbelt, and pushed the car door open. The air outside was cooler than it had been earlier. It carried the clean smell of watered grass and someone cooking something down the street.

I walked up the path and unlocked the front door. The noise hit me as soon as I stepped inside. Not loud, exactly. Just full. The sound of life bouncing off walls that hadn't been built to hold it all. Miles and Alex were both doing different things, but somehow still converged on me the second they saw me like they'd been tracking my presence from another room by pure instinct.

Their voices overlapped immediately.

"Dad! Come see the car track I made!" Miles demanded, tugging at my sleeve with both hands.

"No!" Alex cut in, louder. "You have to defend the house from the orcs!"

I blinked once, the day's sharpness still clinging to me, and tried to assemble a response that didn't sound like I'd been thinking about dead bodies up until I walked in the door.

Claire appeared at the end of the hall, wiping her hands on a tea towel. Her hair was tied back, and she had that look on her face she got when she was pretending she hadn't been waiting for the sound of my car.

"You're home," she said, and there was relief in it that she'd deny if I called it that.

"Yeah," I replied, and then I looked down at the boys. "Alright, alright. One at a time."

Miles tugged harder. Alex squared his shoulders like this was war, which, to be fair, in his mind, he was.

I crouched to their level, spreading my hands out like a referee about to make a bad call. "Okay," I said, letting my voice warm up. "We do the orc defence first, because we spent a lot of money on this house, and I don't want them to destroy it. And then you show me the car track, and we'll have some races."

Alex grinned like he'd won something important.

Miles opened his mouth to argue, then paused, eyebrows pinching together as he weighed whether being second was still worth it if it was guaranteed.

"Deal," he said finally, and then he darted away.

Alex grabbed my hand and pulled me toward the lounge room. Claire moved in behind us, a hand pressing briefly to the middle of my back as I passed her.

The lounge room looked like the end of a weekend. Couch cushions shifted. A blanket half on the floor. Toys in places they shouldn't be and a stack of books that had been dragged out and left open.

Alex shoved a foam sword into my hand. "This is your weapon," he informed me.

"I feel honoured," I muttered, lifting it with exaggerated seriousness.

"You have to stand there," he directed, pointing to a spot near the hallway entrance, "because that's where the orcs come from."

"Of course they do," I said, stepping into position. "They always come from the hallway."

Claire stood off to the side, arms folding loosely as she watched, and her mouth twitched into something close to a smile.

"The orcs are coming," he whispered with wide eyes.

I tightened my grip on the foam sword and lowered my voice. "They picked the wrong house."

Alex giggled, then clapped a hand over his mouth like he'd ruined the mood. We did it properly. I swung the sword at nothing, pretending to be fighting for my life, and Alex made sound effects which I'm sure he'd argue should be used in movies. When the orcs were finally defeated, Alex declared me the hero, and I bowed like I'd earned it.

"Car track!" Miles called, popping back into the doorway like he'd been waiting for his moment.

I stood, flexing my hand as if the foam sword had strained something important. "Alright. Show me."

Miles led me to his room at a sprint, and the 'car track' turned out to be a network of ramps, cushions, and books arranged into something that almost worked. He'd positioned the cars carefully at the top of the ramp, all lined up.

He launched one. It shot down, hit a cushion, and flipped over. Miles stared at it for half a second, then looked up at me. "That one was practicing."

I smiled. "Of course."

His grin widened. "Okay, try the blue one. That one's fast."

I tried the blue one. It did better. It cleared the cushion, hit the book, and made it halfway through before falling off the edge.

Miles cheered.

Dinner came in a blur of noise and forks, and negotiating the correct number of peas to eat before dessert and listening to Miles explain the engineering of his car track.

Claire filled in the gaps without being obvious about it. She kept the conversation moving when my attention dipped. She redirected when the boys started to argue. She placed a plate in front of me and pressed her fingers briefly to my wrist as she did, grounding me without making a thing of it.

After dinner, the night carried on, passing like normal. I stayed present. My mind tried its best to drift, but I didn't let it. Not yet.

As the boy's bedtime approached, we found Miles hiding in his cupboard. No new spot.

"Next time. A new spot next time," Miles said.

"Sure, you are," Alex muttered, but he smiled anyway.

I ruffled Miles' hair, and he swatted my hand away with mock offence, then bolted down the hall toward his room.

Claire and I tucked them in after that. We said goodnight to Miles first. A quick magic trick and a kiss on his forehead. Then we moved to Alex's room. He got the same trick as Miles, but when I was done, he shifted under the blanket and looked up at me with that particular brightness he got when he was about to ask for something.

"Dad," he began.

I stared at him. "Alex."

Alex grinned. "Dad, can I have one more trick before I sleep?"

"One more?" I asked, letting my tone carry the tired humour. "Was that one not good enough?"

"You can do better," Alex giggled, and his shoulders wriggled excitedly.

I glanced at Claire. She gave me a look that said, 'you did this to yourself.'

"Hm." I dragged it out, pretending to consider. "Alright, alright. One more, and then you sleep."

"Yes!" Alex pulled his blanket up to his eyes, only the top half of his face visible.

"We'll do a quick card one," I told him, and moved toward the small bedside table.

I grabbed the deck that sat next to Alex's bed, the worn cards already slightly bent from too much use and too many small hands shuffling them.

"You ready?" I asked, holding it up.

Alex nodded so hard his head bounced on the pillow.

I performed an easy card trick. One I didn't have to think too hard about. One where he picked a card, and I secretly held it in place at the bottom of the deck while I shuffled, then pulled it out like it was random.

When the reveal hit, Alex's eyes went wide. "What?!" he yelped, half sitting up.

"Alright," I said, cutting him off before he could launch into a full interrogation, "now go to sleep."

"How did you do it?" Alex demanded. "Teach me!"

"Maybe when you finish all your homework after school tomorrow," I told him, keeping my tone light but final.

Alex groaned, dramatic and wounded. I leaned down, kissed the top of his head, and stepped back to give Claire space to say goodnight.

Claire and I moved back into the living area after the boys were down. The house shifted into that quieter version of itself, the one that only happened when the lights in the hallway were dimmed, and the doors were closed, and you could almost pretend the world outside had stopped asking for anything.

The television was on. Volume low. Something playing that neither of us was properly watching. Claire sat down beside me and tucked herself in close, shoulder against my chest, her legs pulled up slightly so she could curl into the corner of the couch. She fitted there like she'd done it a thousand times, like muscle memory had claimed the space before her body did.

I kept my arm around her and let my hand rest on her upper arm. She shifted her head a fraction, eyes still on the television even though I knew she wasn't watching it.

"Are you here?"

I swallowed once and made myself answer instead of deflecting. "I am."

Claire waited a beat, then turned her head enough to look at my face. "I thought you would have been here all day."

I let out a slow breath, staring at the flicker of light from the television across the far wall. "I'm sorry. I'm just…"

"Not actually here," Claire finished for me.

The words rang clean because they were true, and because she knew me too well to let me wriggle out of it with humour. Silence settled between us, but it wasn't empty. It was full of the day I'd missed, and the day I'd chosen instead.

Claire's fingers traced once over my wrist, small and absent-minded, then she held still again. "You just need to remember that you have us here," she said quietly.

"I do," I replied, and I meant it, but I heard how automatic it sounded the second it left my mouth.

Claire didn't call me on that. She just breathed out and kept going, voice steady. "You throw yourself into these things. You did it when you worked in medicine. You tend to lose yourself."

I tilted my head back against the couch and stared at the ceiling. "I never got that bad, did I?" I asked, and even as I said it, I knew it was the wrong question.

Claire's mouth twitched as if she'd almost smiled, but there wasn't enough room for humour. "You did have me to pull you out."

I let out a quiet laugh that was more breath than sound. "Fair."

I looked down at her, and she was watching me again, not with anger, but with that blunt honesty she saved for when it mattered. "But there were still bad days," she continued. "Especially before we got serious."

I nodded once. I didn't interrupt because she wasn't wrong, and because those days sat in the back of my mind like an old bruise.

Silence again.

Claire shifted slightly, her shoulder pressing closer into my side. "Those times in the kid's ward weren't just to make them smile," she muttered. Her voice was quiet, but it held weight.

"I know," I said quietly, fighting my mind to not bring up those memories.

The television murmured on, a line of dialogue from whatever show was playing slipping into the room and dying without anyone hearing it properly. The lights from the screen moved across Claire's face as she stared ahead, her brow tight.

"This whole thing, though," I started, and I didn't even know what I meant until the words were already out.

The case. The West. The bribes. Blaze on the carpet. Casey's file being scrubbed. Everything that kept stacking up without giving me an answer.

Claire didn't make me finish it. She just gave me a look that was tired, and affectionate, and done with the world's nonsense. "Sucks."

A breath slipped out of me, almost a laugh. "That's one way to put it."

Claire's eyes stayed on the television, then she looked back at me. "Where did you go today?"

"To try to find out why Blaze was killed," I replied, and I felt my shoulders tighten as my mind automatically retraced the steps.

Claire studied my face. "The look on your face says you didn't find that out."

"No," I admitted. Then I lifted my hand slightly. "But I do have something."

Claire's posture shifted. She didn't move away from me, but her attention sharpened. Less comfort now, more focus.

I took a breath and told her everything. Not in a neat little report. Not in the way I'd talk to Dante. In the way you talk to the person who knows you best, the person who can tell when you're lying by omission, and the person who will ask the questions you've been avoiding.

When I finished, the room sat in the aftermath.

Silence. The kind you needed so your mind could catch up to what your ears had heard.

We could hear the subtle snoring from Alex down the hall, soft and uneven in the way it always was when he'd fallen asleep properly. There was the low hum of the television in front of us, and somewhere outside, a car rolled past on the street without slowing, like the world had never changed.

Claire didn't speak straight away. She shifted her weight slightly, and I felt the tension in her shoulders. "I hate to say what I know you're thinking about doing," she said finally.

I didn't pretend I didn't know what she meant. "You know I can't stop."

Claire's gaze stayed on me, steady and sharp. "I know. You're stubborn. You won't stop until you figure it out. It's one of the reasons I love you." She paused, and the pause mattered. "I just… I need you to be careful."

"I will be," I promised, and I heard myself, heard the way it came out too quick, too reflexive.

Claire didn't let me. "Ryan."

I closed my eyes for half a second. "I know. I know."

Silence again, shorter this time.

Claire drew a slow breath and leaned her head back against my shoulder. "So, what's the plan?"

The question was practical, and that was Claire. She didn't spiral. She didn't let emotion chew through the structure. She put the pieces on the table and asked how we were going to deal with them.

I exhaled and stared at the television again, not seeing it. "Well,

Stephanie is just a thought. Nothing real there. I've still got to work this normally."

Claire's head tilted slightly. "So, no Theresa either?"

"As much as I'd love to," I admitted, because blaming Theresa would have been convenient and satisfying in a way that made me suspicious of myself, "she really only makes sense if it is Stephanie."

Claire's mouth tightened in thought. "I mean, Stephanie is young. She'd have to have an amazing résumé or have known Theresa before getting a job like that."

"We'll keep the idea in orbit," I said, because it was the best way to describe it. Just there, circling, waiting for something to pull it in or fling it out. "For now, I'm going to start with finding out who knew about the money."

Claire's eyes narrowed slightly. "Someone who knew the timeframe for Casey's runs?"

I hummed in agreement, the sound low in my throat. The runs. The timing. The location. Whoever killed Casey hadn't just known what he was a part of. They'd known where he'd be and when he'd be there. That wasn't a random guess. That was information.

"I think I need to have a chat with Wilson," I said, and even as I said it, a tension tightened in my chest.

Dante's warning. No NBI.

Claire didn't immediately argue. She just looked at me, weighing whether I was saying it because it was a smart move or because it was the move that scratched the itch in my brain. "Are you sure he's a part of it?"

I thought back to Wilson's office. Calm, sharp, and deliberate. The way he'd laid down warnings that sounded general if you weren't listening properly. The way he'd made it clear the boundaries existed, and the way he'd waited to see if I'd step over them.

He'd known the file was being buried. He'd known I was looking into it. The chance of him knowing about the money and receiving it was high. There was one sure way of knowing, though.

Angelo.

The thought landed, heavy and immediate, and it shifted something in me. Because Angelo was blunt, and because Angelo didn't play the same games the East did. He didn't pretend the world was clean, and he didn't pretend people did things for the right reasons. And Angelo had already told me more truth in one night than the bureau had in days.

I glanced down at Claire and felt her watching me, reading the change on my face. "Not sure. But I'm going to find out."

14

Names sat on my phone as the road rolled beneath me.

The night wrapped around the car the farther I pushed into it, swallowing the last scraps of streetlight as I left our block behind. Everything always looked different close to midnight. Same buildings, same roads, but fewer people, fewer distractions, and far less pretending.

Claire had gone to sleep.

I'd tried. I'd done the whole routine—lights off, phone facedown, eyes closed, breathing steady like I could convince my head it was tired if I acted tired first—but my mind had stayed lit up. Too full, running too fast, spinning the same images until they blurred: Barb at the barbershop, Lucy's careful words, Stephen's cigarette, and those few words he had graced me with before leaving me standing alone.

Dante had called, waking Claire, though she went back to sleep quickly. He had kept it short and quick, his voice a little rough at the edges, tiredness latching onto it. He'd just finished work.

I'd told him what I could, careful about what I put into words, even over a call, and then asked for Angelo's number. Dante hadn't asked why.

The sigh that came down the line had been heavy enough to answer for him. He'd rather not know, or he already did, and he didn't want to look directly at it. Either way, he'd given me the number without making it a conversation, and we'd agreed to catch up when we could.

As soon as the call ended, I'd sent a message to Angelo. Blunt and simple.

I need names.

The list I'd made on instinct in my head was one thing—a thread, a handful of possibilities, a way to keep my brain from chewing itself in half—but what Angelo could give me was different. Real. Something that didn't rely on my assumptions or my bias. A line I could actually follow without guessing.

The plan had been to try to rest, wait until morning when a response came through, and then act on it with daylight on my side and a clearer head.

But Angelo had responded quickly. Almost immediately.

The notification had lit up my bedside table, and the message had been short enough to read in a single blink. A list of six names. Every time I closed my eyes after that, the names plastered themselves on the inside of my eyelids, sitting there like they owned the space and whispering at me to get up.

So, I did.

I moved silently through the house, feet placing carefully on the timber, so it didn't creak. I paused at the boy's rooms and looked in, letting myself take the sight properly.

Miles was sprawled at an angle that made no sense, and I couldn't understand how he could be comfortable. Alex had his blanket pulled up, his face half buried, breathing steady and soft, with light snores escaping him.

They were peaceful. Lost in other worlds that were much fairer than this one. I took my time taking in the sight of both of them before I forced myself to keep moving.

Claire had stirred as I got dressed. Not fully awake, but not fully asleep either, turning her head on the pillow. "Couldn't sleep?" she'd murmured, her voice thick.

I hadn't lied. I never could to her. "Got a message," I'd told her quietly. "I need to check something."

She'd blinked a few times, and then her eyes had focused enough to find my face. "What kind of something?"

"The kind that won't let me rest," I'd admitted.

Claire had exhaled, slow, a sound that held tiredness and resignation and a little bit of fear.

"Be careful," she'd whispered.

"I will," I'd promised, and I meant it.

She hadn't stopped me. That was its own kind of trust, and it sat heavy as I pulled the front door shut behind me. I sat in the car for a few minutes before turning the key, hands resting on the wheel, letting my thoughts stack up and settle. The house stayed dark and quiet, neat from the outside, soft in the middle, and fragile in the way all good things were when you took your eyes off them.

My phone was propped in its holder, six names looking back at me. Six.

I'd expected more. More hands in the jar, more people dipping in, more names that would make the whole thing feel impossibly large. Six felt almost controlled.

I started the car and eased out of the driveway, headlights washing over the trimmed hedges and the clean footpath as if I belonged there. The streetlamps passed overhead in steady rhythm as I drove back toward the city, and the streets stayed quiet in that late-night way that made every moving car feel like it had purpose.

Close to midnight, most people were winding their weekends down. Making sure they were ready for work on Monday. Alarms set and well-rested.

I knew one person who wasn't doing any of that. And when a message appeared from him on my phone, my jaw tightened.

My office door will be unlocked. Come in.

Wilson.

He didn't know why I had messaged him so late. I hadn't explained, and I hadn't expected a response. I'd asked to meet in private and assumed I'd get silence back, or a delayed dismissal in the morning. The night, apparently, had decided it was going to be generous.

I kept my eyes on the road, but my focus was on the message, burning a little brighter in my mind than it should have. Wilson wasn't the kind of man who did favours for free. He also wasn't the kind of man who met you alone after hours unless he believed he had control of the room.

Maybe he thought he did.

The NBI building loomed as I turned onto its street, its windows dotted with light. Even at this hour, the machine kept working. It always did. The bureau never slept; it just rotated who carried the weight at any given time.

I pulled up to the gate and rolled my window down, turning toward the booth.

A night guard I didn't recognise leaned out, face hollowed by fatigue and the kind of boredom that made you look older than you were. He glanced from my car to my face, then to the badge sitting on the passenger seat.

"Business?" he asked, voice flat.

"Consultant," I replied, keeping my tone neutral.
I held my badge up so he could see it properly. The guard scanned it longer than he needed to, not because he was thorough, but because it gave him something to do. Then he nodded once, hit the button, and the gate slid open with a slow grind. He waved me through.

The lot was almost empty. A few agents and security meant plentiful spaces to choose from, and I took advantage of it, parking near the entrance. As soon as the car was off, I slipped out and moved toward the door, phone in my pocket, badge visible, and shoulders set. The air outside had that cool bite that made you feel more awake than you wanted to be.

I pressed the button at the entrance. A guard inside looked out through the glass. His eyes landed on me, and I lifted my badge again, holding it steady. After a moment he buzzed the doors open.

I'd never been given a security key for after-hours access. That courtesy didn't get passed down to people like me. Consultants came and went at the bureau's convenience, and convenience didn't include letting us wander through the building in the middle of the night.

Still, the night procedure was looser than the daytime. The guard checked me at the desk, took a glance at my ID, asked a question he didn't care about, and then pointed me toward the elevators.

I moved through the lobby, my footsteps bouncing off the walls. The place felt different without the day shift noise: no phones ringing, no shouting across the lobby or beeping security machines, no printers spitting out paper.

The elevator doors opened with a muted chime, and I stepped inside, watching my reflection in the polished metal for half a second. Tired eyes, set jaw, and a face that didn't seem to know how to relax. I looked like I hadn't been able to get a decent night's sleep since Casey had died.

Which I hadn't.

The ride up was quick. When the doors opened onto Wilson's floor, the hallway was dimmer, the lights spaced wider, and shadows sat in corners where they weren't supposed to. I walked past the small kitchen without looking in, past empty desks and dark monitors, and through the bullpen that usually buzzed with noise.

There were no agents around. No movement at the desks, or hot coffees steaming next to someone's keyboard, and no jackets hanging over chairs like people might be back any second.

Dante must have been one of the last to leave. Aside from Wilson.

I moved past the desks, my eyes tracking the line of the hallway and the glass walls of Wilson's office. He would be able to see me before I saw him.

As I reached his door, I raised my hand and knocked. It was the polite thing to do, after all. A second passed. Then Wilson's voice came through the door, calm and steady. "Come in, Red."

I pushed the door open and stepped inside.

Wilson wasn't at his desk. He stood by the window to my left, but the glass was mostly blocked out by a cluster of large boards set up like a barricade. Each one was crowded—crime scene photos, printed reports, evidence logs, and scribbled notes pinned at odd angles like someone had run out of room and patience at the same time.

Some of the photos were from the scene I'd been at with Dante the other day. Others looked similar but different. Different room. Different layout.

The first crime scene.

Same killer.

"Late night?" I asked casually even as my eyes kept moving.

Wilson turned away from the boards and looked at me. The overhead light caught the edge of his face, sharp and controlled, and he didn't look tired. If he was exhausted, he wore it well.

"Just like yourself."

His voice was low and controlled, and maybe that was what bothered me most. More so than usual, even considering what I'd done with the last order he'd given me.

"Got a lot on my mind."

"As do I," Wilson returned, and he gestured at the boards again.

I stepped further into the office and let my eyes wash over it all properly, taking in the details of both crime scenes now they were in front of me.

The bodies.

The cuts—clean and precise.

One cut at the neck. One pierce into the heart.

That was consistent across all three victims. Deliberate. Whoever did it wasn't hacking. They weren't guessing. The blade went where it needed to go, and it went there without hesitation. It was controlled.

The blood at each scene was splattered across the walls and the floor. Messy. It was the one aspect of the murders the killer couldn't control. So, instead, they use it as part of the performance.

My gaze dragged to the photos of the doors—the entrance to whatever room the murders had happened in.

A large number one.

Then a large number three.

The number three I had seen already. Painted to show what was waiting inside.

My eyes drifted some more until I saw something I hadn't been able to see when I was at the scene. Something that I would've seen if I'd done what Wilson told me and gone to the bodies instead of heading off into the West Side to see Angelo.

Carvings.

On the chest, next to the wound that pierced each victim's heart, there were shallow, intentional marks. Not deep enough to be part of the kill. Not random enough to be a slip.

On the first victim, you could've brushed it off. A blade catching. A hand shifting. An accident in the middle of a cleaner cut.

But on the second and third, it repeated.

Pattern.

The killer had marked each victim to show what number they were. A branding, neat and cruel, like it mattered to them that the body itself carried the count.

They weren't just painting the tally on the door.

They were tallying the bodies, too.

"The art of presentation," I remarked, voice low, and it came out drier than I meant it to.

Wilson hummed, then turned and moved back toward his chair. He sat down with controlled ease. He didn't look away from me as he settled in, and that told me he'd been watching my reaction to the boards more than he'd been studying them.

"Please," Wilson said, and he gestured to the chair opposite him.

I glanced back at the boards one more time. Something tugged in my gut, a quiet pull like my mind wanted to keep looking, but I forced it down and took the seat. The leather creaked under my weight, and the office felt smaller with the boards looming to one side like a third person in the room.

"So," Wilson began, folding his hands loosely on the desk, "what can

I do for you, Red?"

I let a few moments pass, watching his face. He was too calm. Too composed. This was a routine meeting and not the middle of the night with a serial killer's work plastered across his window.

"You seem calm after what I did the other day," I said, keeping my tone mild like I wasn't poking at a bruise.

"It wasn't unexpected," Wilson replied without blinking. "You're quite… predictable."

A small breath left me through my nose and leaned back a fraction in the chair

"Especially when you've got someone who sees the future on your side," I added, letting the sarcasm show.

Wilson's mouth shifted, not quite a smile and not quite disapproval either.

"Mia is… unconventional, yes," he said slowly. "But her results speak for themselves."

"So, you don't believe in that crap either, then?"

Wilson's gaze stayed steady. "I believe people are complicated," he said evenly. "And if it gets the job done, then I don't care how they do it." His eyes narrowed slightly, the smallest shift. "It's why I tolerate you."

"Barely," I shot back, and I fought a smile despite myself.

"You're still here, aren't you?"

I let the corner of my mouth lift, small. "That's because I'm more trouble when you don't have a leash on me."

Wilson's gaze didn't move. "Let's be honest, Red. No leash has stopped you before."

"You're not wrong," I admitted, and the words came out easier than they should've.

He held my stare, then shifted forward slightly, dragging the conversation back onto the rails. "So, let's talk about why you're here."

I exhaled deeply before answering.

"Casey Edwards."

"Casey Edwards," Wilson repeated.

We sat in silence. The building hummed around us—air-conditioning, the whir of Wilson's laptop, and somewhere far down the hall a muted thud from what I assumed was a guard. Wilson's office felt sealed off from it anyway, the boards and the closed door making it its own little pocket of pressure.

Wilson's fingers tapped once on the desk and stopped, controlled even in the smallest movement.

"How much do you know?"

"All of it," I replied, keeping my tone even.

"All of it?" His eyebrows lifted slightly, not disbelief so much as irritation at the implication.

"But you only care about some of what I know, right?" I leaned forward an inch, elbows hovering near the armrests. "You don't care about the fact he's dead? You only care about the fact that the bribes and payoffs are known."

Wilson's face changed. It wasn't dramatic. It didn't break him open. But it shifted—guilt first, then fear, then something like regret that he couldn't quite swallow back down. He tried to smooth it into neutrality but didn't manage it. Not fully.

I watched him do it, and the fact he failed was the most honest thing he'd given me all week.

"Do you know who killed him?"

"No," I answered, my jaw tightening. "It's a bit hard when the file is being buried and changed."

"You understand why it is, though?" Wilson asked, and there was something in his tone that sounded like he needed me to understand his side of things.

"To hide the fact the West is paying you all off to stay out?" I held his gaze. "Yeah. You wouldn't want that getting out."

Silence filled the space again. Wilson didn't look away. He didn't flinch either. If anything, he looked tired of the conversation before it had properly started, as if he'd had it in his head a hundred times and hated that I was forcing it into the room.

I shifted in the chair. "You know, we never got along, but I always thought that it was because you were too much of a stickler for the rules," I told him, and my voice sharpened despite myself. "That it was because you had a rod stuck so far up your ass."

Wilson's eyes flashed. "You think I want this?"

"I think you have choices."

"I don't!" his anger flared. Not quick irritation, or the controlled authority he usually wore.

Actual anger, and it carried something else underneath it I couldn't place fast enough to name. He stood up, hands planting firmly on the desk, shoulders squared. His eyes bored down on me as if he could force me back into my chair with sheer pressure.

"Of course I am against this, Red. But the money…" Wilson trailed off, the heat bleeding out of the sentence mid-way.

He dropped back into his chair with less control than before and leaned back, one hand dragging down his face. The movement left him looking older than he had a minute ago. When his hand fell away, he stared at the desk.

"I need it," Wilson admitted.

The words hit harder than his anger had. "This role not pay well enough for you?"

Wilson's voice almost gave out. "Not when I need money for a transplant."

Silence fell again, but it changed shape. It wasn't just tension now. It was something else—something personal that didn't belong in this office.

It didn't belong to me.

Wilson looked away from me. When he spoke again, he still didn't meet my eyes. "My daughter needs a heart transplant."

My gaze drifted without permission, pulled toward the wall behind him. A photo sat there—Wilson and a young girl, no older than eleven, propped in a hospital bed. Too pale. Smiling anyway. Her face had that careful look kids got when they were used to adults treading on glass around them.

When I looked back, Wilson was finally looking at me. His eyes were glassy, and I hated that I was seeing him being vulnerable.

"She has cardiomyopathy," he added, and his voice was steady again, but the steadiness took effort.

I let a breath out through my nose and held the edge of the desk in my mind, something solid to keep my thoughts from slipping. "So, you bury a kid's death so you can keep getting money to help your daughter?" I asked, and I kept it blunt because softening it would've been dishonest.

Wilson didn't look away this time. "Wouldn't you?"

Quiet took over again. The question wasn't rhetorical. He meant it. He wanted me to answer, and I felt the trap in it immediately. If I said yes, I excused him. And if I said no… it'd be a lie.

I didn't answer. "You know I'm not going to stop," I said instead.

Wilson nodded once. Not permission. Not agreement. Just acknowledgement of fact.

"Just help me," I pressed, leaning forward now, hands braced lightly on my knees. "If you know anything."

"I don't know anything about him." Wilson's voice had gone quieter, trying to keep himself contained again.

"Did anyone?" I pushed. "Who dealt with him the most?"

"Red…" Wilson started, and the way he said my name was warning and fatigue wrapped together.

I let my name hang between us, forcing him to sit in it, forcing him to decide whether he was going to shut down or give me something useful. Then I sighed and let a different part of myself take the lead.

"I don't have any strings to pull at St Peter's anymore," I told him, and it hurt more than it should've to say it out loud, "but my wife does. Maybe we can work something out. So, you don't have to do this."

Wilson looked at me properly then. Watching. Measuring whether I meant it and whether I'd hold to it if he gave me what I wanted. "Casey isn't the only one who died," I added, keeping my voice low. "And I don't know why. I need something to hold onto. Just… do the right thing."

The words sat in the room.

Wilson's jaw tightened. He stared at a spot over my shoulder, and for a moment, I thought he was going to stay silent. Then he spoke, quick and sudden.

"Stephanie met with him."

It hit clean. Stephanie.

That name kept circling back like it belonged to the centre of the mess, and my brain grabbed at it immediately, slotting it into the list I'd been building whether I wanted to or not.

"She was the point of contact?" I asked, and the question came out sharper than I meant.

"Mainly, yes," Wilson confirmed.

I stood quickly, the chair legs scraping softly on the carpet, and turned toward the door. The urge to move was immediate, as if staying still would let the information slip away.

"Red." Wilson's voice stopped me.

I paused with my hand near the doorknob and looked back.

"Yeah," I started, "I'll talk to my wife about your daughter."

Wilson didn't acknowledge the offer. Not with words. His expression tightened, and he nodded. "Theresa is keeping an eye on you."

I let a moment pass, standing there with my hand on the door, feeling the weight of that sentence settle into the space between my ribs.

"Yeah, well," I said finally, and my voice came out flat, "she's on my list, too."

Then I walked out of his office without looking back.

I got home in time to wake my boys up for breakfast.

That alone felt like I'd pulled off some sort of magic trick. My body was moving on momentum, the kind that kept you upright while your head ran a separate life somewhere else.

Miles was already half-awake when I knocked on his door. He blinked at me, hair standing up, face creased from the pillow.

"Morning," I murmured, leaning against the frame.

He squinted at me, then rolled over and shoved his face back into the blanket.

Alex was easier. He was always easier in the mornings, mostly because his brain hadn't fully loaded yet. He sat up, eyes half-open. "Do we have school today?"

"It's Monday," I reminded him.

He stared at the wall as if he were trying to remember what Monday was supposed to mean. Then he groaned and flopped back down.

Breakfast happened in the kitchen, with me flipping eggs while also trying to make sure Miles didn't pour cereal straight into his mouth.

Claire came in while I was wiping a spill with one hand and buttering toast with the other. Her hair was still damp from the shower, and she moved with that efficient, practiced calm that made it look like she had more hours in the day than everyone else.

She didn't ask about the night. Not right away. She poured herself coffee, leaned against the counter, and watched me juggle two small humans and a frying pan as if I'd been doing it my whole life.

Miles swung his legs under the stool, swinging too hard on purpose, trying to make the chair squeak.

Claire's eyes slid to me. Just a glance. A quiet check-in without making it a thing. I kept my eyes on the plates.

The boys ate, we did the teeth-brushing battle, we found shoes that had somehow migrated into rooms they didn't belong in, and then we did the final morning scramble where everyone pretended this wasn't a routine and that we weren't going to be late even though we always flirted with it.

Claire slipped her bag over her shoulder, checked her phone, and then moved toward the door. "I'll get the boys from school on my way home," she told me as though she knew I would be elsewhere.

"Alright," I replied, and my eyes met hers for half a second.

There was a question sitting there. She still didn't ask it, just left, the door clicking shut behind her. The house shifted immediately. Quieter. Less organised.

I herded the boys into the car, and we drove to school with Alex telling me something about his friend's new game he got for his birthday, and Miles informing me, very seriously, that he was going to be a dragon at recess.

"A dragon," I echoed, keeping my eyes on the road.

"Yeah," Miles confirmed, and he sounded like that should've been obvious. "But a cool one."

"Pretty sure all dragons are cool."

Drop-off was the usual chaos of kids and backpacks and parents trying to look awake. Miles hopped out, gave me a quick wave before he ran off without looking back. Alex lingered long enough to ask if I'd be there when he got home.

"Yeah, I will," I promised. He nodded, satisfied, and then he was gone too, swallowed by the crowd.

I didn't go back home after. I drove toward the NBI, but I didn't park inside. I didn't go near the gate. I pulled up on the curb about twenty metres from it, just close enough so Dante didn't have to walk too far.

My phone sat in my hand with a message sent to him. A request to come outside. Nothing more. Then I waited.

The building sat there in the morning light as if it hadn't been keeping secrets overnight. People moved in and out. A guard shifted in the booth. Someone crossed the lot carrying a coffee.

Fifteen minutes later, Dante appeared from the direction of the gate, scanned the street, and then headed straight for my car. He got into the passenger seat, shut the door, and exhaled like he'd been holding his breath since he stepped out of the building.

"I am busy, you know," he reminded me, already annoyed.

"I'm aware," I replied, starting the car just to have the engine noise fill the silence between us. "I saw the big board Wilson has in his office. Spooky."

Dante's head snapped toward me. "Do I want to know why you've been in Wilson's office?"

I kept my eyes forward and put on my best version of innocent, which wasn't great. "I don't want you to be mad," I told him, and the way his shoulders tightened said that was a lost cause. "But I may have gone against your wishes."

"Jesus, Red." Dante dragged my name out like it physically hurt him. "I ask you to do one thing."

"Everything is fine," I assured him, waving a hand as if I could smooth this over with the motion. "We're cool. You can keep your pubes neat and tidy and not bunched up."

Dante stared at me like he was deciding whether to climb out of the car and walk back into the building just to avoid being seen with me.

"God. I knew I shouldn't have given you Angelo's number."

"Yeah, well," I said slowly, pulling away from the curb. "We all make mistakes."

He made a noise in the back of his throat that I chose to interpret as reluctant agreement. I drove down the road, letting the car roll us into a lazy loop, keeping us moving because sitting still near the NBI felt like a good way to get noticed.

"You want coffee?" I asked, more to change gears than because I thought caffeine would fix anything.

Dante looked at me and didn't answer. Taking that as permission, I turned into a fast-food drive-through because it was early and because I couldn't be bothered getting out of the car. We joined the queue and waited.

Dante leaned back in the seat, rubbing his forehead. "So?" he prompted, the word sharp.

"So," I echoed, and I let the silence stretch just long enough to annoy him. Then I sighed. "I need to get Stephanie on her own."

Dante's laugh came out without humour. "Good luck with that. She's basically sewn at the hip to Theresa."

"That's comforting," I muttered, tapping my fingers on the steering wheel, then stopping because it was irritating me. Lack of sleep would do that.

We crept forward a metre.

"Why?" Dante asked, eyes narrowing. "What do you know?"

"Well," I began, keeping my voice light because it was better than the alternative, "she has a limp."

"Yes," Dante replied flatly. "We've established that."

"And," I continued, watching the back of the car ahead to give me something to focus on, "Wilson told me she was one of Casey's main contacts."

Dante went still. "Collecting the money."

"She would know the schedule," I said, and it felt like saying it out loud made it more real.

Dante's jaw worked once. "Why would she kill him, though?"

"Well," I replied, and I couldn't stop the edge from creeping in, "that's what I'd like to find out."

We moved up the queue again. The speaker box was close enough now that I heard the person in front of us ordering.

Dante's gaze stayed on me. He wasn't letting this slide. "What's the personal angle?" he asked. "What's the Blaze angle?"

"Things are a work in progress here, Dante," I told him, and I made sure he heard the frustration under the humour. "I'm trying to pull answers out of my ass."

Dante snorted quietly. I pulled forward, ordered two coffees without asking what size he wanted because I already knew he'd complain either way, then rolled to the next window.

"Casey came from the East," I said, and the words still didn't fit right. "And ever since he was young, an older woman would come and visit him and an unidentified kid."

Dante's eyes sharpened. "These two people are from the East?"

"The woman is," I clarified. "The kid… I'm not sure. No one seems to know who they are, and no one seems to have ever seen their face properly."

The barista handed the coffees through the window. I took them, thanked her, and set them in the cup holders with more care than I felt.

Then I pulled out and decided on doing a lazy loop around the block instead of heading straight back. I needed the movement. I needed the space to talk without the NBI building staring at me.

Dante watched the coffee, then looked back at me. "But your mind is making the leap that Stephanie is the kid," he said, his voice steady.

"The ages would match up," I replied, and I held up a finger, ticking it off. "The limp checks out, and the connections make sense."

"It's still a leap," Dante reminded me firmly.

"She is worth talking to," I insisted, keeping my tone controlled.

"You won't be able to," Dante countered immediately. "Not without Theresa being around."

"And no doubt Wilson has let her know that I know about the money," I added, because that was the part that kept curling in my stomach.

Dante's head snapped toward me again. "You told Wilson you knew about the money?"

I glanced at him. "Honestly, I thought you had already made that connection."

Dante made a sound that was half groan and half curse. "Fuck me."

"Claire wouldn't like that," I muttered automatically.

Dante stared at me, then shook his head, and finally took a sip of coffee like he needed something to stop himself from yelling. A few seconds passed, and the only sound was the car rolling over uneven road.

Then Dante's tone shifted slightly, less annoyed and more thoughtful. "If Stephanie is the kid," he said slowly, "do you think she would know who the woman is?"

"Maybe," I replied, and I hated how much that word carried. "At this point, whoever that kid is most likely killed Casey. Stephen said they were with Casey not long before he died. Limp and all."

Dante's fingers tightened around the cup. "Which means they knew Casey well enough to know Blaze, to know the woman, and to think Blaze knew something that meant he needed to die."

"And," I added, and the thought came out colder than I meant, "it also means that whoever this woman is may also know something that means she needs to die."

The sentence landed and stayed.

Neither of us spoke. Dante stared out the window, and I watched the road without seeing it properly.

Then Dante nodded. "Even if she doesn't know something," he muttered, "Casey's killer might think she does."

I swallowed. "It may mean… anyone else who was close to Casey may also be a target."

Dante turned back toward me. "You think Angelo?"

"They were 'family'," I said, and didn't like that I was saying it.

I looped back toward the NBI and pulled to the curb again near where I'd parked before, keeping the car idling because I wasn't ready to stop moving yet, even if the car wasn't going anywhere.

Dante sat back, thinking. "Alright," he said finally, and his tone went practical again because that was how he survived this job, "what if Stephanie is the kid, but not the killer?"

I looked at him. "Then I need to find someone else with a limp."

Dante's stare held mine, and the exhaustion in it wasn't just from lack of sleep. He took another sip of coffee, then exhaled. "Okay," he said, voice low. "So how do you plan to get Stephanie alone without

Theresa smelling it from across the building?”

I shifted my grip on the wheel, eyes flicking toward the gate, toward the guards, and then back to the street.

“I’m working on that,” I muttered, and realised how much it wasn’t an answer yet.

Dante sat in my passenger seat like he’d been welded there against his will, coffee between his hands, eyes forward, jaw tight enough that his teeth were grinding. The car idled under us, the curb and the gate to the NBI sitting just ahead, close enough to see the security booth through the windscreen.

The air inside the car had cooled, but the tension hadn’t. It clung to the space between us, and I felt Dante’s patience thinning by the second, which was impressive considering the man had made an entire career out of staying calm while people lied to his face.

“What’s on for your day?” I asked, keeping my voice casual.

“Following some leads that aren’t actually leads.”

“Sounds thrilling. What time are you planning on going home?” I asked, and I let it sound like small talk even though it wasn’t.

He caught on. “What do you want, Red?” Dante asked, finally turning his head enough to look at me properly.

“A casual check-in with Angelo,” I said, watching his face for the reaction I knew was coming.

“That’s cute. You worried about him now?” Dante asked, and he sounded like he hated that the question wasn’t entirely a joke.

“I just want to know if he knows anything about the woman or the kid. And I feel like I’ve pushed my luck with him. And with Stephen.

Think if he sees me heading that way again, he'll cut me."

Dante rolled his eyes and got out of the car. I did too. The morning air hit me immediately, cooler than it looked, carrying that faint city smell of exhaust smoke and garbage, and the NBI building sat ahead like it always did—too clean, too tall, and too confident that it owned the world beneath it. I stepped around the front of my car and fell in beside Dante, matching his pace.

"What're you doing?" Dante asked, not slowing down.

"Going to work," I said, like it was nothing.

"You're kidding?" Dante asked, and he finally stopped long enough to look at me, hoping I'd blink and admit it was a joke.

I held up my badge. Dante's face shifted through about five expressions in one second—shock, irritation, disbelief, and then that familiar tired anger that always arrived when I made a decision he was against.

"Red, please don't—" Dante started, and he sounded like a man trying to talk someone down from a ledge.

"It'll be fine. I'm sure I can distract Theresa for a little," I said, and I heard how confident it sounded. I had no idea where that confidence came from.

"Oh, shit," I said, and it hit me fast—that little mental snap when you remember a detail too late.

I moved to stop Dante from moving any further, stepping into his path with a hand half lifted, not touching him, but making him pause.

"Rochelle."

"Who?" Dante asked, his eyebrows drawing together.

15

"She was a waitress at Mamma's. She knew Casey. And… she died before Casey did," I said, letting the sentence run out my mouth quickly.

"Okay?" Dante asked, and he sounded like he was trying very hard to be patient with me and failing.

"Just more questions to sprinkle in when you talk to Angelo."

"I hate you," Dante said, and he didn't sound like he meant it, but he also didn't sound like he didn't.

Dante continued to walk toward the NBI, and I followed. We moved together across the footpath and toward the pedestrian entry, the gate and security booth sitting slightly to our right, and the building's main entrance looming ahead. People were already filtering in, a slow stream of agents and staff, faces set into that morning seriousness.

"Alright, I'm heading out that way around lunch 'cause I'm stopping around to see mum. So, I'll see what I can do," Dante said, and his voice had shifted into work-mode, practical, forcing himself to focus on the doable parts of the day instead of the mess I kept creating.

"Aw, and how is Melissa doing?" I asked, still trying to keep things light.

"Swell. Look…" Dante started, and the single word carried a warning, the kind that meant he'd humour me for exactly one sentence before he snapped. We stopped at the pedestrian entry, waiting for the people ahead of us to head through security before us. "How long are you planning on playing around in here for?" He didn't look at me when he said it, his eyes tracking the line ahead.

"Kinda depends on how it goes," I said, and it was the truth, unfortunately, because I didn't have a neat plan. Just an instinct.

"Things are a little tense in there at the moment with this new case. And my team is… well, somehow, they hate you even more now," Dante said, and I caught the way his mouth tightened as he admitted it.

"I'm guessing it's been labelled as serial," I said, and my mind flicked back to Wilson's boards, to the numbers on the doors, and to the clean cuts and carvings.

"Yeah. So, maybe, just steer clear of that floor while you're here. Especially, if you're already going to cause a problem with Theresa," Dante said, and he finally looked at me, the warning clear in his eyes.

"I will keep that in mind," I said, which was not a promise, but it was as close as I was willing to give.

We moved to go through security. Showing our badges and being waved through. The guard barely glanced at Dante—he didn't need to—and then his eyes lingered on me a beat longer, taking in the consultant badge, the fact I wasn't in suitable bureau attire, and the fact I looked like I hadn't slept properly. He waved me through anyway.

We walked to the front entrance of the NBI in silence and went through security in the lobby together. The lobby was already alive with movement: agents guiding perps toward holding, witnesses being signed in, and a few civilians hovering near the desk looking lost.

Once we were on the other side of it, Dante stopped me. He turned slightly, so we weren't blocking traffic, but the move still made it feel like he was putting himself between me and the rest of the building like he could physically prevent me from doing something stupid if he stood in the right place.

"Stephanie is fine. But do not go to Theresa. Let's just… feel it out for the moment," Dante said, and he kept his voice low.

"You should not be feeling it out at work," I said quickly, and Dante's mouth twitched before he caught himself.

"Red," he said, and that single word carried my full name without him having to say it.

"Fine. Fine. No Theresa. But if she finds me, that's not my fault. Hades doesn't keep her around for no reason," I said, and I watched his face for a flicker of amusement that never came.

"Hilarious. Be good," Dante said, and it was the closest thing to affection he was willing to offer me at this time.

Dante turned away from me and headed to the elevator, leaving me standing alone.

I didn't move. Not yet—just watched him disappear into the crowd, the elevator doors swallowing him. Then I let my attention shift outward, taking in the lobby properly. The security, the flow of bodies, the rhythm of the place, and the way everyone seemed to know exactly where they were going except the ones who didn't, and those were the ones that stuck out.

People walked in and out. Agents moved with perps into holding, and witnesses entered and left. A guard laughed at something quietly, a receptionist answered a phone with a bright professional voice, and somewhere near the scanners someone dropped a folder and cursed under their breath, scrambling to pick up the pages.

I had to get Stephanie away from Theresa long enough to talk to her. I let my mind move on its own and let an idea form, and it wasn't a good one, but it was something, which was enough.

I walked over to the reception desk and leaned my elbow on it. The receptionist looked up as if I'd interrupted his entire existence, and the tension in his posture told me he wasn't used to people approaching him without an appointment or a form.

"Hi," I said, and I made my voice pleasant enough to be disarming.

"Uh, hi, how can I help?" the man behind the desk asked, and he sounded like he was already bracing for whatever this was.

I read his name tag. "Jordan."

"That is me," Jordan said, and his eyes flicked to my badge, then back up to my face.

"Sorry to bother, I need to use the phone there. I left mine at home," I said, and I kept the request casual, like people did this all the time.

"I'm sorry I can't—" Jordan started, but I cut him off before he could finish.

"Consultant stuff. Pretty important. It's about that big case Agent Wilson Barnes is on. I won't be a second," I said, and I watched the lie land, not because it was convincing, but because it sounded official enough to make his brain short-circuit.

"Uh," Jordan said, and he looked around the lobby nervously.

His eyes darted to security, to the flow of agents, and to the elevator bank, trying to figure out who would notice him letting me use the phone and who would punish him for it.

"I'm going to go to the toilet. I'll be really quick," Jordan said, and the words came out too fast. "You can use it."

He quickly jumped up from his seat and almost ran from behind the desk and down the hall that sat just to the left of the desk.

"Weird kid."

I moved around the back of the desk and kept my posture like I belonged there and found the phone quickly. I lifted the receiver and let it rest against my palm for half a second, eyes sweeping the mess of sticky notes, laminated procedure cards, and a plastic stand holding a list of extensions.

My gaze snagged on it immediately.

A neat column of names and numbers. I tracked down the list slowly, not wanting to miss the one I wanted. Then I found it. Theresa's office.

And beneath it—Stephanie.

I punched it in. The keypad clicked under my fingers, each press a little too loud in my head, and the ring tone started on the other end, dull and repetitive, like the building itself clearing its throat. I stared straight ahead, expression neutral, while the lobby moved around me in its usual rhythm—security scanning people through, agents cutting across the tiles, and civilians hovering in that awkward space where they weren't sure where to stand.

She picked up on the third ring.

"This is Theresa's office, Stephanie speaking," Stephanie said professionally.

Her voice was crisp, young, and practiced, and it had that particular edge people got when they worked for someone who didn't tolerate wasted time. I shifted my stance slightly, angling my body away from the lobby, trying to shield the call from noise, then did my best to alter my voice.

Nothing over the top. Just lower and flatter in that bureaucratic way that made you sound like you'd been born to do this job.

"Stephanie. Agent Barnes has some files for Theresa, but he is a little pre-occupied at the moment. Are you able to come and get them?" I asked evenly.

"May I ask what they're in regard to?" Stephanie asked cautiously.

There was a pause in her tone, the kind that didn't feel like suspicion so much as procedure, and I pictured her at a desk somewhere upstairs, pen already in hand, ready to write down whatever I said.

"Agent Barnes' current case," I replied plainly.

I let the answer sit there without elaborating, counting on the weight of Wilson's name to do the work for me. People didn't pry when a senior agent was involved, not unless they wanted to become part of the problem.

"Oh, of course. Um, yes. I will head down now to collect them." Stephanie answered quickly.

"Perfect. Thank you," I said, keeping it short, and then I hung up before she could ask anything else.

The receiver clicked back into place. I stood there with my hand still hovering over it. It felt like I was waiting for alarm bells that never came.

I looked across the lobby and caught a security guard staring at me. He wasn't rushing over. He wasn't calling anyone. He was just watching as if he'd clocked something unusual and couldn't decide whether it was worth caring about. His posture was loose, but his eyes were sharp.

I shot him a smile and waved, raising my badge up, before moving out from behind the desk and moving toward the elevator. I kept my pace steady, shoulders loose, eyes forward, and I let the lobby move around me back into its flow. The badge stayed visible as I crossed the tiles, my fingers resting against it in case I needed to flash it again.

The elevators sat ahead, chrome doors reflecting the lobby in warped slices. I pressed the button, and when the doors opened, I stepped in with a couple of other people and stood near the back, letting them take the front positions like they mattered more. The ride up was quiet and quick, with only a few stops.

I slipped out on Wilson's floor. The hallway was empty, but I heard the clacking of keyboards ahead in the bullpen. Not wanting to upset Dante and make a scene with his wonderful team that love me, I quietly moved down the hall and into the kitchen.

It was small, corporate, and tired. A fridge humming in the corner, a coffee machine that needed to be cleaned, and a couple of chairs pulled under a table that had seen too many sad lunches. No one was there, and no one from the bullpen could see me.

Good.

I leaned back against the counter and waited, keeping my face blank while my mind ran through the timing. Stephanie had said she'd head down now. That meant she'd be leaving Theresa's orbit, and I would have a small window to intercept.

I waited. Hoping no one wanted to come get a coffee or a sandwich.

The building was quiet in a way that made every distant sound feel amplified. A printer whirring somewhere down the hall. Footsteps fading and returning. I kept my eyes on the doorway and resisted the urge to pace.

It wasn't long before one of the elevators dinged, and Stephanie strolled past.

She moved with purpose, not rushed, but not casual either. Dark clothes, clean lines, hair pulled back, and that knee brace sitting against her leg like it belonged there. The limp was subtle, but it was there. She didn't glance into the kitchen as she passed. Her gaze stayed forward.

I stayed still.

I let her go, counting the seconds and listening to the faint sound of her footsteps fading down the corridor. A few minutes went by, and Stephanie came walking past again, muttering to herself.

Her head tilted slightly as she moved, eyes narrowing like she was doing the mental maths of being summoned for nothing. The muttering wasn't loud enough for me to catch every word, but the tone was clear: irritated, frustrated, unimpressed.

That was my opening. I hurried out of the kitchen and fell in step behind her, keeping enough distance not to startle her and not so much that I'd lose her if she turned a corner. She didn't look back. She just walked with purpose toward the elevators.

Once she reached them, she hit the button with more force than necessary and stepped inside the first one that opened. I followed her in a second later, slipping into the space beside her. The doors closed.

"Why call me if there's nothing?" Stephanie muttered harshly.

She still hadn't turned to look at me. She aimed the question at the air, at the building, at the universe, at whoever had wasted her time, and it made me almost smile because the anger was pure.

The elevator started moving, the floor indicator lit up, and the gentle hum of the elevator filled the small space between us. Stephanie's shoulders stayed squared, her jaw set, and the annoyance rolled off her in waves.

"That may have been me," I finally admitted.

Stephanie turned to face me as I hit the emergency stop on the elevator. The motion was quick and deliberate—my hand moved, the button clicked under my finger, and the elevator gave a soft mechanical protest before it obeyed. The momentum eased, the hum dropped, and then everything went still.

The elevator came to a halt.

Stephanie didn't stumble. She didn't flinch. She just stared at me, eyes flat, and then her expression shifted into something even less charitable. I read it as something close to hatred.

"Oh, good. It's you." Stephanie said dryly.

She didn't reach for the panel. She didn't press any buttons. She didn't even glance at the emergency stop. She didn't make a move to get the elevator started again.

"What do you want?" she asked bluntly.

"Just to talk without Cerberus breathing down our necks," I replied, keeping my tone even, and I watched her face at the mention of Theresa.

Stephanie's mouth tightened a fraction. "And this is your solution to that?"

"Would you have come down if I had asked nicely?" I asked, letting a sliver of humour in.

"Touché," Stephanie mumbled. Her gaze stayed on me.

"I would rather not do this in an elevator, though. So, now you're here, why don't we go for a walk?" I asked, keeping my tone light and friendly.

Stephanie let out a long sigh. Something flickered across her face. I could've read it as guilt, but I wasn't sure I wanted to yet.

"Fine. But I don't have long." Stephanie agreed shortly, followed by a huff.

"Perfect." I smiled faintly.

I reached back to the panel, hit the button to get the elevator to move again, and pressed the button for the lobby.

16

The elevator doors opened, and we stepped out.

I let Stephanie lead the way, mostly because she was already moving like she'd decided this was her hallway and I was just an inconvenience trailing behind her, and partly because if I tried to take control too early, she'd clamp down and turn into Theresa's shadow again.

Instead of heading toward the entrance, we cut down the hall adjacent to the elevators, away from the lobby's noise, and away from the front desk.

We didn't talk.

The corridor thinned out the further we went, the lighting turning harsher and flatter, and the walls losing that polished, public-facing finish the bureau liked to show the world. This part of the building felt like something they had forgotten about.

Halfway down, Stephanie slowed, glanced once over her shoulder, checking if I was still following, and then she turned into a door that looked like it hadn't been opened in months. I followed.

She stepped inside and reached back, pulling the door shut behind us with a soft click that made the outside world feel suddenly far away. The room was a storage graveyard. Old computers stacked in uneven towers, cables coiled in tight knots, whiteboards leaning against tables, folding chairs piled in a corner, and cardboard boxes labelled in fading marker with dates that were not recent.

Dust sat on most surfaces. The lighting overhead buzzed faintly, and the air carried that dry, forgotten smell of plastic and dampness. Someone had once tried to organise the room and failed, leaving behind half a system that had collapsed into clutter.

Stephanie didn't bother looking around. She'd clearly been here before. She stopped near one of the tables, turned to face me, and folded her arms. "My patience is already running thin, so you don't have long."

I took that in, then let my eyes flick over her posture, the tightness in her jaw, and the way she held herself. "God, it's like she cloned herself."

Stephanie gave me a warning look, and I lifted my hands in defence. "Alright. Fine. We'll make it quick. I'll be nice to your patience."

I waited a moment, letting the room settle around us and letting her feel the silence instead of rushing to fill it. No doubt, Theresa had taught her how to handle pressure.

"How well did you know Casey Edwards?"

The question sat between us. She didn't answer. Her face went through changes in the space of five seconds—surprise first, then calculation, then that flicker of annoyance that came from being dragged into something she'd hoped was finished, and finally a calm that looked practiced enough to be rehearsed.

Then she lied. "I only know him from the case file."

I nodded slowly as if I believed her, and then I turned the knife a fraction. "Right. The one you sent a message to Dante about."

Stephanie nodded. The motion was small, but it wasn't relaxed.

"And why did you send that message?" I pressed.

"I just do what I'm told." Stephanie clenched her jaw, then forced herself to relax.

"From Theresa?"

"Obviously."

Her tone stayed sharp, but there was a faint tightness behind it, the kind that didn't come from confidence and didn't come from anger either. It came from loyalty that had been trained into her so thoroughly she didn't know where it ended and where she began.

"So, when she told you to meet with Casey and collect the money, you just went and did it? No questions asked," I said evenly.

Silence.

In that quiet, I watched her eyes shift and watched her mouth tighten. I watched the tiny movements that told the truth even when the words didn't.

"I don't know what you're talking about," Stephanie said flatly, chin lifting a fraction. Panic crept across her face, not huge and dramatic, but there in the corners—behind her eyes, in the tension in her cheeks, and in the way her shoulders sat a fraction higher like her body was bracing for impact.

I let it run its course—watched her sit in it until her breathing changed and her control had to work harder to keep up.

"Come on, Steph. You know I can tell when you're lying," I said quietly.

She didn't say anything. She just watched me, trying to decide whether I was bluffing, whether I had proof, and whether any of it mattered if she simply refused to engage.

"If it makes you feel any better, Wilson knows I know," I continued, keeping my voice calm, "and Theresa probably knows by now, too. So, it just hadn't trickled down to you yet."

Her eyes narrowed, and the panic shifted into something sharper. "What? You're trying to separate us now?" she asked, her voice harsh.

"I'm just trying to get the truth," I said simply, holding her stare.

I waited again. The air felt dry, and the room seemed smaller than it was. It felt as if the old equipment was listening.

Stephanie's gaze dropped briefly, then returned to my face, and her lips pressed together like she'd made a decision she hated. "I met with him," she said at last, the admission forced out.

"That much I already know, but thank you."

Her jaw flexed at that, and I saw her irritation flare up. "If you want to know if I knew him, I didn't," she said quickly. "I went to the meeting spot, did what had to be done, then left."

"You never spoke to him?" I asked, tilting my head slightly.

16

"What would I speak to him about?" Stephanie snapped, one hand lifting in a small, frustrated gesture before dropping again.

I didn't answer, because any answer would've given her a path to walk down and a story to build, and right now I wanted her standing in uncertainty instead. I watched her knee brace when she shifted her weight and the subtle limp she tried to minimise. She shifted her posture to take the weight off her knee.

"You met up with him two weeks ago. Wednesday night."

Stephanie's face shifted again, and she nodded.

"How did he seem?"

"Like someone doing something illegal," she said immediately.

"Is that how you felt, too?" I pressed.

Stephanie's eyes hardened. Her voice stayed controlled, but there was a tremor underneath it, the tiniest tell. "I have a good job," she said, as if that settled it.

"So, that's a yes."

Stephanie scoffed, turning her head slightly.

"From what I can tell, you were the last person to see him alive," I said, watching her reaction.

"Aside from you," she shot back, and she aimed it like a jab.

I smiled despite myself, because she wasn't wrong. "You saw the original report."

"It's my job to know a lot," Stephanie replied, shoulders squaring a fraction. The way she said it made it clear she took pride in that. She'd earned her competence, and she didn't like being treated like she was only someone's lackey.

"Well, do you know that someone else close to Casey died?" I asked, letting it hang.

Her face shifted again, and this time it wasn't calculation or irritation. It was genuine surprise.

She didn't know.

"As much as I'd love to bring this money thing out in the open," I said, voice low, "I don't think it's the reason Casey or his partner died."

"So why are you talking to me?" Stephanie demanded. Not defensive, exactly. More like she wanted to know what role she was being forced into and how to get out of it. I glanced down to her knee, and the brace stared back at me.

"I'm just trying to figure out who knew Casey," I said, looking back up at her.

"Well, I didn't," she said fast.

Too fast.

There was something beneath her words, written across her face in the split second after she spoke, before she could smooth it away. It wasn't exactly a lie, but it wasn't the full truth either. The kind of statement that could be technically accurate while still hiding the real shape of things.

I held her gaze. "No," I said simply.

Stephanie's mouth tightened. Her eyes narrowed. "Your five minutes is up," she said, her voice flat.

She turned slightly, already angling toward the door as if she were done and had given me enough, and as if she didn't care that I hadn't gotten what I wanted.

"You've heard a lot about him, though, haven't you?" I asked, keeping my tone light but my eyes fixed on her.

She stopped mid-turn and glanced back at me. "What?"

"Someone spoke about him to you. More than just about the money."

The words landed, and the room went still around us while Stephanie stood there deciding whether she was going to keep walking or humour me for a little longer.

"And who would that be?" Stephanie asked, but her tone had shifted. Less dismissal, more sharpened interest.

"My guess is Theresa."

Stephanie fully turned to face me again, arms still crossed, but the set of her shoulders changed. Defensive now. Protective.

"And why would she do that?"

"I don't know," I admitted. "But you do know more about Casey than you're saying. I can see it."

She let out a short breath through her nose, the closest thing to a laugh without humour. "Jesus. You and Mia should start a club."

I scoffed. "Cheap shot."

Her eyes narrowed, trying to work out if I was joking or if I was actually bothered.

"I just can't tell how personal you were with him," I said softly. "That's the part you keep avoiding answering."

"I wasn't," Stephanie insisted.

"But he wasn't just a file to you. I can see that," I pressed. "He wasn't just someone you went and grabbed the money from."

Her jaw flexed, and she shifted her weight. "And you think Theresa whispered in my ear about him?" Stephanie asked, voice rising a fraction. "Why would she do that?"

"You tell me."

We watched each other.

"Why don't you go and ask her yourself?" Stephanie shot back.

"You know what? You're right," I said, and I made my voice light like I wasn't watching every micro-shift in her face.

I shrugged and moved to walkit around her, angling toward the door.

She moved fast. Not a lunge in panic, but a decisive step that cut off my path. "Wait."

I stopped and turned slightly to face her, leaving my body half-turned.

"She mentioned him," Stephanie admitted.

The words shouldn't have weighed as much as they did for how small they were. She'd been trying to keep that sentence trapped behind her teeth for weeks. I faced her fully.

"We talked about him as more than just part of the deal," she added, letting out a long breath.

"And you're telling me this now… Why?" I asked, keeping my tone even.

Stephanie's throat bobbed when she swallowed. "Because I did know him."

I let that sit. It changed her face. There was more to it now—hurt, yes, but also fear that hadn't been there before, or maybe it had and I'd missed it.

My eyes were quite heavy, so it was possible.

"From what you and Theresa spoke about?"

She shook her head quickly. "No."

"I saw him outside of the deals," Stephanie said, the words coming out slower.

"As friends?"

"No. No." She shook her head again, sharper this time. "Just… sometimes. He'd be in the East, and we would see each other."

East. Not the Strip. Not the West. Not the meeting points.

"Why are you worried of me getting information from Theresa? Why stop me?"

"I'm not. I'm—" Stephanie started, then stopped. She drew a breath like she'd forgotten how. This wasn't irritation anymore. This was fear. "I just don't want Theresa to know," she finished, voice quieter now, almost a plea she didn't want to sound like.

"That you knew him?"

She nodded once. "How much I know."

"Why?"

Stephanie's gaze flicked to the door behind me like she expected it to open. She expected Theresa to appear in the frame without making a sound, smiling politely while she cut the throat of the conversation.

"The one time she mentioned him," Stephanie said slowly, "it was… different. Like she was planning something. It was like it slipped out and she wasn't supposed to say it."

"You didn't ask questions?" I asked, and I kept my voice careful because I felt her pulling back already.

Stephanie's mouth twitched, sharp and bitter. "I keep my job because I don't ask questions."

I watched the panic start to rise again, controlled but real, sitting behind her eyes like storm clouds

"Why are you scared?"

"I'm… I'm not," she lied, and it was a bad one.

"What did she say?" I pressed.

Stephanie hesitated, and then she forced it out. "She mentioned something about Casey talking to her about a girl."

My mind jumped immediately, snapping to the outline it had been building since Stephen's story. The kid. The one no one could name. The one who'd been there since the beginning. "What about the girl?"

"I don't know," Stephanie admitted, frustration bleeding through. "It was just a quick thing. Theresa seemed… angry, almost."

There was a moment where the room felt too still, like the old computers and dead monitors all had eyes. "Then she talked about the schedule he followed for the runs," Stephanie continued, and her voice flattened. "And that was it."

My chest tightened. "You think she did it."

The words came out suddenly before I had time to measure them. Stephanie stared at me with her mouth slightly open.

Then she closed it, quick and hard.

It looked like she wanted to say something but couldn't, like the words were stuck behind whatever Theresa had built into her—loyalty, fear, training, or all three at once.

Her hands unclenched at her sides, then clenched again. "No," she breathed, but it wasn't an answer.

"No… you don't think she did it?" I asked quietly.

"I—I don't," Stephanie said, but her voice didn't have any conviction in it.

I watched her, taking in all the subtle movements of her face. The way her eyes moved, and how her mouth twitched, as well as how she tried to keep her eyebrows steady.

I still couldn't get a read on her, though. Either I was too tired to translate all the movements, or she had so many thoughts stacked up they cancelled each other out. "Could she have?" I pushed.

"Don't," Stephanie warned, and her jaw tightened as she held my stare.

"Do you know where she was on Saturday? After we had our little reunion in the lobby?"

"Why does that matter?"

"Because that's when Casey's partner died. I need to know if she could've done it."

Stephanie's eyes flicked, quickly, checking to make sure the room still held only us. "I don't know. I—I went to run errands," she said, and the stutter sounded less like nerves and more like she was choosing her phrasing carefully.

I thought back to that day, sitting in my car as I watched Stephanie and Bryce leave the building and Theresa get left behind. The memory came back in clean frames, the kind that stuck because my brain had filed it away without asking why.

The timeline matched. The motive didn't.

But if she was the woman who visited Casey on The Strip when he was a kid, the personal connection was there. I just needed to find out why. "I'm going to have to talk to her," I said, more so to myself than to Stephanie. Maybe it was the lack of sleep talking, but I thought it was a good idea.

"No," Stephanie said immediately, the word cutting through the room like a knife.

"I won't mention you," I promised.

"She'll know I said something," Stephanie insisted, and her voice lifted at the end as if it wasn't an argument so much as a fact she'd learned the hard way.

My mind rushed to Blaze and how he was most likely killed because he knew something he shouldn't have. It was possible Stephanie was in the same situation. If Theresa was the one pulling the trigger, I would have to move fast.

"Do you trust me?"

"No," Stephanie said without missing a beat.

"Okay. Fair."

We stood there, and I watched the realisation settle into Stephanie piece by piece. Not a flash of understanding. The slow, sinking kind that changed a person's eyes when they finally saw there was no clean way out.

"Nothing will happen to you," I said firmly, like volume and certainty could make it true.

Stephanie looked at me, and I knew she didn't believe a word of it. Just as she drew breath to argue, her phone sounded. She quickly checked it. "It's Theresa. I need to go. I've been gone too long already."

"Shit," I mumbled.

Stephanie moved to the door quickly, then paused, fingers hovering over the handle as if it were hot. She looked like she had one more thing to give me and couldn't risk it. Then she made her choice and slipped out, leaving me alone.

My mind ran.

It sprinted through Theresa's face, the lobby, the timing, the way Stephanie's fear had sharpened the second I said I'd talk to her, and the way Blaze's death sat in the background like a warning I couldn't ignore.

Then I sighed. I couldn't leave it. Not now. I waited a minute or so, then moved out of the room.

The hallway outside was too bright after the storage room's stale dimness, and my footsteps sounded measured and deliberate as I headed back the way I had come.

It was time to move on to the next name on my list.

17

My steps were heavy as I walked through the NBI toward the elevators. The weight sat in my calves, in my shoulders, and behind my eyes, where sleep had started to feel like a rumour.

My direction was clear. I needed to go to Theresa. Stephanie's fear and what she had said had led me in this direction, and I needed to follow it through. There were other routes I could've taken. Safer ones. Routes that didn't involve walking up to an Assistant Director of the NBI and announcing myself.

I was concerned, though, because I had no idea what I was going to say to her. I didn't even know if I'd be able to get in to see her. And then, if I did, I had no idea what would happen.

Theresa wasn't someone you cornered in a hallway. If she didn't want to see me, I'd end up trapped with somebody else, a polite smile, and security that didn't mind throwing me face-first into the pavement. I knew I couldn't go in there and accuse Theresa of murder. But I needed to get some information from her.

My main goal was to confirm if she was the woman who visited Casey, and if she was, why? The why kept repeating itself like a low alarm. Because if she was connected to Casey when he was a kid, then the money, and then the runs, it all started to be a long list of coincidences if she wasn't involved in his death.

I continued down the hall and came to the elevators, and just as I was about to hit the button, someone caught my eye.

Bryce.

He was just coming through the lobby's security. Carrying himself the same as he was last time I saw him. Entitled. The way he walked was almost identical to his mother.

He didn't slow for security. He didn't look at the guards as if they mattered. He moved as if the building was his, and security was just a formality.

Then an idea started to form. It didn't arrive like inspiration. It came together like a lock clicking into place. Theresa was a fortress, and Bryce was a side door she'd left propped open because she couldn't imagine anyone daring to use it.

I moved away from the elevator and headed toward the middle of the lobby, intercepting him. I adjusted my pace so I hit his path at the right angle. I let the lobby noise swallow the edges of us, the phones and footsteps and distant conversations giving me cover.

"Bryce, right?" I asked as I approached him.

He looked at me like I wasn't worth his time but nodded anyway. "Yeah," Bryce said flatly.

"Ryan," I said, and I stepped closer, holding out my hand, which he didn't take.

My palm hung there longer than it should've, long enough that the refusal was obvious to anyone watching, and then I let it drop. Bryce didn't even pretend to be polite about it. No awkward smile or apology. Just a blank look that said he didn't see me as a person, only as a nuisance.

"I know. We met," Bryce said, his eyes flicking past me.

"Just seeing if I was memorable," I said, and I kept the faintest curve in my mouth like this was all harmless.

Not a laugh, or smile, or even a twitch of the mouth. He was his mother's son.

"What brings you to the building?" I asked, keeping my tone casual. "What brings you here? Didn't you ditch the case they gave you?" Bryce tilted his head like he'd caught me doing something embarrassing and smirked at himself.

"We'll say I had a change of heart," I said evenly.

"Right. Well, I'm actually here to train, so if you don't mind." Bryce stepped around me and moved toward the elevators.

I followed. "What're you training for?" I asked, letting the question land like small talk.

He glanced at me and wore a look of disgust on his face. It wasn't subtle. "Don't you have, like, other people to annoy and be old around?"

"I'm in my late thirties," I mumbled, mostly to myself. Then I lifted my gaze to him again. "Come on, just because your mother flies to work on a broom doesn't mean you have to… swoop up there, too."

That earned a twitch of the mouth. The smallest crack in the entitlement. Not quite amusement, but it was something.

"I'm doing shooting down in the basement," he said as though it was a quirky hobby he had picked up.

"Looking to join the team at some point?" I asked, keeping my voice interested.

"Haven't thought about it much. But it is pretty fun to shoot."

The way he spoke was almost boyish.

"Oh, yeah. It sure is," I said dryly.

"You shoot?" Bryce asked, and he finally looked at me properly.

When the elevator arrived, the doors slid open with a soft mechanical sigh, and the mirrored walls caught our reflections, doubling us, multiplying our faces into angles I didn't need to see. Bryce stepped in first, and I moved in after him, staying near the side panel.

"Yep," I lied. "Actually, was heading down there myself."

"You have your own gun?" Bryce asked, and the way he said it made it clear he thought this was the normal question adults asked each other.

"Nah. I just… check one out when I'm down there."

Bryce clicked the button to go to the basement and nodded. "Yeah, same. Mum won't organise for me to have one. Not unless I become an agent."

"How unfair," I said, keeping my face straight.

"At least Dad lets me use his to practise sometimes," Bryce added, and his tone softened just slightly, like his father was a loophole he enjoyed.

"Oh, yay. Parent of the year."

We fall silent as the elevator comes to a stop and the doors open. Sound hit us immediately as agents were already in training. The basement range was its own world. Bright lights, hard surfaces, and noise that didn't echo so much as it punched. Shots cracked down the lanes in staggered rhythm, sharp and clean.

Bryce's posture changed the second we stepped into it. His shoulders loosened and his jaw unclenched. This was somewhere he wanted to be.

I moved with him, keeping pace as we approached the counter. The window to our right was thick glass with a narrow opening at the bottom, and behind it was a man who looked like he'd been here long enough to stop reacting to anything human. He slid a clipboard toward Bryce without looking up. Bryce took it, grabbed a pen, and started writing with the lazy confidence of someone who'd never been questioned about his name.

I follow what Bryce is doing because I have never been here in my life.

Once Bryce finished signing his paperwork, the guy behind the counter disappeared for a moment and returned with a case. Bryce watched it with open interest, like a kid watching a present get unwrapped. He signed something else, took the case, and then moved off toward the lanes with the same entitled stride, already scanning for an open spot.

He didn't glance back at me. He didn't ask if I was coming. He assumed I'd either keep up, or I didn't matter.

The guy behind the counter looked at me, and I shook my head.

"I'm supervising," I said as though that was enough of an explanation.

He grunted. It was a sound that meant he didn't care what I did as long as I didn't make it his problem. I leaned slightly closer to the opening in the glass, lowering my voice. "I do have a favour to ask, though," I said carefully.

He looked at me, waiting. Head tilted slightly and eyebrows raised.

"Can you call Assistant Director Theresa Langer and tell her Ryan Red is with her son," I said, pitching it like a harmless request.

The man's brows lifted a fraction more. "Is that something that matters?" he asked, sounding like he already knew the answer and didn't like it. "Something she gotta know?"

"Oh, yeah. She's gonna lose her fucking mind," I said, and I let the faintest humour into it.

The guy sighed heavily then shrugged and moved to the phone. He didn't ask for my badge. He didn't ask for a reason. He just picked up the receiver.

I smiled to myself and grabbed a pair of earmuffs and moved down the lanes, looking for Bryce.

The earmuffs were heavier than I expected, stiff plastic with padding that smelled faintly like sweat and disinfectant. I hooked them over one hand as I walked, weaving between bodies and benches without bumping anyone. The lanes ran long and narrow, each one boxed in by dividers that made you feel like you were both protected and trapped.

Bryce was easy to find. Not because he stood out physically—he didn't—but because he moved like he didn't belong to the same rules as everyone else. He didn't wait. He didn't hover. He stepped into his lane like he'd paid for the whole range and the rest of us were just borrowing it.

I stopped not far behind him, close enough to watch without looking like I was hovering and put the earmuffs on.

He shot. Bryce held the gun with confidence, but his posture looked off. I didn't know much about it. I had never shot a gun before, but from what I'd seen when Dante had shot, Bryce's stance was a little weird. As though he was compensating for something.

His shoulders were slightly uneven, and his elbow locked harder than it needed to. He was overcorrecting. He seemed to hit the target, though, so I guess it didn't matter.

Bryce lowered the gun, breath steady, and glanced sideways. He caught me immediately and narrowed his eyes. He took off his earmuffs, and so did I.

"You not shooting?" Bryce asked, raising his voice over the noise.

He hit the button to bring the target toward him, eyes still on me. The target mechanism whirred and started to reel the paper back toward him, sliding along the lane with a smooth, mechanical pull.

"Oh, no. I lied. I don't shoot," I said dryly.

Bryce stared at me like he'd misheard, brow raised. "Then why are you here?"

"You'll see soon."

His lips twitched, half disgust, half amusement. "You're insane, dude."

The target reached him, and he took it off and looked at it. He held the paper up, admiring it. There were tight clusters in the centre mass, but a few stray holes that told me his stance *did* matter, even if he didn't want to admit it.

"Didn't miss. I'm getting better," Bryce said, and there was real pride in it.

"Yippee," I deadpanned.

Bryce snorted quietly, then set up another target and hit the button to send it away.

The fresh paper slid out, gliding toward the far end with a whir. He didn't put his earmuffs back on yet. He turned slightly toward me, leaning his hip against the bench as if we were having a conversation at a café and not standing in a firing range.

"I heard about what happened with you last year," Bryce said casually.

"Oh, yeah?" I replied, keeping my face neutral.

"Kind of insane they kept you around."

"Well, they didn't really."

"You can still get in the building," Bryce pointed out.

"And how joyous that is," I said, glancing around the range.

Bryce's gaze didn't move. His attention was fully on me now, even though his target was set up and waiting.

"Was it a part of your scheme to almost get those agents killed?" he asked. The question was too clean and rehearsed. Not in the wording exactly, but in the way it came out. Like he'd heard a version of the story and decided it was true because it was entertaining.

"Funnily enough, no," I said evenly.

Bryce's brows lifted a fraction. "How'd you get into the perps house anyway?"

There was curiosity under the snark. He wanted the story. He wanted to picture it. He wanted to understand the line between stupid and impressive.

"Picked the lock around back," I said, and then I flicked my eyes to the target still sitting downrange. "You gonna shoot?"

Bryce glanced toward the far end, then back at me. He didn't reach for the gun yet. "Would you have felt bad if they died?" There was no cruelty in the question, which made it worse. It wasn't a trap. It was genuine curiosity.

I exhaled slowly. "As a normal human, yeah. I would have," I said, and I let my tone stay almost conversational. "I'm happy to say even from when I was a doctor, I've never been the cause of someone's death."

Bryce's eyes sharpened. "But you've seen people die. Got blood on your hands."

That wasn't a question, but Bryce's face was filled with genuine curiosity. "Yeah," I said, and my shoulders rose and fell in a small shrug. "Kinda came with the job."

Bryce stared at me, absorbing it. He looked like he wanted to ask more, but he couldn't quite find the right question. Before he could find one, though, the air changed.

"What the hell do you think you're doing?" Theresa's voice ripped through the air. It cut through the range noise like a blade, sharp enough that even with shots cracking in the distance, heads turned.

"And that is why I am here," I said to Bryce with a smile.

I turned away from Bryce to see Theresa standing near us, hands on hips and a sharp glare pointed in my direction with a few security guards positioned behind her.

She looked like she'd been poured into her outfit and hardened in place. Hair perfect. Face composed. Anger precise. The guards behind her weren't subtle. Two in plain clothes, one in a darker uniform. Their hands hovered near their belts, not resting, or threatening, just ready. Theresa didn't need muscle to look intimidating, but she brought it anyway.

A reminder.

Bryce turned, eyes widening slightly at the sight of her. Then his expression shifted into mild annoyance.

"He said he was allowed to shoot guns, Mum," I said sarcastically, pointing at Bryce, who let out a small chuckle.

Theresa didn't look amused. Her gaze stayed on me, steady and unblinking. "After your stunt the other day, I'm surprised you're comfortable walking into the building," she said coolly.

"It does make me feel a little hot," I said lightly, "but nothing compared to how you would feel walking into a church, I'm sure." Theresa's face didn't change, but her eyes narrowed by a fraction, the kind of fraction you noticed only if you'd spent your life watching and reading people.

"Bryce. Practice," Theresa said, and her voice turned a notch colder.

She gestured toward the target, and Bryce rolled his eyes but did what he was told. He slid his earmuffs back on with exaggerated annoyance, then turned back to the lane. The moment the earmuffs covered his ears, his shoulders relaxed again.

"Unlike you, I am quite busy," Theresa said, her gaze still fixed on me, "so, whatever reason you needed to lure me down here for, let's get it over with."

"You're right, I'm sorry," I said, and I lifted one hand in a small, almost apologetic gesture. "But could I maybe bribe you to be a little less condescending?"

Theresa's face didn't change. She didn't move at all. Everything about her stayed the same. She held still like a statue, and that stillness did more than any gesture could've. It said she didn't need to fidget. She didn't need to perform. She was in control, and she wanted me to feel it.

Just then, Bryce started shooting, and I scrambled to put the earmuffs on. I fumbled them for half a second; the plastic slipping against my fingers. The shots cracked hard. Without the earmuffs, it would've been painful. Even with them, it was a dull thud in my bones. I forced the earmuffs down over my ears properly, adjusting the seal until the noise dampened into something manageable.

Then I lifted my eyes back to Theresa, who signalled for the security guards to leave.

It wasn't dramatic. She didn't look back at them. She barely moved her hand. A small flick of her fingers like she was shooing away dust. The guards hesitated—checking if they'd understood—then one of them nodded and they peeled off, moving back toward the entrance with practised neutrality.

Theresa waited until they were out of earshot, her gaze still on me the whole time. Her patience was a weapon. She didn't waste it on people who didn't matter.

Which meant, for the moment, I mattered.

When Bryce stopped firing, I took the earmuffs off. The world rushed back in, not just sound but all the sharp little details the padding had dulled—the mechanical whir of targets sliding, the murmured instructions from trainers down the line, and the dull slap of paper being clipped onto holders. Even the air felt different without the seal pressing against my head, cooler against my ears, thinner somehow.

My ears rang anyway. "That's loud," I said, and I shook my head once as though I could knock the ringing loose.

"So are you. You should really keep that in check," Theresa said coolly. She didn't raise her voice, not even down here. She didn't need to. Her tone had that controlled edge that cut through the range noise better than shouting ever could.

"Zing!" I said, putting on a grin.

Theresa's gaze didn't even flicker. "What do you want, Red?"

"We can do this somewhere else," I said, glancing toward the lanes. Bryce was still there, gun down, listening harder than he pretended.

"Here is fine."

We let the range noise fill the gap between us, and I watched her face for anything—an irritation, a tell, a shift in her focus—but she held herself like a woman who didn't offer micro-reactions unless she meant to.

"How well did you know Casey?" I asked, keeping my tone even.

Bryce's head turned slightly as if he were about to speak, but Theresa held her hand up to him without looking away from me. The gesture was small. Total control. Bryce stopped immediately, lips pressing together as he swallowed whatever he'd been about to say.

"More than any file will say."

A clean admission. No hedging. No pretending. "He used to meet a woman in The Strip when he was young. You know about that?" I asked, and I let the question sit on the edge of accusation without tipping into it.

"I do. His father died in a car accident, and his mother used to abuse him. I helped him where I could."

"You're being very forthcoming," I said, and I tried to keep the surprise out of my voice.

"Why lie to you, right?" Theresa said, as if the answer was obvious.

Her face still didn't change. I didn't even know if I could tell, even if she was lying. That was the problem with people like Theresa. If she were lying, she'd do it in a way that made the truth irrelevant. If she were telling the truth, she'd do it in a way that made it feel like she was in control of what it meant.

The only thing that changed was her posture, which shifted slightly. It was subtle. A redistribution of weight. A tiny adjustment in how she stood.

I looked down and noticed her shoes. The same as she was wearing on Saturday. They were polished enough to catch the overhead lights.

17

Expensive and sharp. The kind of heels that clicked and let everyone know who was coming.

Then I noticed again. The left heel was slightly longer than the right.

It wasn't dramatic. It wasn't obvious unless you were looking. But once you saw it, you couldn't unsee it. The angle of her foot. The way her weight sat uneven. A built-in correction. I looked back to her face.

"Why help him as a kid?"

"I knew his father," Theresa said. It came out smooth and rehearsed. It was a sentence she'd used before.

"You felt like you owed him or something?" I asked, watching for any sign of irritation.

"I felt it was the right thing to do," Theresa said calmly. "But there's only so much one can do. For a while, he stayed with his grandmother in The Strip. But eventually, he turned further into the West and look what happened."

I glanced over at Bryce. He was looking at the target he'd just shot, though he was clearly listening to us. His body stayed angled toward the lane, but his attention wasn't on the paper. His head was slightly turned, chin lifted just enough that I knew he was catching every word through the muffled chaos.

I looked back at Theresa. "You don't feel responsible for his death?"

"Why should I?" Theresa asked, and her tone didn't shift. "People die all the time. You worked in a hospital; you should know that better than anyone."

She said it like it was normal. It was the kind of statement you made when death was a statistic, and you'd trained yourself not to see the faces. I continued to watch her face and felt my jaw clench. I could not get a reading off her at all.

"We done?" Theresa asked, and impatience started to creep into her voice. She had decided we had come to the end of what she was willing to give me.

"Where did you know his father from?" I asked, not letting her close the door yet.

Theresa held my gaze. She was deciding whether the answer mattered.

"Levison Ridge," she said finally.

The name hit with a strange weight. "Fancy suburb," I said, keeping my tone neutral.

Theresa smiled, though it didn't reach her eyes. "Make sure you don't bite off more than you can chew. Again." She turned, and the movement was unhurried and elegant.

But before she walked away, she glanced over her shoulder. "And don't pull Stephanie away from her job again," Theresa said, her tone sharpening just slightly on Stephanie's name.

That was a threat. Not overt or loud. But pointed. It told me she knew exactly where Stephanie had been, exactly how long she'd been there, and exactly what the conversation was about.

Theresa walked away and I watched after her, eyes staying on her uneven heels. The longer heel clicked differently. A fraction slower and heavier. The kind of detail you'd miss if you weren't looking, and the kind that would matter if you were trying to place someone in a memory. I stayed still until she was out of sight, then I shifted my weight and let out the breath I'd been holding.

"Ooh, you stole Steph away from her? That's a no, no," Bryce said, and there was amusement in his voice now that his mother's attention had moved on. He'd taken his earmuffs off again. His hair was slightly flattened where they'd pressed, and he looked younger without them. Less polished. More like a kid playing at something serious.

"Yeah, well, she was friends with Casey," I mumbled.

The truth slipped out before I could stop myself. I was trying to sort everything in my mind.

Bryce's eyebrows lifted. "He was the one who died in the park?" There was real interest in his question.

"Yeah," I said. I grabbed the earmuffs and started toward the counter. They felt heavier this time, not because they'd changed, but because I was carrying that sliver of information and trying not to drop it.

"Enjoy your shooting," I said over my shoulder.

I didn't wait for a response and quickly took the earmuffs back to the desk, then moved toward the elevator. My pace picked up without me deciding it. Not a sprint. Just faster. Purposeful. My mind was already ahead of my feet, building connections, checking timelines, dragging old memories through new light.

The elevator doors were a short walk away, but the building felt longer now. Like the hallway had stretched out while I wasn't looking. My mind rested on what information Theresa had given me.

Levison Ridge. A suburb in the East. Not too far away. Where Casey had been before he left for The Strip. A life before. Somewhere a mystery kid could've come from. Or where Theresa's motive lived.

18

"You're not meant to be behind here." Jordan's voice was quiet, half-amused, and sounded as though he was not particularly invested in the rules being followed as long as nobody made a scene.

I paused my typing and glanced over at him. I was sitting in the seat next to him at the reception desk. He sat with his shoulders relaxed and one elbow leaning on the desk while he watched me with careful eyes.

He was right. I was not meant to be here. But I needed a computer, and it was the easiest place I could get one without heading to the floor I did work on and deal with people who did not want me there. At least Jordan seemed nice.

"You abandoned the desk before for no reason," I said, keeping my voice light as I turned back to the screen.

Jordan grimaced and then shrugged. He turned back toward his own computer. Though, I felt him still watching me from the corner of his eye.

My eyes trailed back to the monitor, skimming over the time. It was almost four in the afternoon. I let out a small sigh, then continued typing.

Levison Ridge.

Casey Edwards.

The database interface looked like it hated me personally. Pale background, harsh fonts, too many tabs, and a search function that seemed designed to punish curiosity. Every click brought up three more menus. Every menu offered ten fields that could mean anything.

I was trying to find a history of him in the suburb. An old address. A school. A parent record. Anything that said he'd existed there in a way that mattered, and not just as a name on a file that people in power had decided to bury. Where his family had lived, if they still lived there, or if anyone connected to him still did.

The database did have some information, but none of it was recent. A couple of address entries that ended years ago. A handful of cross-references that led to other dead tabs. A note about a family services involvement that didn't give details, just a date stamp and a reference number. And from what I saw, his mother no longer lived in the area.

That was the part that kept throwing me. If Theresa's story was true, Casey's childhood had been messy enough for an Assistant Director to notice and 'help where she could,' which meant there would've been noise. Paperwork. People involved. Neighbours complaining. And yet all I had were old addresses and silence.

The one thing I did find was about his grandmother, whom Theresa said he lived with in The Strip for a while. I found a death certificate dated six years ago. Which would have put Casey in his late teens.

I leaned back in the seat and ran my hand down my face. My palm dragged over my cheek and jaw, fingers catching on the day's stubble, and I held it there like pressure could reset my brain. My eyes burned from staring at the screen too long and having no sleep, and my thoughts were moving faster than my body could keep up with.

"Hi, excuse me?" a man's voice entered my ears, and I looked up.

He stood at the desk with the tentative posture of someone who didn't know if he was allowed to take up space here. Middle-aged, balding, and dressed in clothes that did not match the building he was standing in. His eyes darted toward the signs, then toward the elevators, then back to us.

He looked like he had stumbled into the wrong building. "Oh, I can't help you," I said automatically, throwing my gaze over to Jordan.

The man blinked. "Oh?" he said, confused.

Jordan shifted smoothly into that customer-service mode he probably hated but wore well. He rolled his chair forward a fraction, squared his shoulders, and gave the man a smile that was professional without being fake.

"Sorry, sir. He's… in training," Jordan said, and then he tilted his head in a polite question. "How can I help?"

The man gave me a questioning look, then moved to the desk slightly to talk to Jordan. Jordan listened, nodded, and tapped at his keyboard with the easy rhythm of someone who'd answered the same question a hundred different ways. He pointed once, then slid a small visitor pass across the desk, and then gave the man directions.

Once he had got the information he needed, the man nodded with relief and moved on, disappearing into the lobby traffic. Jordan watched him go, then turned back toward me with a look that was half curiosity and half entertainment.

"What do you do here?" Jordan asked. His tone wasn't suspicious. It was almost friendly. Like he'd decided I was a break in the routine, and he didn't mind that.

"I'm a consultant."

Jordan made a small noise in the back of his throat—something between a laugh and a scoff.

"So, why are you not… consulting?" Jordan asked, and he leaned back in his chair, swivelling slightly to face me more fully. "Or with the team you work with?"

"That's a good question," I said, and I tapped a key hard enough that it clicked louder than the others. "I'm not going to answer, but it's a good question."

Jordan smiled at that, just slightly as if he respected the commitment to being difficult.

He didn't push. Instead, he glanced back at his own monitor, then back at mine, then finally at my hands.

I leaned forward again and began looking for more information. I changed the date range. I widened the search fields. Nothing gave me a clean line. Everything fractured into references and dead ends.

Jordan rolled his chair a little and looked at what I was doing. He didn't try to hide it. He just slid closer like this was normal. "Do you need help?"

I paused and looked at him. He was watching the screen, not me, which somehow made the offer feel less like an intrusion and more like a favour.

"Don't you have your own stuff to do?" I questioned.

Jordan gestured vaguely around the reception area with one hand, palm up, presenting the thrilling landscape of his responsibilities.

"I'm a receptionist. What do you think I do?"

"I actually don't know."

Jordan's smile widened by a fraction, like that answer entertained him more than it should've. "What're you looking for?" he asked. "I know my way around the database pretty well."

I hesitated, then shrugged to myself. "Uh, looking into a kid named Casey Edwards," I said, keeping my voice low.

Jordan nodded as though that was all the information he needed.

"May I?" he asked, and he gestured at the computer.

I tilted my head in agreement and shifted out of the way, sliding my chair back a few inches so he could move closer. Jordan rolled forward more and began typing. His fingers moved fast, confident. Not the hesitant tapping I'd been doing. He knew where things lived. He knew which fields mattered and which ones were decorative.

"Your account has clearance for this stuff, right?" Jordan asked without looking up.

"Yeah, sure," I said, even though I had no idea.

Jordan paused briefly and glanced at me. His expression was open, but his eyes were sharp.

"Don't worry," I said, and I kept my tone dry. "If I'm involved no one will blame you for anything if it goes wrong."

Jordan's eyebrows lifted. "Is something going to go wrong?"

"What? No. Probably not," I said quickly, then made a small dismissive wave with my hand.

Jordan didn't turn back to the screen yet. He waited a moment, still looking at me. I saw the question sitting behind his eyes now, bigger than the database. Bigger than Casey. A question about who I was, and what kind of messes I usually walked into.

I exhaled slowly and pinched the bridge of my nose. "I am on a bit of a time crunch here," I said, letting the honesty slip in under the sarcasm. "Kinda concerned someone might die if I don't hurry it up."

Jordan's face changed. It was subtle, but I saw it. The little recalibration that happened when something stopped being hypothetical. His eyes sharpened, and the corners of his mouth flattened, not into fear exactly—more into attention. The half-amused energy he'd been running on drained away, replaced with a quiet seriousness that didn't need to announce itself.

"Right, right. Sorry," Jordan said, and the apology came quickly.

He didn't ask follow-up questions. He didn't make a joke. He just turned back to the screen and committed to it, shoulders shifting forward slightly as he leaned into the work. The chair wheels squeaked once, then stopped. The keyboard taps became more rhythmic and less casual.

18

The light from the monitor caught on his face and made the concentration look harsher than it was. He blinked slower, eyes tracking across lines of text, then flicking to a new field, then another. His fingers didn't hesitate over the keys. When he paused, it was only long enough to decide what to do next, not long enough to doubt himself.

My own restlessness started to build and prickle under my skin, the urge to move, to do something physical instead of sitting here waiting for a system to spit out a name.

"How'd you learn this stuff anyway?"

"Gets pretty boring here," Jordan said with a shrug. "Kinda help out when I can and learn."

He straightened in his chair again, rolled a little closer to the desk, and turned back to the screen. His fingers started moving again, and the bored receptionist energy was truly gone now. If nothing else, Jordan knew how to lock in when there was a task in front of him.

As I watched him work, my phone started to vibrate in my pocket. I pulled it out and checked who was calling. Dante. About time. "Good afternoon, handsome," I answered, my voice light.

On the other end of the line, Dante exhaled like he'd been holding his patience all day and I'd just made him spend some of it. *This is why people thought we were dating growing up,"* Dante said flatly.

I shrugged even though he couldn't see it, and I flicked my eyes toward Jordan, who was listening to me, though trying hard to pretend he wasn't.

"That's not true. I'm way out of your league," I said lightly, then leaned back in the chair, keeping my posture casual. "How was

Melissa?"

"She was good," Dante said, and there was a faint shift in his voice that always happened when he spoke about his mother. *"Had to fix one of her doors. Not why I'm calling, though."*

"Angelo?" I asked, and my tone sharpened without me meaning it to.

"Yeah," Dante confirmed. *"Was meant to call earlier but had to go talk to some witnesses."*

"Well, I don't care about that," I said, tapping the edge of the desk once with my knuckle. "What did Angelo say? Did he know anything about Rochelle?"

"Yeah."

There was a pause. Long enough that my skin tightened a fraction, and my mind started filling in the silence with worst-case options.

Then Dante spoke again, and it was worse than what my brain was coming up with.

"Casey killed her," he said.

The lobby noise seemed to dull, like my brain had turned it down to make room for the words. I let his sentence settle.

Casey killed Rochelle.

I ran it through my head once, then again, watching it bump into the other pieces I already had—Theresa's name, The Strip, the mystery kid, Blaze, and the timing of everything.

"How certain is he of that?" I asked quietly.

"Not entirely, to be honest," Dante admitted. *"That's just what he heard."*

"Does he know why?"

"No," Dante said. *"He wasn't very talkative. Only reason he said anything was because I told him you sent me."*

I huffed out a breath, something close to a laugh. "Look at me, making friends."

Dante didn't respond to that. He was thinking. I heard it in the way he was breathing. *"Do you think it has anything to do with Casey's death?"*

"I don't know," I said, and the truth of it sat heavy in my mouth. "It could've been payback. Maybe this mystery kid was dating Rochelle."

Even as I said it, I felt the idea hook into place. It was thin, but it was still something.

"Then why kill Blaze?" Dante asked.

I glanced at Jordan again. He was still typing, eyes flicking between fields, and he looked like he'd found a groove.

"Cover up?" I said, more to myself than Dante. "If Blaze knew about it, guess he could suspect who killed Casey. Go after them. Or tell someone."

Dante made a low sound of agreement. *"Makes sense."*

Then Dante's tone shifted, and I recognised the change immediately. He was checking if he needed to do damage control.

"How'd your… well, whatever you did go?" Dante asked. I smiled faintly into the phone. Whatever he thought I'd done, he didn't want to give it a name.

"Oh, yeah," I said, and I made the words light. "You're not gonna be happy."

There was a brief silence, and I didn't need to see him to know his expression. His eyes narrowing. His jaw clenching. The exact look he got right before he told me I was an idiot.

"What did you do?" Dante asked.

"Just talked to some people," I said casually. "It's no biggie."

On the other side of the desk, Jordan's eyes flicked up from the screen. "He went to school in Levison Ridge for, like, a year or two when he was a kid," Jordan said, speaking like he'd been waiting to drop the line at the right moment.

I pulled the phone from my ear slightly. It wasn't that the information surprised me. It was that Jordan had found something tangible in the middle of all my dead ends. "Can you find who went to school with him?"

Jordan nodded quickly, already leaning closer to the keyboard like the next step was obvious.

"Alright. Here, send me a list of names when you have them."

I grabbed a pen from the desk and a scrap of paper from the desk tray—some old note someone had left behind, half-blank and unused. I scribbled my number down fast, then slid it across to Jordan.

He took it, eyes dropping to the digits, and his brows lifted slightly. "You're leaving?" There was something almost disappointed in it.

"Yeah," I said. I pushed the chair back with my legs and started gathering myself. "I gotta check something out. Thanks. You're a good kid."

Jordan snorted softly at that, but he didn't argue. He just tucked the paper near his keyboard. I got up from the seat and moved around the desk, stepping back into the public side of reception.

"What was that?" Dante asked through the phone.

I adjusted my grip and brought it back to my ear as I walked. "Just outsourcing some help," I said, keeping my tone calm. "I'll tell you about it later."

Dante exhaled again. He didn't like not knowing. It made him antsy. *"Right,"* he said, forcing himself to move on. *"So, what're you doing now?"*

I angled toward the security line, weaving between a couple of people waiting to be checked in. "Gonna head to Mamma's. Find out more about Rochelle."

"Mamma's?" Dante repeated.

"Yeah," I said, and I kept walking, eyes scanning the lobby out of habit. "There's a waitress there who knew her. Wanna come?"

There was a pause, then Dante answered as if he'd already known his decision before I asked. *"Nah,"* he said. *"I gotta get back to the office. I'll swing by your place later, yeah?"*

"Alright," I said. I slowed slightly as I approached security, then stepped forward when the line cleared. "Buzz kill."

The line went dead. I lowered the phone and stared at the screen, then shoved it back into my pocket. Dante's words sat in my mind, trying to slot in with everything else.

I moved through the lobby and passed security, my mind disconnected from myself physically. Casey killed Rochelle. The words were only a rumour, but I couldn't shake the idea that they held more information than that.

I pushed through the exit, and the outside world slammed into me. The sound of traffic and people moving out of their workplaces and schools. The heat of the late afternoon wrapped around me and clung to my skin.

I paused, closed my eyes, and took a deep breath. I almost had to pry my eyes open again as the weight of the sleepless night held them down. When I did get them open, I set them ahead of me. I couldn't stop now. I had too much momentum.

19

My brain wouldn't shut up.

It kept replaying everything in fragments—Stephanie's face tightening when Theresa's name came up, Theresa's calm in the range, Dante's voice going flat on the phone, and that boy's blood soaking into my hands. None of it came in order. It just cycled, overlapping, stacking, and scraping at the inside of my skull, trying to force a pattern into existence.

The East was a slow crawl at this hour, the kind where everyone in a car looked like they'd made peace with sitting in the same place forever. Streetlights blinked on as I moved through it, one by one, casting that artificial glow over the road. I kept my eyes on the cars ahead and kept my foot steady, but my head was somewhere else.

Somewhere between Theresa and Casey.

Somewhere between Rochelle and Blaze.

Somewhere between a rumour and a body.

The thing that wouldn't leave me alone was how separate it all seemed on the surface.

It all felt unrelated. And yet it didn't.

Theresa threaded through it all like a wire. She'd been there in Casey's childhood, if she was telling the truth—something I couldn't quite read from her. She'd been there through the runs, through the money, and through the people around Casey. She was there now, still polished and unmovable.

Why? That was the part I couldn't get my brain to stop circling. Why would she kill Casey? Why would she kill Blaze? Unless she was protecting someone. Stephanie came to mind again. The mystery kid. The limp. The fear of Theresa.

Rochelle sat amongst it all like a weight.

She'd died before Casey. Before Blaze. Not long ago. Close enough that it didn't quite look like a coincidence. If Casey had killed her—if that rumour was even half true—then it could have set in motion everything that followed. Or she was a ghost I was chasing because I didn't like how little I could pin down about Theresa.

I stopped at a red light and checked my phone, thumb flicking over the screen without thinking. Nothing. No message from Jordan. I stared at the empty notifications like they might change if I watched hard enough, then let out a slow breath and dropped the phone into the console.

The clock on the dashboard told me I was closing in on five. That felt wrong. It felt like the day had been going for three days.

I dragged my hand down my face and caught myself in the rear-view mirror—eyes a little too heavy, jaw tight, and that faint grey tone you got when you were running on adrenaline and nothing else. I looked away before I could start thinking about it.

The light changed. The line moved. I kept driving.

The sky was darkening properly now, the last of the blue bleeding out behind the buildings. The East still looked clean at this hour— trimmed hedges, tidy street corners, houses set back from the road like they needed breathing room—but there was nothing soft about it. It was just quiet in a way that made you forget other places existed.

Then I hit the edge of The Strip, and the whole mood shifted. The streets narrowed. The buildings crowded in. The signs changed. The people changed. The Strip didn't care if the sun went down—it just started switching on its other face. Neon signs buzzed and stuttered to life, some of them bright and confident, others flickering like they were on borrowed time.

I cut down a side road and parked where I could—wedged between a battered sedan and a van with paint peeling off the side. I killed the engine and sat there, listening to the outside world through the closed windows. Voices and muted laughter that cut off too quickly. Light traffic that never quite stopped.

I got out and locked the car. The heat of the day still hung in the air, though it was slowly making way for the night's breeze. I moved out of the side street and onto the main road, walking with my head down and eyes up.

Down the road, I spotted Stephen. He was talking to someone near the edge of the street; body angled in a way that made it look casual while still controlling the space. His hands moved when he spoke, small gestures, nothing dramatic. The person he was talking to kept their head tilted close.

Stephen didn't acknowledge me. Maybe he hadn't seen me. Maybe he had, and he'd decided I wasn't worth his time. I kept walking, letting him stay in my peripheral as I passed.

The Strip tonight felt the same as it had the other day. On edge. It wasn't panic. It wasn't chaos. It was the quiet readiness in people's shoulders, in the way they stood with their weight balanced, in the way doorways weren't empty even when they looked it. The kind of alert you got when something had happened recently, and no one knew if it was finished.

I kept going until the familiar front of Mamma's came into view. The place sat there like it always had—dim lights and smudged windows. Inside, a couple of people were scattered through the tables, keeping to themselves.

I paused outside for half a second, letting my eyes scan the room through the glass. Habit. A quick read. Two people in the corner booth, shoulders angled inward, talking low. A guy near the window staring at his drink. Someone near the counter hunched over a plate, eating quickly. Then my gaze landed on the waitress behind the counter.

Lucy.

She looked tired in a way you couldn't fake—eyes dull around the edges, movements efficient but heavy, like every step was a decision. She was still doing her job, wiping down the counter, stacking dishes, and checking tickets and receipts. It was the kind of working that happened even when your brain was already at home.

I pushed the door open and stepped inside. The bell overhead gave a small, dull chime. The air inside was warmer, and it smelled like fried food and coffee that had been sitting too long. The noise level was low, but not silent—cutlery, dishes being done, someone murmuring to another. I headed straight for the counter.

Lucy's head snapped up the moment I was close enough. Her eyes found me and stayed there, flat and unwelcoming, as if my presence was a problem she'd already dealt with once and didn't want to deal with again. "Can I help you?"

"We spoke the other day," I said, keeping my tone even.

"Yeah. I remember," Lucy replied, and she didn't bother pretending it was a pleasant memory. "What do you need?"

"I just want to talk about Casey," I said, then added the other name carefully, watching her face. "And Rochelle."

Lucy's expression tightened a just a fraction. It wasn't a full reaction—nothing most people would clock—but it was there. A small shift in her focus, like the second name had dragged a different weight into the room.

"Well, I'm kind of busy," Lucy said flatly.

She stepped out from behind the counter and moved toward one of the tables nearby, grabbing a cloth and a spray bottle on her way, giving herself a reason to leave the spot where I could stand too close. She started wiping the table with quick, irritated strokes.

I followed, but I kept a little distance. Close enough to talk, far enough that it didn't look like I was crowding her. "Were you close to Rochelle?"

Lucy let out a long sigh, shoulders lifting and dropping as if the question had landed exactly where she didn't want it to. "We were all close."

"And Casey? You didn't know him?"

"I knew him," Lucy said, then corrected herself like she didn't want me to misunderstand. "Well, I knew about him. Personally, didn't have much to do with him."

I let a beat pass, then asked the thing that had pulled me here in the first place. "Do you know how Rochelle died?"

Lucy had moved to another table and paused as she was wiping it down. Her hand just stayed there, cloth pressed flat against the laminate like she'd forgotten what she was doing. Her attention snapped hard in my direction as if I'd crossed a line.

"What're you trying to do?" Lucy asked, and the question wasn't curious. It was defensive.

I looked at her properly then. Not just at the tired posture or the impatience. At the details she wasn't trying to show anyone. The redness in her eyes that wasn't from being up too late but from crying. The slight puffiness around them that came from doing it more than once and wiping your face too hard afterward. The shadows under her eyes told me she hadn't had proper sleep either.

Her shirt sleeve rode up when she shifted her grip on the cloth, and my eyes caught it automatically. Just below the cutoff of her sleeve was a bruise. Faded, but large. The shape wasn't accidental. Too wide. Too specific. Fingers had gone around her arm with enough force to leave a memory on her skin.

"Three people died within two weeks around here," I said, keeping my voice low and steady, "and I think they're all connected. I'm just trying to find out why."

Lucy kept her eyes on me, held there. She glanced once—quick and sharp—to her arm, then back to my face. She'd clocked that I'd seen it.

She shifted her stance, subtle but deliberate, angling her body so the bruise disappeared behind the line of her torso. Her hand tightened on the cloth.

"So, you don't care about the fourth?"

My chest tightened. "Fourth?" I repeated, and I heard the edge in my own voice before I could smooth it out.

Lucy didn't stop. She moved to the next table as a customer stood up, leaving a couple of bills and sliding out of the booth without looking at anyone. The money lay there like a small offering. Lucy picked it up, tucked it into her apron without counting it, and kept wiping.

"Rochelle's boyfriend was killed as well," Lucy said, and her tone stayed flat like that was the only way she could say it out loud.

My brain stalled for a fraction of a second, trying to catch up. "When?"

"The same night she did."

I went still. I couldn't decide which part to focus on. The fact that there was another body nobody had mentioned, or the fact it had happened the same night.

Lucy kept moving the cloth over the table. Back and forth, back and forth. The laminate already looked clean, but she scrubbed anyway, like motion was the only thing keeping her from cracking open.

I stayed silent long enough for the noise of the café to fill the gap. A fryer hissed somewhere behind the kitchen doors. A low murmur of conversation drifted from the corner booth.

Lucy didn't look up. I could hear in the way she breathed—tight and measured—that this wasn't easy for her. She was talking anyway. Fatigue did that.

"Do you know what happened?" I asked carefully.

Her shoulders rose a fraction, then dropped. A tired motion that didn't carry relief. "Look…" she started. Her voice caught slightly on the word before she forced it back into that controlled flatness. "I really need to clean all this up."

It wasn't a refusal exactly. It was an escape route. Something she could point at, so she didn't have to keep standing in the middle of the café talking about death.

"Did Casey kill them?" I asked anyway.

The question made the air shift between us. Lucy stopped wiping. Not for long, but long enough that the cloth stayed planted on the table and her fingers went still around it. She looked at me again, searching.

"From what Rochelle told me about him," Lucy said slowly, "he wouldn't hurt anyone."

It wasn't a declaration. It wasn't certainty. It was what she wanted to believe. She wanted to believe her friend.

"Lucy!" a voice called from the kitchen. Sharp. Impatient. The kind of shout that belonged to someone used to being obeyed. "Come to the back!"

Lucy's head snapped toward the sound. The tiredness slipped and something else took over—automatic obedience, or the instinct to not cause problems, or both. She turned back to me quickly, eyes flicking to my face like she didn't want to leave the conversation unfinished but couldn't stay.

"Look, I'm off in a few hours. If you still want to talk," Lucy said under her breath.

Then she moved past me before I could respond, slipping around my shoulder with practised ease and heading toward the kitchen door without looking back.

I nodded to myself and slid into one of the booths. The vinyl seat gave a soft squeak as I shifted my weight, and the table edge pressed into my forearms when I leaned forward. My exhaustion hit the second I stopped moving, like my body had been waiting for permission to remember it was running on nothing.

I let my shoulders drop. Let my spine settle back against the booth. Let the weight come off my feet, and I just sat there, staring at the table in front of me, listening to the small noises of Mamma's—plates being stacked and the low hum of conversation.

I leaned back and closed my eyes. The darkness behind my eyelids was full. Rochelle and her boyfriend, killed on the same night. Casey dead. Blaze dead. Theresa's name sitting under all of it like a stain. And Stephanie. All of it circling. All of it muddled together. I sat there and my mind keep working, rolling over itself and letting the noise slot in around me.

"You good?" Lucy's voice came suddenly.

My eyes snapped open, and I jerked upright. For a moment, I didn't know where I was. The booth seat stuck faintly to the back of my shirt, and my neck complained when I moved. The table in front of me was the same scratched laminate as before, but now it looked different as my eyes adjusted. I blinked a few times.

The café was empty aside from Lucy and someone else working in the back. Everything seemed a lot cleaner than it had before. The kitchen door swung once and clicked shut again, and I caught a glimpse of movement—someone stacking something or washing something.

I glanced out the window onto The Strip and saw the night had fully taken shape. Neon bled into the glass. A cluster of people moved past outside, their silhouettes broken by the signs, the streetlights, and the occasional car creeping through like it didn't want to commit to being here.

Shit. I'd fallen asleep.

"Yeah," I muttered, clearing my throat. "I'm… I'm good."

Lucy didn't look convinced. She stood with her arms folded, keys in one hand, and her apron untied but still hanging around her waist. "I'm off. I can walk and talk if you want."

I shook my head as if that would rearrange time. It didn't. All it did was make my skull throb, and my eyes sting harder. Then I nodded. "Yeah," I said, pushing my palms against the edge of the table. "Yeah, alright."

19

I shoved myself up, feeling my body fight to stay down. My legs felt heavy, and my spine popped in a way that made me want to pretend it didn't. I rolled my shoulders, trying to wake up the muscles that had decided the booth counted as a bed.

Lucy watched me with that same measured look. "You sure you're all good?" Her voice stayed light, but her eyes didn't.

"I'm fine," I told her, even though my eyelids felt like they had weights stitched into them. "Been a long few weeks."

Lucy nodded like she understood that kind of long. Then she led the way out of Mamma's. She moved like she'd walked these streets a thousand times and didn't expect anything to surprise her.

The air outside was cool and refreshing, and the sounds of The Strip rushed into my ears. It hit me all at once. Music from somewhere nearby and voices layered over each other. The coolness helped. It cut through the sticky tiredness clinging to me and made my lungs feel like they could actually do their job again.

Lucy stepped onto the sidewalk and adjusted her shirt. I followed half a pace behind, still shaking the last of the sleep out of my hands and face.

"So," she said after a moment, glancing at me from the corner of her eye, "you're like a cop, yeah?"

"Nah," I replied, keeping my hands out of my pockets so I didn't look too comfortable. "Just… trying to find out what happened."

She let out a small breath through her nose

"Why?" Lucy asked. "Do you care, I mean?"

We walked slowly and carefully. Not because we were taking our time, but because The Strip didn't reward people who moved like they weren't paying attention. Lucy kept to the edge of the footpath, not hugging the wall, but not straying too far into open space either. She moved with quiet awareness, eyes scanning, and her keys gripped between her fingers like a weapon.

"I was there when Casey died," I said, and the words came out flatter than I expected. "Tried to help him."

Lucy's face shifted at that, the tiredness tightening around her eyes. "You couldn't."

"No," I admitted.

I felt the answer sit in my chest the way it always did. The moment of it. The feeling of doing everything you could, and it not being enough.

"You feel responsible?" Lucy asked.

I shook my head. "No. There wasn't much I could do except be there."

Silence followed my words. Lucy kept walking, and I kept walking with her, neither of us rushing to speak.

She was the first to, though. "I sometimes feel responsible for Rochelle's death."

I turned my head toward her. "Were you there?"

Lucy shook her head. "No." She kept her gaze forward, but her shoulders pulled in slightly like she'd braced for judgment. "But I knew what was happening."

My tiredness sharpened into something else. "What was that?"

Lucy swallowed.

"Her boyfriend used to hit her," she said quietly. "I tried to step in but… well, you saw my arm." She didn't gesture to it. She didn't need to.

Another moment of silence. Not the comfortable kind. The kind where you could feel the weight of what she'd just said settling between us as we walked.

"I wish it was only him that died," Lucy said, but her voice wasn't cruel. It was tired. It was angry in that quiet way that didn't have anywhere to go.

I let my breath out slowly, keeping my tone careful. "You don't think Casey did it?"

"I don't think so," Lucy said, and she sounded more certain about that than anything else she'd told me. "I know Rochelle used to say Casey joked about doing something about her boyfriend, but she always said it as if that's all it was. A joke."

I nodded. "I was told Casey had another friend from the East," I said after a beat. "Did Rochelle ever mention anyone?"

Lucy's lips pressed together as she thought. "Not really," she said slowly. "She used to mention they met up with people in the East when Casey came to get her. But…"

"You assumed it was the woman," I finished the sentence for her, and she nodded.

"Yeah."

The street shifted as we moved—different faces, different corners, different pockets of noise. Lucy kept her pace steady. I kept mine with hers, letting my eyes roam without lingering on anyone.

"Do you think Rochelle's death had anything to do with Casey?" I asked eventually, because the question wouldn't leave me alone. "Because other people seem to think so."

Lucy's jaw tightened. "Casey was one of the last people to be in their apartment when the gunshots went off."

"One of?" I repeated.

Lucy nodded. "I was told someone ran out before he did."

My tired brain tried to assemble a picture and kept dropping pieces. "Does anyone know who?"

"No," Lucy said, and there was frustration in it now as though she'd asked the same question and gotten the same answer. "Sorry. All I heard is that they fell. Apparently ran down the street limping."

There was the limp again. My mind reeled. A jolt of recognition that made the edges of the night sharpen.

If Casey didn't kill Rochelle and her boyfriend, he was definitely there when it happened. He was with whoever did it. Maybe that was what he spoke to Theresa about. The girl. My thoughts tried to jump ahead, and I forced them back down.

One thing at a time.

My mind kept linking Theresa and Stephanie, filing them as the same coin just different sides. One polished. One bruised. One untouchable. One scared. I didn't like the way that it looked.

"Anyway," Lucy said after another stretch of quiet, "this is me."

We came to a stop outside a laundromat with apartments above it. The laundromat windows were bright from the lights inside, and the hum of the machines pressed out onto the street even with the door closed. Above it, the apartments sat back from the edge, dark windows, a narrow stairwell entrance with chipped paint on the rail and a buzz panel that looked like it had been punched more than once.

Lucy shifted her weight and took a small step toward the entrance. "I hope you figure it out," she said, and then she glanced up to my face with something that almost looked like sympathy. "And I hope you're able to get some sleep."

"Thanks," I said, and I meant it. Then I added, because it felt like the only decent thing to say, "I'm sorry about your friend."

Lucy gave a faint smile. It was the kind that showed up out of habit, not because she felt it. It didn't reach her eyes, but it softened her face for half a second before she pulled it back into place. Then she turned and walked inside the building, leaving me alone on the footpath.

I watched the door swing shut behind her, and I watched the space she had been, listening to the muffled hum of the laundromat and the street noise around me. The one thing I knew she was right about was that I needed sleep. My body felt like it was running on fumes. My head was thick, and the thoughts didn't connect cleanly anymore. I had pieces. Too many pieces. Pieces that looked like they fit, and pieces that might be tricking me.

I felt like I had everything I needed but couldn't put it all together properly because my mind was too foggy. That was the part that scared me most—not the danger, not the threats, not Theresa's eyes on me, but the fact my brain was starting to lag behind my instincts. That was how mistakes happened.

So, sleep was the next piece I needed to put in place—before I made the kind of mistake I couldn't take back.

20

The door clicked shut softly behind me, and the quiet of the house hit like a wall. Warm and heavy. The kind that settled into the corners and waited for you to either match it or ruin it. I dropped my badge and keys onto the hall table and then moved into the living room.

Claire and Dante were there. Claire was on her feet the second she saw me, and I didn't need to be good at reading people to know what she was thinking. It was all in the set of her mouth, the way her eyes tracked my face.

She didn't say anything, though. She just crossed the space between us and wrapped her arms around me. I stood there too long before my body remembered what to do. Then I folded into her, my hands settling at her back, my forehead hovering near her shoulder like it wanted to rest there permanently. She held on tight.

Behind her, Dante stood up. "Thought you were going for a quick visit to Mamma's?"

Claire pulled away slowly, but she didn't step back. Her eyes stayed trained on me, searching. I glanced from her to Dante, then back again.

"Yeah," I said, my voice rougher than I meant it to be. I cleared my throat and tried again. "Turned… turned longer than I expected."

Claire's expression softened in that way it only ever did when she was trying not to scare me off with the truth of what she felt.

"I'm sorry," I added, quieter, and meant it.

She gave me a small, sympathetic smile, then guided me toward the lounge with a hand at my arm as if she didn't trust me to make it there without collapsing halfway. I let her. I let myself sink down, the cushions taking some of the weight I'd been carrying all day, and then she moved away into the kitchen without a word.

She could tell how exhausted I was. The kind of exhaustion that didn't just sit in your muscles—it rewired your whole face.

"I was almost going to come looking for you," Dante said.

"You worried about me?" I tried to make it sound like a joke.

"When it hit ten, yeah, I was."

I blinked. "Yeah. I may have dozed off in Mamma's for a second."

"That's because you're pushing yourself too much," Claire called from the kitchen.

I tilted my head slightly, just enough to see her moving around— opening the fridge, pulling something out, closing it with her hip, then shifting to the microwave like this was a routine she'd done a hundred times for me.

"You're not young anymore, you know."

I let my head fall back against the lounge, then I nodded once, eyes half-closed. "I love you, too." A small sound came from the kitchen that might've been a laugh.

I looked back to Dante. His eyes were careful in that way that meant he'd been sitting here with Claire, waiting, and they'd both been getting more annoyed the longer I wasn't here. "Was it worth the trip?"

"Casey was there when Rochelle died," I said slowly. "I don't think he killed her, though."

Dante's mouth tightened. "So, yes."

I shrugged, rubbing my hand down my face. My palm dragged over stubble and tired skin, and it didn't help "Rochelle and her boyfriend died on the same night. Someone else was there with Casey. And, surprise, they were limping."

"Same person," Dante said immediately.

"Things do be pointing that way."

"The kid?"

I gave Dante a vague gesture with one hand, like my body didn't have the energy to commit to words.

Dante leaned forward slightly, elbows on his knees, locked in now. "So… who killed Casey?"

I stared at him, letting the question hang. Letting the weight of the answer settle before I said it out loud.

"I don't know," I admitted. "I have a name. You're not going to like it."

Dante didn't blink. "Say it."

"Theresa."

Dante's face changed so fast it was almost impressive.

"Are you fucking serious, Red?"

"Language," Claire said sharply, and then, without missing a beat, "and volume. The boys are asleep."

Dante took a breath through his nose, forced it down. "Sorry, Claire."

"Told you," I muttered.

Dante's eyes narrowed at me. "Did Stephanie tell you something?"

"Kind of. But also…" I exhaled. "And, again, you're not going to like this."

Dante's jaw clenched. "You spoke to Theresa." He cursed under his breath, quiet but vicious.

Claire came back into the living room with a plate, setting it down on the coffee table in front of me. The smell hit a second later— reheated food that still somehow felt like care. She placed a fork beside it with the same calm precision she used when she was trying not to show how worried she'd been.

"After this," Claire said, looking directly at me, "you're going to sleep."

"Yes, ma'am," I said automatically.

Dante stared at me. Mouth slightly agape. "Are you insane?"

"We both know the answer to that."

He blew out a breath, then leaned back, palms on his thighs, holding himself still. "Whatever. You obviously got something from it. So, what is it?"

"Theresa is the woman who visited Casey," I said slowly. "She knew him from when he was a kid. Knew his family."

Dante didn't argue right away. That was how I knew he was taking it seriously. He just sat with it, eyes fixed on me, running the implications through his head.

"Okay…" he said finally. "That's something. Doesn't prove anything."

"I'm pretty sure she has anisomelia."

Claire's head snapped up. "LLD?"

Dante frowned. "What? What's that?"

"It's… a discrepancy in limb length," Claire said, the explanation coming quick and clean. "Leg length discrepancy."

"She wears shoes that compensate for a shorter leg. I noticed it. Different heel height."

Dante's brows knitted tighter. "So, she has a limp."

"In a manner of speaking," I said, and finally picked up the fork. I ate a mouthful of the food. It was warm. It grounded me for half a second. Not enough to make the day make sense. But enough to remind me I was home.

Dante sat forward again, elbows on his knees. "So, what's the reason for killing Casey?"

I stared down at the plate, fork hovering, thoughts lining up and then slipping out of place again.

"Well," I said slowly, "Casey's mystery friend most likely killed Rochelle and her boyfriend. Casey told Theresa about it, maybe. He spoke to her about a girl. I'm assuming it was Rochelle. So, maybe Theresa killed him to protect the other kid."

Dante didn't react the way people normally did when I said something insane. He just took it, eyes narrowing, and then pushed it further. "What if the girl Casey told her about wasn't Rochelle?" he asked. "What if it was Stephanie?"

The room went quiet in a way that made the fridge hum too loud. I let it sit there, that name, and felt my brain catch on it like a hook. Stephanie's face in the storage room.

I swallowed once and looked up at Dante. "It would fit," I admitted, and my voice came out flatter than I expected. "The way she acted. The way she didn't want Theresa knowing what she'd told me. If she was the one with Casey that night… and Theresa killed Casey to protect her… that's one reason to be afraid."

Dante's jaw tightened. "The limp would line up."

I exhaled through my nose and leaned back slightly, letting the edge of the lounge press into my shoulders. "I would understand killing Rochelle's partner," I said, and the words felt sharp in my mouth. "He was abusive. They want to save their friend from it. Why kill Rochelle?"

No one answered immediately. Claire sat on the opposite side of the coffee table, still, hands resting in her lap, eyes on me, listening to the words and the gaps between them.

Silence stretched.

"Unless Rochelle was an accident," I said finally. "A fight. A struggle. Collateral. Something goes wrong. Then guilt makes Casey tell someone. And that gets him killed."

Claire's brows drew together. "So, you have two killers?"

"Unless the mystery kid—or Stephanie—has nothing to do with it," I said, and I hated how thin that sounded compared to how heavy it felt.

Dante's gaze sharpened again. "You think Theresa killed Rochelle?"

I hesitated, then nodded. "I mean, height-wise, she's the same as Stephanie. She would pass as just a friend in the right clothes. If someone saw somebody with Rochelle and Casey in the East… they'd assume it was the same circle. Not a fancy looking East side lady."

"Right," Dante said, but it wasn't agreement. It was him slotting it into his own mental board.

A pause hung between us while the house stayed quiet around the conversation. The boys asleep down the hall. The kind of quiet that felt fragile.

Then Dante started building the sequence out loud. "Casey tells Theresa about Rochelle and the abusive boyfriend. Wants to help. Theresa says she'll handle it. They go. It gets out of hand. Two people die."

I nodded slowly. "Casey gets nervous about it. Maybe wants to tell someone what happened. Theresa kills him."

Dante's eyes flicked to mine, catching the thread. "Then kills Blaze," he said, "because maybe Casey told him about it."

"The timelines would match up," I said, shifting my food around on the plate. "The day Blaze died, Theresa was left on her own. She had enough time to get to the West."

Claire's expression shifted, a small frown deepening as she tried to picture Theresa in that world. "She would know about Blaze?"

"She knew Casey since he was a kid," I pointed out. "I'm sure they would've spoken about their personal lives. Or Casey could've mentioned him in passing."

Claire's mouth tightened. "So, she visited him growing up, helped him, and then killed him because he's a loose end?"

Dante's gaze didn't soften, but his tone stayed controlled. "Statistically, people who are closest to the victim are the ones who kill them."

I gave a small nod. "She would've made it in time to kill Blaze, too. We just need to find out if she would've made Casey's. And Rochelle's."

Dante held up a hand slightly, not to stop me, but to slow the momentum before it ran away. "Let's not get ahead of ourselves. We can pull NBI security and credential movement. See if she left the building the day Blaze died."

Claire looked between us. "You can do that?"

Dante's mouth twitched like he didn't love admitting what he could and couldn't do. "I can try. I don't think pulling the thread matters much anymore."

He looked at me then, and the look said what his words didn't. *Since you've already run rampant.'*

I didn't argue. I just lifted my shoulders in a small shrug like I didn't have a defence that didn't sound stupid. "You could talk to Wilson.".

Dante's eyebrows lifted immediately. "Why would Wilson want to help us? He's part of the whole money thing."

"Trust me," I said, and it came out too sure for how little sleep I'd had.

Dante held my stare, then shook his head, exhaling. "Whatever. It'll be easier to get access if I go through him anyway."

Claire's voice cut in, quiet but firm. "You two need to be careful."

Dante and I both looked at her. She didn't raise her voice. She didn't dramatize it. She just stared at us. And in the silence that followed, I realised she wasn't asking. She was warning us.

"This is the Assistant Director of the NBI you're talking about," Claire continued. "If she thinks you're going to be looking into this stuff and it *is* her, she'll shut it down."

Dante nodded, gaze fixed somewhere past the coffee table, already picturing the chain of approvals and locked doors. "She'll catch on quick if we're pulling movement logs. Even if it's through Wilson."

"Not if she's preoccupied," I said quietly.

Dante turned his head slowly, eyes narrowing. "What? You're gonna create a distraction?"

"I am very good at that."

Dante shook his head as I finished the last of the food on my plate. "Yeah, and that always goes well."

Claire looked between us, then let out a quiet breath. "I think the both of you should sleep on it."

"You're right," Dante muttered. He pushed himself up from the couch, rolling his shoulders once, then he looked down at me. "You know after we deal with this, there's still the money problem."

"One corruption at a time," I mumbled. "I've still got Angelo's list of names."

Dante huffed out a short laugh despite himself, like his body betrayed him on reflex. Then his face reset into something more serious, and he nodded.

"I'll walk you out," Claire said. She stood, and Dante fell into step with her. They moved out of the living room toward the front door while I stayed where I was, shoulders sinking into the lounge cushions now that nothing immediate demanded movement. I let the quiet settle. Let the pieces sit where they'd landed.

The front door closed with a soft click. A moment later Claire came back into the living room, and she paused in the archway. "The boys were devastated you weren't home."

My gaze dropped to my hands. "I'm sorry," I said quietly.

"And I was incredibly tired after work," Claire added, and her tone made it clear that this wasn't a guilt trip.

It was a fact. I pushed myself up from the lounge and walked toward her. "How can I make it up to you?"

Claire's expression softened just slightly, but her eyes stayed steady. "Promise me you'll be here to tuck them in tomorrow."

"I promise."

"You're lucky I'm not working tomorrow," she said, and there was a dry edge to it that sounded like her trying not to smile. "Means I can sleep all day to make up for this afternoon."

"I promise," I repeated, and I stepped closer, voice firmer. "I will be here to tuck them in tomorrow."

"Good."

I leaned down and kissed her, pulling her close by instinct, like contact could reset whatever I'd disrupted. She kissed me back, brief, then pulled away before I could sink into it.

"How about you go and say goodnight now," Claire said, already turning toward the coffee table. "I'll clean this up, and we'll get you cleaned and in bed, yeah?"

"You make it sound like I'm a child," I said with a chuckle

"You are," Claire replied without hesitation.

We smiled at each other, then separated completely. Claire moved to grab the dirty plate, and I turned and headed down the hall.

The corridor was dimmer than the living room, the light softer, and the wooden floor carrying my footsteps. Halfway down, I slowed automatically at the cupboard.

Miles' cupboard.

It was slightly ajar, no doubt from when Claire had found him tonight. The sliver of darkness inside felt like it was staring back at me. I moved past it before my brain could build a story around it and walked to Miles' room, opening the door gently, hoping it didn't creak.

It didn't.

I stepped inside and navigated around a few scattered toys on the floor, lifting my feet higher than necessary so I didn't kick anything and wake him up. Miles was sprawled across his bed, completely out, one arm flung above his head and the blanket twisted at his legs like he'd fought it and lost.

I stood there just watching him breathe. Then I bent down and kissed his forehead, gentle, lingering for a moment. "Goodnight, buddy."

He didn't stir. I straightened and slipped back out, pulling the door closed softly behind me, then moved down the hall toward Alex's room.

I pushed the door open, and as I stepped in, Alex lifted his head slightly. "Dad?" he mumbled, voice thick with sleep.

"Hey, pal," I said quietly. "You're still awake."

He blinked at me, eyes heavy and unfocused, but he stayed upright like he'd been waiting for the proof I was actually here. "I couldn't sleep."

I walked across the room and stopped beside his bed, then sat gently on the edge, careful not to jostle him too much.

"You weren't here," Alex said quietly, a little hurt in his voice.

"I know. I'm sorry. I got held up."

Alex's face shifted as he tried to decide what to do with that. "Was it important?"

I paused, looking down at him. "Yeah," I said, and then I corrected myself. "But not as important as you."

Alex watched me, then his shoulders lowered like something in him had unclenched. "So, does that mean you'll be here tomorrow?"

"Yeah. Of course."

I leaned in a little, voice dropping softer. "And I tell you what. I'll teach you how to do one of those card tricks."

"Two of them," Alex bargained immediately.

I chuckled. "Alright, alright. Two of them."

Alex smiled. His eyelids drooped again, but the rest of his face looked lighter, content in that simple way kids were when a promise felt solid.

"For now," I said, and I tapped the blanket lightly near his shoulder, "you gotta get some sleep, okay?"

"Okay," he murmured. Then, quieter, "I love you, Dad."

My throat tightened a fraction. "I love you. Goodnight."

"Goodnight," Alex whispered back, the word faltering as he said it, already sinking into his pillow. I waited until his breathing steadied and his head settled properly, then pushed up from the bed and stepped out of the room.

Claire was waiting in the hallway, leaning lightly against the wall, arms folded. Her expression was amused before she even spoke. "Two tricks?"

"He'll be a magician in no time."

Claire's smile stayed, small but real. She unfolded herself from the wall and reached for my hand, her fingers closing around mine with that familiar steadiness.

"Alright," she said, voice quiet. "Let's get you cleaned and into bed. Seems like you've got a big day tomorrow."

She led me down to the end of the hall toward our bedroom, and her words sat at the front of my mind like a countdown.

Tomorrow, I was going back to NBI.

21

The engine of my car ticked as it cooled.

I sat in the driver's seat, eyes on the NBI building. It hadn't changed. Same glass, same concrete, same ugly look. The clock on the dash rolled over. Four in the afternoon.

I'd stayed home all day. Doing everything around the house quietly while Claire tried to catch up on sleep. Laundry. Dishes. Cleaning. The slow, boring maintenance of life. I'd picked the boys up from school and made sure they were fed, clean, and distracted enough that Claire could actually lie down without feeling like they would bring the house down around her.

Now it was time to put a plan in motion. The thought should've made me feel focused. It did, sort of. Mostly, it made my stomach tighten. My eyes lingered on the time again, and my chest pulled in around it.

I needed to be home for the boys' bedtime.

I exhaled, long and slow, then lifted my hand and killed the remaining silence by opening the door. Cool air slid in immediately, that late-afternoon shift where the heat starts giving up. I stepped out and shut the door. I started across the lot. My hands were loose at my sides, and my posture was casual enough that I didn't look like I was here to cause problems. Even though I was.

Inside, the building met me with the usual chaos that came with this time of day. Witnesses sitting too straight in chairs that didn't support anyone properly. Security standing like furniture. Agents moving with purpose, or pretending they were. A couple of people in suits who looked like they'd been born in conference rooms.

I blended in with them as best I could, which mostly meant I kept my head down, my badge visible, and my face set in a neutral expression. Security waved me forward. The guard barely looked at me. I was checked. I moved through. As I cleared the checkpoint, my eyes slid across to the reception desk automatically.

Jordan was there. Not slouched. Not staring at the ceiling. He was sitting up, shoulders slightly forward, typing with both hands like his life depended on it. His jaw worked once as he read something on the screen, then he tapped again, faster.

I hadn't received a message from him yet. That fact sat in the back of my head. I angled toward the desk. Jordan noticed me when I was close. He glanced up, then back down, then up again as if he'd had to confirm it was me.

"Afternoon," I said, keeping it light.

"Oh, hey," Jordan said, a small smile played on his lips.

I stopped at the desk and leaned gently on the desk. "I didn't hear from you."

Jordan's mouth pulled to one side. "Sorry. I kinda got kicked out when my shift ended."

"Fair. Any luck this morning?"

He hesitated. Not a long hesitation, but enough that I noticed the way his fingers curled around the edge of the desk. "Uh… it sort of got flagged?"

"Is that… a question?"

"Sorry, no," Jordan said quickly, then sat up straighter. "It did get flagged. And I may have got spoken to for looking into that guy."

My brow furrowed before I could stop it. "Who spoke to you?"

"Some agent. Didn't say his name."

"Okay," I said carefully, keeping my voice steady. "But you don't need to use the system to look into who he went to school with."

Jordan's eyes flicked down again, then back to me. "I know… I just…" He trailed off, shoulders tightening as if the rest of the sentence was stuck behind his ribs.

I watched him and let the quiet sit between us just long enough to make it easier to tell the truth. "You're scared you'll lose your job."

Jordan let out a small breath, the kind you made when someone said the thing you didn't want to admit. "Yeah. That one."

"Alright." I straightened slightly and lowered my voice. "Can you just look into it. Please. Call the school. Or something. Your job will be fine. I promise."

Jordan stared at me briefly. He was still young. Still new enough that the building hadn't trained the kindness out of him yet. He was nervous, and it showed in the way his foot bounced once under the desk before he forced it still. But under that nervousness, he wanted to do the right thing, and he did think this was the right thing.

He swallowed, then nodded. "Okay. I'll… give myself twenty minutes, but then I'm stopping."

That was more than I'd expected, and less than I wanted, which meant it was probably the perfect compromise for a receptionist who'd already been told off once today.

I offered him a small smile. "Thank you,"

Jordan returned it, quick and a little embarrassed, then dropped his gaze back to the screen like he didn't want anyone seeing him be nice. At least to me.

His fingers started moving again immediately. He clicked through something, then opened a new window, eyes narrowing as he read.

I inhaled through my nose and felt the air hit that clean, cold part of my lungs that always made me feel like I was back in a hospital corridor. Then I stepped away from the desk. The lobby kept moving around me. People cutting across paths and voices overlapping. Someone laughing too loudly near the security line.

I headed toward the elevators with my pace steady. At the elevators, I stopped and waited, and while I waited, I pulled my phone out. My thumb hovered over Dante's name for half a second, then tapped.

Heading up. Three minutes.

I sent it, watched it deliver, then shoved the phone back into my pocket before I could overthink it. The elevator dinged, and the doors slid open.

I stepped inside with a few others—an agent with a folder tucked under his arm, a woman in heels who smelled like expensive perfume, and a guy with a lanyard who looked like he'd rather be anywhere else. I stood near the back, eyes on the panel, and hit Theresa's floor.

The elevator started up. The ride was slower than I wanted. It stopped. People got off. People got on. Voices came and went in slices. Somebody checked their phone. Somebody cleared their throat. I kept my hands still. By the time it stopped on the second-last floor, I was the only one left.

The doors shut, and for the first time in the ride it was quiet. Just the hum of the cables and the faint whirr of the motor. I rolled my shoulders, then let them settle back into place.
The elevator finally reached Theresa's floor. The doors opened. I stepped out.

The floor was open in a way the lower levels weren't. Not crowded. Less noise. The kind of space that had been designed to feel calm and powerful at the same time. On my right, a large kitchen sat in the open— stainless steel surfaces, clean counters, and a coffee machine that looked like it belonged in a café. There were mugs lined up neatly like nobody here ever left anything out of place.

On the left, a conference room with large windows wrapped around it. The blinds were half-open, letting the late afternoon light cut across the table inside. The chairs were pushed in under the empty table.

Straight ahead was a glass wall with all the blinds drawn, and a door with a nameplate that didn't pretend to be modest.

Assistant Director Theresa Langer.

Even in golden letters, it felt like a warning.

A little off-centre and to the right sat another small open-plan office. Stephanie. She was seated at her desk, posture too controlled to be casual. Hands near the keyboard, paperwork aligned, and her face angled toward the hallway like she'd been expecting someone.

Her eyes locked on me. Even from this distance, I could read her expression easily. *'What are you doing here?'* The question sat on her face, in the set of her brow and the way her mouth flattened just slightly, and for a moment I stood there with the elevator doors closing behind me, knowing I'd crossed into the part of the building that didn't forgive mistakes.

And I still had to be home for bedtime.

I moved carefully into the space, letting the carpet swallow the sound of my steps.

"You don't have an appointment," Stephanie said flatly.

"Good to see you too," I said, and kept walking until I was close enough to stop in front of her desk.

Stephanie sat at her small desk like she'd been bolted there. The same neatness as always. Computer angled. Pen cup lined up. A legal pad with handwriting that looked like it had never made a mistake in its life. Her gaze stayed on me, unblinking.

"You okay?" I asked, pitching it casually.

21

She clenched her jaw. "I'm fine. I can't let you in there."

"Sure you can," I replied, and I let the faintest smile tug at my mouth.

Her hand shifted slightly on the edge of her desk. The movement was controlled, but the tension wasn't. "I really—" she started.

A door opened. Theresa's voice carried out before she fully stepped into view, smooth and unhurried like she'd been listening the whole time and had decided now was when the scene should begin.

"It's okay, Stephanie. I'll humour him."

I turned my head toward the sound. Theresa stood in her doorway like she'd been framed there on purpose—hair perfect, posture set, and expression calm. Her office light spilled out behind her, warmer than the rest of the floor.

"Did you feel all that cold air when she opened the door?" I asked, giving a fake shiver.

Stephanie didn't react. She held her face steady the way people did when they weren't allowed to be human.

Theresa's mouth curved slightly. "Funny. Would you like to come in?"

I shifted my weight and faced her fully, letting my shoulders loosen. "It'd be my pleasure." I moved toward her, and as I reached the doorway, I widened my smile into something exaggerated and bright, the kind that made me look harmless and insufferable in equal measure.

Theresa stepped aside without moving much. It was almost impressive how little she needed to do to make space. I passed her, and the office swallowed me.

Behind me, Theresa's voice cut clean through the air again.

"Stephanie, can you please go organise dinner," she said, then added, "and take some to my home for Bryce and Lawrence."

Stephanie's head dipped as she mumbled an agreement. She pushed back from her desk and stood, smoothing her skirt with a hand that didn't quite look steady. I tracked her movement without turning fully. I didn't need to see much to know she was moving fast. Not rushed, but eager to get out of this space. She collected her things with the efficiency of someone who had done this hundreds of times—phone, keys, bag—and then moved toward the exit.

Theresa waited until Stephanie was almost out of sight, then turned back into her office and closed the door behind her. The click landed heavy.

We were alone.

My phone was already in my hand as I walked deeper into the room. I kept it low against my thigh so it wouldn't look like I was waving it in her face, and my thumb moved fast over the screen.

Time to move. I sent it to Dante.

Theresa moved around me like I was furniture and crossed the room to her desk, which sat in the far right corner. She sat down with the same composed ease as always.

Her office was large. Not just spacious but designed. A couch sat in the middle with a glass coffee table in front of it, the kind of setup that wasn't meant for comfort so much as control. There were plants in heavy pots that looked too expensive to be kept in an office. Paintings lined the walls—abstract enough that you couldn't accuse them of meaning anything but chosen well enough that you could tell someone had been paid to pick them. Trophies, medals, and framed certificates sat along the cupboards and cabinets, each one positioned as if it belonged exactly where it was and nowhere else.

It was an office that said: I have earned this, and I will remind you.

A large board was poised in the middle of the far wall, next to her desk. It was sleek. Magnetic. Clean lines. Information arranged in tidy sections with headings that looked like they'd been printed by someone who'd never had to use their hands for anything else.

It looked like various information on the different teams within the NBI. Names, roles, current tasking, and high-level case tags. I scanned down it, and my eyes caught Wilson's team.

LOCAL.

Even the tagline felt like a label slapped on something messy to keep it contained. I walked further into the room, my eyes staying on the board. As I did, I felt my phone vibrate. I didn't look at it. I kept moving toward the board.

The closer I got, the more the detail sharpened. Wilson's section had the serial killer case under it. No cute nickname, no media-friendly title. Just a case number and a brief descriptor.

And then, off to the side—separate from everyone else, like a footnote that didn't quite fit the structure—was my name. Not under a team. Not under a heading. Just there. A loose thread.

Casey's name sat with it.

My throat tightened, and I forced myself not to let it show. I kept my expression flat, like this was just another bureaucratic attempt to make chaos look organised.

Behind me, Theresa's voice slid into the quiet. "Two days in a row. I seem to be popular."

"Well, you know me," I said, still looking at the board. "Just trying to be thorough."

"You're trying to get under my skin."

I let out a small breath through my nose. "I would never."

Theresa's chair creaked softly as she settled back, and I didn't look up. I could picture how she was sitting. Hands placed neatly. Spine straight. Eyes on me like I was just another problem to solve.

"You know," Theresa said, "we kept you around because you're useful to us."

I didn't respond right away. I kept my gaze on the board, letting my eyes move across the names and tags, the clean divisions that pretended the building wasn't full of secrets.

"You close cases," she continued. "In fact, you have managed to close every single case you have ever worked here. That's impressive. I think you're the only person who can claim that."

I turned my head slightly toward her, enough that my voice carried back clean. "Is that a genuine compliment, I hear?"

Theresa's mouth did that small, controlled curve again. It wasn't warmth. It was restraint. "Would you like me to follow it up with: you're a pain in the ass?"

I shrugged, then faced the board again, letting my eyes sit on my name and Casey's. I pictured the report. My recount of events. My words sitting in there, scrubbed away.

I let my shoulders drop, and I spoke without turning. "When did you know I was looking into Casey's death?"

Theresa didn't hesitate. "Dante should know the logs are checked. Even if something isn't flagged, we can still see movement. And I knew the only reason he'd be looking at it was if it involved you."

I swallowed once. "Because I was on the report."

I turned my head toward her properly then. Theresa gave a small nod. It wasn't smug. It wasn't apologetic. It was just fact.

"So, you try to swipe me away from it," I said, keeping my tone even. "Because you knew I'd figure out about the money."

Theresa's gaze didn't flicker. She didn't lean forward. She didn't do any of the things people did when you accused them of something true. "Oh, I don't care about the money. Whether it stops or keeps going."

I stared at her. The casual way she said it made my stomach tighten. "There's no actual proof of it," Theresa continued, voice still calm. "Besides, bigger conspiracies have been covered up by the NBI before. Long before I came along."

That was the part that made my mouth go dry. Not the admission of corruption. Not the shrug at it. The ease. As though it was a history lesson. Like she was proud of the institution's ability to swallow its own rot.

I exhaled slowly and let my gaze slide back to the board, to the clean labels and the tidy case tags and the neat little boxes. "Good to know the system works."

"The system is for the people," she said smoothly. "We send people in places when they are not wanted, do you know how many deaths will come from that? How many innocent people will die?"

I stayed facing the board, eyes fixed on the neat headings. Silence held between us, filled only by the soft hum of the building.

"I am trying to clean this up," Theresa continued, and her voice didn't lift or crack. "We're not the first changing of guard to get the money. But I am hoping we're the last. I'm not the bad guy here, Red."

"Not the bad guy," I echoed, and the words came out dry. "Right." A scoff escaped me before I could swallow it back. I turned from the board, letting my eyes settle on her properly now. Theresa sat at her desk as if she owned the air in the room, shoulders relaxed, hands placed neatly, gaze steady.

"So, if the cover-up wasn't about the money, why bury Casey's death? I mean, three shots to the torso could hardly be a suicide."

Theresa's smile thinned, and her eyes stayed on mine. "Clearly, you've come here with your own reason," she said carefully. Her tone didn't accuse. It assessed. She watched me, waiting for the point where I'd slip and tell her something useful.

Even with the sleep I'd gotten, I still couldn't get a clean read from her. Theresa held herself too well. She didn't fidget. She didn't overplay calm. She simply existed in it.

I shifted my body to face her fully and moved closer to her desk. The chair opposite her sat perfectly aligned, as if nobody was allowed to sit wrong in this room. I positioned myself behind it instead, hands resting on the back, keeping the furniture between us.

"Do you know Blaze?"

For the first time, Theresa's face changed. It was subtle, quick, and then gone. A small tightening around her eyes, a flicker of recognition she didn't have time to bury completely.

I saw it. She did know him.

"Casey's partner," Theresa said, and her voice stayed even again, not reacting at all.

"You and Casey spoke about him?"

Theresa's gaze held steady. "We spoke about a lot."

My phone vibrated again in my pocket. A short buzz against my thigh that felt louder than it should've. I ignored it. "Did you know Rochelle?"

Theresa's eyes flickered again. More recognition. "I had heard about her. Not much, though."

"She was a friend of Casey's."

"That much I know. I also know she had an abusive partner."

I didn't move. My fingers tightened slightly on the back of the chair. "Had…" I echoed. "You know they died?"

Theresa's expression shifted again, sharp this time, and then she forced it back under control. "I do."

"Casey told you."

Theresa's gaze stayed on mine. "Casey also told Blaze," she said, and there was something jagged in her voice now. "He had a habit of not keeping his mouth shut."

My stomach tightened. "That's why Casey died."

Theresa didn't blink.

"That's why Blaze died."

The words hung between us, and I watched her face for the slip that would confirm it. The flinch. The irritation. The satisfaction. Anything.

She looked away from me. My phone vibrated again. I exhaled

through my nose and pulled the phone out.

One message from Dante. Two from Jordan.

The screen glowed in my hand, harsh against the warm lighting of Theresa's office. I glanced down at Dante's message first.

It was short and direct. *She didn't leave.*

My eyes snapped back to Theresa before I could stop myself. She was looking at me again. Her face was different. Not neutral. Contorted in a way I hadn't seen on her yet. Confusion and concern, real enough that it didn't look rehearsed. Her brows drawn together, her mouth tense, her gaze locked on me like I'd just said something insane.

"Blaze is dead?"

The question landed like a brick. My brow furrowed. I didn't answer her right away. I couldn't. My brain was still catching up to her expression, to Dante's message, to the fact that Theresa looked… blindsided.

I glanced back down at the phone. Dante's message didn't change. *She didn't leave.*

I lifted my eyes slowly. "You didn't do it," I said, and the words came out quietly.

Theresa stared at me. "You thought I killed them?" she asked, and her voice had lost its edge. It sounded smaller than it should have in this room.

I didn't respond. I looked back down at my phone and opened Jordan's messages.

I got a list of classmates.

I read that first. Then I read the second message. Slowly and more than once. I read it again, and then again, like my brain needed repetition to accept what it was seeing.

Theresa's son went to school with him when he was a kid.

The words sat there. Plain. Truthful. My throat went dry.

I rolled it through my head, the pieces shifting without me touching them. Theresa and Casey. The visits to The Strip. The mystery kid. The limp and the corrected shoes.

My mouth opened before I could fully decide to speak. "Bryce was friends with him."

Silence. Not the polite kind. The kind that made the room feel suddenly smaller.

Theresa didn't answer.

I looked up at her. There was no neutrality on her face anymore. Her eyes had gone sharp, and her mind was moving fast. I saw it in the way her eyes moved, not around the room, but inward, replaying memories and ordering them into something she didn't want to see.

"Bryce was the kid," I said, and my voice hardened as the sentence formed. "The one Casey went to visit."

"No."

It wasn't firm. It wasn't a command. It was disbelief. It came out small, and it sounded like she was trying to reject the idea before it could become real.

I stared at her, and my stomach dropped.

"Fuck," I muttered, and the swear tasted bitter in my mouth. "The limp. Anisomelia. It's genetic."

The words spilled out as my brain kept connecting dots, dragging them into place whether I wanted them there or not.

Everything started sticking.

Saturday. Bryce leaving the building when I left, the way he carried himself, the set of his shoulders, and the stride that had felt just slightly off if you knew what you were looking for. Exactly like his mother.

Bryce in the range, stance confident but compensating, elbow locked, shoulders uneven. He'd looked like someone who'd learned to stand a certain way so nobody would notice the difference.

His father's gun.

He would've known Blaze. He would've known Rochelle. He would've known everyone Casey knew, because Casey was the thread that tied them together.

I looked at Theresa, and for the first time, she looked like a person, not a title. Her breath was shallow. Her hands had shifted, fingers curled slightly on the edge of her desk as if she needed something solid to hold.

"Were you burying it for him?"

Theresa shook her head once. Too quick. Too desperate for someone who usually moved like she had all the time in the world. "No. He didn't."

The denial didn't sound like strategy. It sounded like a mother.

For the first time, I saw Theresa coming apart at the seams. There was no sobbing or anything dramatic, but the control that had sat on her like armour was slipping. The cracks were in the small things—her eyes widening, her jaw tensing, her posture leaning forward like she needed to get closer to the truth so she could stop it.

"He thought Casey was going to tell you what happened," I said, and my voice stayed steady even as my chest tightened. "So, he killed him. Then he killed Blaze as a loose end."

Theresa's head shifted slightly. She wanted to interrupt, to correct, to shut me down, but her mouth didn't form anything convincing enough to say.

I kept going, because the momentum was too strong now. I let everything move around in my head until it landed on one last piece.

"Stephanie."

The day in the shooting range. My own words to Bryce. *'She was friends with Casey.'* The truth slipping out of me like it had been nothing and falling on Bryce's ears.

Theresa's eyes flicked up sharply. She had sent Stephanie right to him.

"If he thinks she knows…" I started, and my voice trailed off because I didn't need to finish it.

Theresa's face drained of colour.

I didn't wait. I turned on my heel and ran out of the office.

22

"It's Bryce."

My voice came out sharp and rushed into my phone's receiver as I stepped into the elevator. Theresa was right beside me, moving with that same controlled urgency she'd worn in her office—except now the control looked like it was being used to keep something from falling apart. The doors started to close.

"What?" Dante's voice snapped back through the line.

"I don't have time," I said, eyes on Theresa's hand as she reached for the panel. "We think Stephanie is in danger. Organise agents to go to Theresa's home now."

There was a beat of silence on the other end that wasn't confusion; it was Dante recalibrating. Then, *"On it,"* and the line went dead.

Theresa pressed a sequence of buttons, fast, and the elevator responded like it recognised her as law, the doors sealing and the carriage dropping without that usual stutter of stops. No pause. No polite dinging on every second floor. Just motion. The descent made my stomach lift slightly.

Theresa didn't speak. Neither did I.

The hum of the elevator motor filled the silence, and the lights in the ceiling panel made everything look paler than it should have. Theresa stood with her shoulders set, chin lifted, eyes forward. If I didn't know better, I would've mistaken it being calm.

I'd seen her face a hundred different ways in the last few days. Neutral. Amused. Cold. Calculating. This wasn't any of those. This was new.

The doors opened at the lobby. We moved out together, and the shift was immediate. Even the lobby felt different with her in it—like the air remembered hierarchy. People moved out of our line without being told. Agents stepped aside. Visitors stared and then looked away. Security straightened like they'd been caught doing something wrong.

Theresa didn't acknowledge any of them. She kept walking. It was odd moving through that space with her. I'd been in this building enough times to know its rhythms, the way it swallowed tension and spat it back out as bureaucracy, but she didn't move like a person inside the machine. She moved like the machine moved around her.

We hit the doors and pushed through into the outside. The sun was low, burning orange along the edge of the sky, but the air had already started to cool.

"I'll follow you."

Theresa didn't respond. She gave a single, tight nod and headed for her car. I broke into a jog toward mine, cutting between rows of vehicles, shoes scuffing gravel and painted lines. My keys were already in my hand. I got in, slammed the door, and turned the ignition.

The engine kicked over. I glanced at the time on the dash. Twelve past five. I forced my eyes up. Theresa's car was already moving, turning out of the lot with purpose. I pulled out after her. She flipped her siren on, red and blue lights spilling across windshields and concrete. Traffic hesitated, then shifted, and she took the gap like she owned the road, too.

I followed as close as I could, leaning on my horn when someone looked too slow to understand what was happening. The noise sounded wrong coming from my car—too ordinary compared to the authority screaming from hers. In the rear-view mirror, I saw other cars pulling out behind us, lights flashing as they joined the line.

The lights lit up the street as the sky darkened properly, reflecting off shop windows and the sides of cars, turning the world into a pulsing smear of colour. Theresa cut through intersections like she'd already decided the consequences were worth it.

We headed deeper into the East. The houses started changing. More space, bigger fences, wider driveways, and greener lawns. The kind of place that pretended nothing bad ever happened.

Theresa turned down a side street and didn't even bother with the driveway. She ran her car up onto the curb hard enough that the suspension bounced, jumped out before it had fully settled, and started moving.

I followed, skidding my own car into a stop behind hers, not as aggressive but close, then I was out too, feet hitting pavement and momentum carrying me forward. The street was quiet in that East-side way—no kids in sight, no groups on corners, no noise except engines cooling and the distant hum of traffic on the main road.

Theresa hit her front path at a run. We reached the door together and she shoved it open. "Lawrence!" Theresa's voice tore through the house like a command. She disappeared inside immediately.

I moved slower as I crossed the threshold, my body finally remembering I wasn't armed. No way to defend myself. Just my hands, my instincts, and the fact I'd followed a woman into her own house after accusing her of murder. Then her son.

The entry foyer was too grand, too polished. Tile floors that looked spotless, reflecting the light from a chandelier that didn't belong in a home so much as a hotel. The air smelled clean—faint citrus, expensive fragrance, and something floral that didn't feel natural. Everything in the space was arranged as though it was waiting to be photographed.

Theresa's footsteps thudded somewhere deeper in the house, fast and harsh, and I heard her call again—sharper this time. Behind me, the front door stayed open, and the first agents spilled in, moving with practised efficiency. They flowed past me like I wasn't there, splitting directions without needing to speak.

"Clear left."

"Kitchen clear."

"Stairs."

The sound of boots on tile echoed, and the house didn't feel like a home at all. It felt like a scene being secured.

Dante came in behind the second wave. His eyes found me instantly. "You good?"

"Yeah, yeah," I said, keeping my voice low. "Go."

He didn't argue. He nodded once and moved, slipping into the stream of agents clearing rooms. My eyes tracked the movement, then flicked toward the driveway visible through the open door.

Stephanie's car wasn't there. I stepped back out onto the front path, then down onto the lawn. The street had filled fast. Flashing lights painted the trees and the parked cars and the pristine façade of Theresa's house. Neighbours had appeared—front doors cracked open, a few people stepping onto porches in robes or casual clothes, faces pulled tight with that mix of curiosity and fear people got when law enforcement turned their street into a spectacle.

The grass under my shoes was too soft, too even. No patches. No dead spots. I kept my eyes down at the path and lawn as if the ground might tell me something. From inside, voices continued to call out.

"Clear."

"Clear."

"Clear."

Each one landed a little harder than the last. I tried to force my mind into simple timing, because timing was something I could use. Stephanie had left the NBI when Theresa sent her out. Dinner for Bryce and Lawrence. An ordinary task. A routine task.

How long would it take to get here from the building? Traffic at five.

East side roads clogged with people heading home, kids being picked up, commuters angry at each other for existing. Even with intention, she would've been stuck in it. Even with shortcuts, there was only so much you could shave off.

She wouldn't have made it yet.

The last of the daylight slipped lower, and the air cooled another degree. The red and blue lights kept pulsing, washing the neighbourhood in alternating colour. Somewhere inside, a voice called Theresa's name.

She didn't answer immediately. Then I heard her, distant, the sound rawer than it had any right to be.

"Lawrence!"

My stomach dropped in a way it hadn't yet. Because that wasn't the voice of a woman managing a situation. That was the voice of someone whose life was coming apart I kept my eyes on the neighbouring houses.

"Where are you?" I muttered, hoping the universe would answer.

Dante's voice came from behind me as he joined me on the front lawn, his steps flattening the grass as he came to a stop beside me. "Only Theresa's husband is in the house. No Bryce."

I turned, letting my eyes land on the front door. On the movement of agents inside. On the shape of the windows that told you nothing because the lights behind them were too bright.

"Someone should try to contact Stephanie."

"Someone's already on it. We've been trying since the NBI. No response yet."

We stood there with the sirens washing the street in colour and the neighbours pretending they weren't staring. The cold had slipped in properly now, creeping through the thin spots in my shirt and settling against my skin.

Dante didn't look at the house. He looked at me. "Are you sure it's him?"

I nodded. "He went to school with Casey. That's why Theresa helped him. It was for Bryce."

Dante's mouth tightened, the pieces clicking in behind his eyes. "He would've been friends with Rochelle as well."

"Tried to stop the abusive boyfriend. Accidentally killed them both."

Dante shifted his weight slightly, jaw working. "Why would he be after Stephanie?"

"He knows Stephanie was friends with Casey. My fault. I'm assuming he thinks she knows about what he did."

Dante stared ahead, eyes narrowing. "Last loose end."

I hummed in agreement.

Troy came into view in the doorway, moving out onto the lawn. "Can't get a hold of her." He stopped a few feet away, phone still in his hand, screen glowing against his palm. "BOLO has been sent out."

I didn't look at Troy. I didn't need to. The words sat where they landed, and my mind ran past them, already searching for the next thing.

"I'll go talk to Theresa. See if she might know where he'd go," Dante said.

I nodded, but my head wasn't really with him. It was already somewhere else. My gaze slid down the street, past the patrol cars, past the cluster of neighbours at their fences, past the corner where the road dipped out of sight.

Bryce wouldn't know she was coming here. Unless it was routine. I dragged my eyes back to the house and forced my brain to stop sprinting in ten directions at once.

Habit. Theresa was a person of habit. The way she moved in the office. The way she spoke. The way she ordered her space. People like that didn't improvise unless they were cornered. They defaulted to what was familiar.

I thought back to the night Casey died. Bryce had known Casey would be in the park. He'd picked the time, the place, the angle. He'd chosen a location where the noise of gunshots could be swallowed by distance, darkness, and trees.

Premeditated.

Then Blaze. The house he died in. Calling him to it. Planned.

Bryce didn't wing it. He didn't panic and lash out. He set things up, then stepped into them. Which meant if he was going after Stephanie, it wouldn't be random. It would be a part of a schedule. Somewhere she'd go because Theresa told her to go.

My mind snapped back to the moment in Theresa's office. Theresa telling Stephanie to organise dinner. To take some to the house for Bryce and Lawrence. No address given. No explanation. Just an instruction delivered as if it were routine.

Because it was. Theresa wouldn't need to tell Stephanie where to go. Stephanie would already know.

I turned sharply and jogged back across the lawn, the grass soft under my shoes. The noise of the street muffled as I moved into the house, the warmth hitting me immediately, thick and expensive. Voices bounced off high ceilings. Agents moved in practiced lines, stepping around furniture as if they'd been trained to respect property while they tore through a home.

Theresa and her husband were in the large living room to the left of the entrance foyer. Lawrence stood rigid, hands slightly raised. Theresa sat on the edge of a chair, posture too straight, face controlled, but her eyes were frantic in the way she kept tracking the movement in the room.

Dante was there too, half-turned toward her, speaking low.

I didn't slow. I didn't soften my approach. "Where did Stephanie go to get food?"

Dante's head snapped toward me. "What?" he said, thrown off by the question.

I ignored him. My eyes stayed on Theresa. She looked at me like she didn't understand why I was asking something so small in the middle of something so big, and then she seemed to understand exactly why. "She goes to Amoretti's. Every Tuesday."

My pulse jumped. I turned to Dante immediately. "Go there."

Dante's expression shifted, the same click of logic tightening his face as he followed the leap I'd just made. He didn't argue. He didn't ask how I knew. He just moved, already pulling his phone up again as he started toward the hallway.

Behind me, the house kept humming with controlled chaos, but my focus narrowed until it was just that one name sitting in the air. Amoretti's. If Bryce was going to intercept her, that was where he'd do it. Because that was the schedule.

I spun on my heel and headed back out of the house, keeping my pace steady even though my pulse had already started doing laps. Dante and a few agents fell in behind me without needing to be told twice. The foyer swallowed us back into its too-bright cleanliness and then we were out through the front door and into the cold of the early night.

Police lights painted everything in rotating colour. Somewhere behind us, Theresa's voice rose and fell with another agent, but I didn't turn back.

Dante caught up beside me as we cleared the front steps. "You think he's there?"

"He planned for Casey and Blaze," I said, and I kept my eyes on my car as we moved. "If he's going to get to Stephanie, he'll have planned that, too. He'll know where she's going."

Dante didn't answer, but I knew he accepted it.

We split at the curb. Dante angled toward his car with Troy and two others, keys already out. I went for mine, cutting across the lawn and taking the shortest line through the cluster of flashing lights and parked vehicles. My hand was shaking as I fumbled for the door handle, which annoyed me more than it should have. I got it open, slid in, and shoved the key into the ignition.

I pulled off the curb hard enough that the tyres gave a small complaint against the asphalt, and then I was falling in behind Dante's car as he pulled out ahead of me, lights already on. The street narrowed with cars and people and corners, but the red and blue carved us a path anyway. Traffic did what traffic always did when sirens hit it—hesitated, panicked, then scrambled out of the way at the last possible second.

The suburb flew by as we tore through it. Houses with lit windows and trimmed gardens blurred at the edges. Street signs snapped past too quickly to read properly. My hands stayed locked on the wheel, knuckles pale, shoulders tight. I kept my distance from Dante's bumper, but not by much. Close enough that nobody could slip in between us. Close enough that if he hit the brakes, I'd be in trouble.

My mind tried to do three things at once—track the road, track Dante, and track Bryce in the invisible space in front of us. The idea of him sitting somewhere calm with a plan felt wrong, and yet it fit too well. He'd been calm at the range. He'd been comfortable with a gun in his hands. Comfortable in a way you didn't learn overnight.

We hit a stretch of heavier traffic and Dante leaned on his siren harder. Cars peeled aside reluctantly. A few suburbs over, the landscape shifted. Less open space. More small shops with signage and tired lighting. A handful of people on foot turning their heads as the convoy went past, curiosity flickering across their faces.

Then I saw it. Amoretti's. A small Italian restaurant tucked into a strip of businesses. Warm light spilling through the front windows. A couple of cars in the lot.

Dante swung into the parking lot fast and took a hard angle, pulling up near the front. He was out of his car before the engine had even fully settled, door slamming behind him. Troy and two agents followed immediately, moving in a line toward the entrance like they'd done this a thousand times.

I pulled in behind and killed my engine, then got out and moved away from my car, not rushing, but not wasting steps either. The cold hit my face, and the smell of the place reached me even from here—garlic and oil and bread, warm and harmless.

I stopped partway across the lot. I didn't go in. I was useful in a room when people needed someone to talk. Out here, I was just another body to trip over.

So, I waited.

The windows were large enough to see into the restaurant clearly; the inside lit warm and yellow. Dante and the agents pushed through the door, and the atmosphere inside changed instantly—heads turning, bodies stiffening, the usual ripple of fear and curiosity that came when law enforcement walked into a place that had nothing to do with them.

Dante moved fast, sweeping his eyes across tables and corners. Troy split to the left with an agent. The other agent moved right. It was clean and practiced.

And then I saw her. Stephanie.

She was near the counter, a paper bag on the surface in front of her, her posture rigid in that controlled way she always wore like armour. Her head turned sharply toward the door as Dante entered, eyes briefly widening.

My shoulders loosened slightly. Not relief exactly. More like the pressure in my chest shifted enough that I could breathe properly again. I took a slow breath in through my nose and let it out carefully.

Then I felt cold metal press into my back.

It was sudden and intimate. A firm point against my spine through my shirt, right where the muscles were tight. My body locked immediately, every instinct screaming to move and not move at the same time.

A voice came close to my ear. "Get in your car," Bryce said quietly.

His tone wasn't loud. It didn't need to be. It was controlled, but it wasn't calm. I didn't turn my head. I didn't move my hands. I kept them loose at my sides and forced my breathing to stay steady.

"I'm not going to do that, Bryce," I said, and my voice came out flatter than I expected.

The gun pushed harder. "I will shoot a fucking hole in you."

I swallowed. "I'm sure you would," I said slowly. "But then what?"

Bryce didn't answer. He just drove the gun in harder, forcing me forward a fraction. The pressure hit bone. My body reacted before my brain could stop it, a flinch I hated myself for. I lifted both hands slowly, palms open, bringing them up where he could see them without making it look like a sudden grab for anything.

"There are three agents in there who will hear the shot," I said, keeping my tone low and measured. "They'll come running. And you can't go home. Everyone knows, Bryce."

He let out a breath that shook on the way out. Not a sob. Not a full crack. Just the kind of unsteady exhale you made when you were trying to hold yourself together and failing.

"Stephanie told you. That's why you came to the gun range with me. To figure me out."

The accusation hit wrong because it was too close to the truth without being actually true. "Stephanie doesn't know what you did." I kept my gaze forward; eyes fixed on my car and the space between us.

22

"You would've killed her for no reason. Just like you killed Rochelle."

"I didn't—I—" Bryce stammered, and the composure slipped properly then. His voice fractured.

I turned slowly, careful and deliberate, hands still raised. Bryce didn't stop me, but as I rotated to face him, he pressed the gun hard into my gut. The barrel was cold through my shirt. The pressure made me tense, abdominal muscles tightening as if that would do anything.

Bryce's face was different up close. Not the clean, confident kid at the range. Not Theresa's polished extension. His eyes were wet and red. His jaw clenched so tight it looked painful. He held the gun with a grip that was technically correct, but there was a tremor in it now, a small shake he couldn't fully hide.

"You made a mistake."

"It was an accident," Bryce said quickly like he'd rehearsed the line until it felt like a shield.

From inside the restaurant, I heard a shout. "Red!" Dante's voice cut through the glass and spilled into the lot.

Another voice followed, sharper. "On the ground, Bryce!" Troy yelled.

Bryce's eyes flicked toward the door for half a second, then snapped back to me, pupils wide and wild. The gun stayed in my gut, unwavering in direction even if his hand shook.

"Casey wasn't an accident," I said quietly. "Blaze wasn't."

Bryce's throat bobbed as he swallowed hard. He looked like he wanted to argue, but the words weren't lining up right. His breathing was too fast. Too shallow.

"No one…" he started, then stopped and tried again. "No one would've known."

"Yeah," I said, and I didn't soften it because he didn't deserve soft. "Maybe. But now everyone does. So, what're you gonna do?"

Bryce's eyes locked on mine, glassy and furious and scared all at once. "I could kill you."

"They'll shoot you."

His mouth twisted. A strange, bitter expression that didn't match his age. "Maybe I want them to."

I looked at his face properly then. Not just the anger, not just the fear. The guilt sitting behind it. It had eaten a hole in him. Tears clinging to his lower lashes, refusing to fall.

"Fear makes you do stupid things," I said, keeping my voice steady. "Don't make this one of them."

The shouting behind me got louder. I heard movement now, quick footsteps on pavement, the scrape of a door opening. I didn't turn. I didn't break eye contact. If I looked away, Bryce would feel it. He'd either bolt or fire. Both were bad options.

So, I kept my eyes him. His finger hovered too close to the trigger. His breathing hitched. His lips parted like he might speak, then he didn't.

I heard my own heart in my ears. Could feel the sweat breaking at my spine despite the cold. My hands stayed up, palms open, fingers spread, and I hated how aware I was of how exposed my chest felt. How fragile my throat felt. My voice stayed even because it had to. But inside, I was falling apart. I was shitting my pants. I didn't want to be shot.

"Lower the weapon!" Dante shouted.

Bryce's eyes snapped behind me, flicking between Dante and the agents spread across the lot. Their guns were up, bodies angled, voices layered over each other in short commands. Bryce flinched at each one, but then his gaze dragged back to mine and locked there.

He kept the gun pressed into my stomach hard enough that it felt like it was trying to leave an imprint.

"You don't want to do this."

"Shut up!" Bryce hissed.

His breathing was loud, uneven, pulling too much air in and not getting enough back out. His hand shook, and he hated it. I saw it in the way he set his jaw like he was trying to clamp the tremor out of his body.

"I didn't want—" he started, and his voice cracked on the edge of the sentence.

"I know."

The words hung between us, and the pressure of the barrel eased, not because he meant to, but because his grip faltered with the admission. I kept my hands where they were and kept my body still as if stillness could make me less of a target. I paused and let the noise of the lot rush back in.

"So, this is where you stop."

Nobody moved. Not me. Not Bryce. Not the agents. The air held tight, like the whole scene was balanced on the thinnest thread, and everyone could feel it.

My mouth was dry. My heart was loud in my chest. I felt the pulse in my throat, in my wrists, in the spot where cold metal met skin.

"I want to get home to my family," I said, and my voice came out steady in a way my body did not deserve. "Please."

Bryce stared at me, trying to find a lie in my face. If he could prove I was manipulating him, he'd get his footing back. His eyes searched mine, darting across them, then holding again, and for a moment, I watched him fight himself.

He took a shaky breath in. Then another. His shoulders dropped, barely, like the tension had finally started to leak out of him. Slowly, his hand lowered. The gun slipped away from my stomach, the cold pressure disappearing so suddenly it made my muscles twitch in relief. He hesitated with it halfway down, wrist trembling, and then he let it fall.

It hit the asphalt with a sharp, ugly clatter.

Time snapped back into motion. Troy and another agent rushed in. Orders came fast and loud—hands up, turn around, on your knees— and Bryce followed them like a man walking through heavy water. He dropped to his knees without resistance, arms lifting, empty hands shaking.

The agent yanked his wrists behind his back. The cuffs clicked. That sound did something to my lungs. It reminded them they were supposed to work. I finally exhaled properly, the air leaving me in a slow, ragged stream I hadn't realised I'd been holding.

I took a step back.

Dante moved to my side immediately, close enough to anchor me without touching me, his presence a solid line in my peripheral. His voice came low, controlled, aimed at me and not the chaos. "You good?"

I nodded, because it was easier than explaining what my legs felt like, what my hands were doing, how my stomach still thought there was a gun pressed into it.

"Yeah," I managed, and watched as Bryce was hauled to his feet, face slack with shock and grief and something that looked like relief he didn't know how to admit to.

They guided him toward the car. As they moved him across the lot, Troy looked back at me. No smile. No nod. No acknowledgement. Just a quick check, eyes scanning me like he wanted to confirm I was still alive. He turned away again and shoved Bryce into the back seat. The door slammed.

Dante's voice cut in again, closer, now he'd decided the immediate threat was over and he could finally be annoyed. "You're gonna have to come back to the NBI for this."

"Yeah," I said. My gaze slid past the flashing lights and the agents, and the watching faces, back to the restaurant.

Stephanie stood near the entrance, half in the light, half in shadow. Her posture was stiff, shoulders drawn up like she'd braced for something that hadn't happened and didn't know how to unclench now that it was over. Her eyes locked onto mine. Confusion sat all over her face. Shock, too. She looked like someone who'd just watched a familiar world tilt on its axis.

I lifted a hand and gave her a small wave. She didn't return it.

I drew in another shaky breath, felt it scrape through my chest, and swallowed hard.

"I think I'll drive you."

I let out something that was almost a laugh and almost a groan. "I might need new underwear."

"Can't help you with that one," Dante said with a small chuckle.

I dug my keys out and handed them to him without arguing, then started walking toward my car on legs that didn't quite feel like mine. My fingers curled against my stomach as I moved, pressing lightly as if I could erase the sensation by force. I could still feel it. The cold metal. The pressure. The certainty of it.

It didn't ease.

23

Work at the NBI kept ticking around me like it didn't know how to do anything else.

Phones rang. Printers coughed paper out in steady bursts. People moved around me with purpose before disappearing down the hall or to the elevators. Some of them spoke as they passed. Asking questions.

"You alright?"

"You need anything?"

I guess being held at gunpoint made people forget why they disliked me. At least briefly.

Forms sat in front of me. A pile of them, all slightly different, all asking for the same information with new boxes so the system could file it away properly. I wrote my name more times than any human should have to. I initialled, dated, and signed until my signature started looking like someone else's handwriting. A pen rolled between my fingers as I waited for the next sheet to slide across Dante's desk.

I was on Wilson's floor, parked in Dante's chair, shoulders pressed into the backrest, and my knee bouncing under the desk because I still hadn't been able to bleed out the adrenaline.

Across the bullpen, Lavern sat at her own station, spine straight, hands moving over her keyboard with a controlled rhythm. She didn't look at me. She didn't talk to me.

That was fair. Some people still held onto the past.

My eyes kept finding the clock on the wall. Eight nineteen Eight twenty-two. Eight twenty-four. Every minute landed like it had weight.

I needed to leave soon. I needed to be home. I'd promised.

The forms kept coming. I kept filling them out. It wasn't just for tonight. It was for the entire file on Casey. Things that were swept under the rug and forgotten were being dragged back up, and because I was the one doing the dragging, my name had to be all of it.

My eyes drifted back to the clock.

Eight thirty-one.

My fingers were steady, which was the lie my body always told first. Everything else lagged behind.

A ghost-pressure still sat against my ribs where the muzzle had pointed, like my skin had memorised it. I kept swallowing like there was something stuck in my throat. There wasn't. Just the aftertaste of fear and the lingering awareness of how fast everything could've ended.

I dragged a hand down my face and felt how stiff my skin was, like the day had dried there. My jaw ached from holding tension too long. My stomach still remembered cold metal in a way it shouldn't have.

The subtle sound of doors opening came from my right, and Wilson stepped out of his office. He crossed toward me, pulled a spare chair from the side of Dante's desk, and sat down close enough that his knee nearly hit the desk leg. His eyes didn't quite land on mine. They hovered somewhere between my hands and the paperwork like he didn't want to watch my face while he said whatever he'd come over to say.

"How're you holding up?" Wilson asked quietly.

I didn't bother pretending. "I want to go home."

Wilson nodded once, slowly. The kind of nod that acknowledged the truth without doing anything about it. "Soon."

I stared at him, then tilted my head. "You didn't come over here to check on me."

Wilson's mouth shifted. He exhaled through his nose—something between a sigh and resignation. "I was the one to bury it." His voice was low enough that it belonged to the space between us, not the bullpen or the building.

"I know."

Wilson's eyes flicked up then—just briefly—and I saw the tiredness there. "I just had to—" he started.

I cut him off. I didn't need to hear his excuses again.

"I understand why," I said, and my voice came out rougher than I wanted. I cleared my throat and tried again, slower. "You were scared. You don't know how deep it goes. You were looking out for your family." I paused. "This… this doesn't have to happen." I gestured between the two of us.

Wilson nodded slowly. Twice. Three times. We sat there in the noise of the bullpen, the building breathing around us.

Wilson cleared his throat and pushed up from his chair. He didn't pat my shoulder. He didn't say anything. He just stood and moved through the bullpen, heading down the hall toward the kitchen. His back stayed straight. His pace stayed even. But something about him looked smaller as he went.

I watched him disappear, then leaned back in Dante's chair and stared at the ceiling. All I wanted was confirmation I could leave Agents filed in and out of the bullpen. Some looked at me. Some didn't. Everything kept moving.

Dante came in a few times. Each time, he had another question. Another angle. Another detail they needed nailed down because now that Casey's death was officially reopened and completed properly, the whole timeline had to be reconstructed.

Dante didn't interrogate me like a stranger. It was worse than that— he questioned me like a colleague who needed the report to survive scrutiny.

Dates, times, locations, why I was where I was, and what I saw. The kind of details lawyers would care about.

He kept his pen moving, kept his voice level, and every so often he'd pause just long enough to remind me this wasn't only paperwork. It was a body. It was blood I had washed from my own hands.

We backtracked the night at the park. The night with Blaze's body. Everything that led up to the scene at Amoretti's. Bureaucratic crap. I answered anyway. Dante wrote it down, clarified, double-checked, and kept his face neutral. He already knew most of it. He was just checking boxes.

At one point, he disappeared for twenty minutes and came back with a new form, like the building had decided the last five weren't enough.

I signed. I initialled. I stared at the clock. Eight fifty-two. I let out a slow, controlled breath.

Then Dante came in again, and this time he didn't bring paper. He stepped up behind me and clasped my shoulder with his hand, firm and grounding. "We're good to go."

I turned my head slightly, relief cutting through. "Thank God. This building is suffocating."

Dante's mouth twitched. He waited until I pushed myself up from the chair, then fell into step beside me as we headed toward the elevators. My legs felt stiff from sitting down for so long.

"I guess it is a good thing you don't listen to me."

I glanced at him. "I always listen to you."

Dante snorted softly, then gave me that sideways look he'd perfected over the years. "You go behind my back all the time to do shit I tell you not to."

"That doesn't mean I don't listen. It just means I ignore."

Dante shook his head as we reached the elevators. He hit the call button, then looked back at me.

"Yeah, well," he said, "I guess it works for you."

I let out a breath that might've been a laugh if I'd had more energy. "I wouldn't say almost getting shot is something that works for me."

Dante's eyebrows lifted. "Hey, at least this time it wasn't two agents you almost got killed."

I stared at him, then huffed. "Yeah. I'm slipping. Gonna have to up my game again. Find my footing again."

The elevator dinged, doors sliding open. We stepped inside, and Dante hit the lobby button. The ride down felt longer than it should have, even without stopping. My mind kept trying to replay the parking lot at Amoretti's—Bryce's face, the tremor in his hands, the gun falling to the asphalt. When the doors opened at the lobby, I stepped out with Dante beside me and the noise of the building washing over us again.

"You think they're gonna call you again?" Dante asked as we drifted toward the exit.

"Maybe. I mean, where would they be without me?"

Dante made a sound that was half amusement, half pain. "I'm gonna have to wear earmuffs all the time if you and Mia work together."

"I think I might have to go to another team."

Dante laughed, short and genuine.

"Besides," I added, "maybe you'll be in the big office. If this money thing becomes something, Wilson might not be in there for much longer."

Dante's expression tightened again, reality sliding back in. "Somehow, I don't think the NBI are gonna let that one get out."

We walked past security and pushed out into the night air. The cold hit my face, clean and sharp. The sky was fully dark, and the parking lot lights made everything look too bright and too flat. I thought back to what Theresa had said about the money and what the NBI had buried before.

"You're not wrong."

Dante didn't answer straight away. He stopped instead, turning to face me. His eyes flicked over my expression, my posture, the way my hands were sitting at my sides.

"You sure you're all good?"

I stopped too. "Yeah," I said, and tried to sell it. "Not the first time I've had a gun pointed at me."

Dante nodded, deadpan. "You've just got one of those faces."

"You make it sound like you've thought about it."

"I've dreamt about it." Dante chuckled at himself.

I felt a smile tug at my mouth. "Alright. I need to get home to tuck the boys in."

I reached out and shook Dante's hand. It was firm, familiar. We said goodbye, then I turned and headed for my car. I slid into the driver's seat and kicked the engine over, the dashboard lights washing my hands in pale green. My eyes went to the clock immediately. It was just after nine O'clock. I was cutting it close.

I pulled out of the lot and hit the road. The suburbs blurred past, streetlights streaking across the windshield in regular intervals. Traffic was light—people heading home from dinner, couples in cars with quiet music, and people who had worked late heading home. My hands stayed tight on the wheel. My brain stayed busy, trying to outrun the quiet.

It wasn't long before I turned onto my street. My driveway came into view, and I eased in. I killed the engine and sat there for half a second, staring at the house. The lights were still on inside.

But there wasn't any movement.

I exhaled, slow, and felt my chest tighten like a fist closing. I may have missed it. I got out of the car; the night air colder than it had been at the NBI. I walked up the path toward the front door.

As I got close, I heard something muffled from inside, and a smile lifted on my face before I could stop it. Maybe I wasn't too late. I stepped inside and shut the door behind me. The sound sharpened immediately. A phone ringing. Old-fashioned. Insistent. The kind of ring that belonged to a landline.

Something we didn't have.

I stood there, listening, the sound cutting through the house like a blade. I looked into the living room. Empty. The television off. No toys on the floor. No Claire on the lounge with that exhausted, patient look on her face.

The ringing was coming from down the hall.

My mind went straight to the bedroom. To our room. The television in there. The place Claire went when the boys were too worked up, and she needed to calm them down in the dark with soft voices and the sound of something mindless on the screen.

I swallowed. I had been late. If the boys had been upset, she would've taken them in there. I stepped toward the hallway. The ringing grew louder with each step, filling more of the space, pushing everything else out.

As I entered the hall, my eyes lifted toward the end. Our bedroom door sat closed. And as my gaze locked on it, it felt like the whole world dropped away around me, like someone had turned the volume down on everything except that ringing.

And I didn't have to open it to know what was on the other side.

SEEING RED
THE FIRST CALLING

WRITTEN BY

FINN